ALSO BY THE AUTHOR

The Bone Season series

The Bone Season
The Mime Order
The Song Rising
The Mask Falling
The Dark Mirror

The Pale Dreamer
The Dawn Chorus
On The Merits of Unnaturalness

The Roots of Chaos series

The Priory of the Orange Tree
A Day of Fallen Night

AMONG
THE
BURNING
FLOWERS

AMONG THE BURNING FLOWERS

A Roots of Chaos Tale

SAMANTHA SHANNON

BLOOMSBURY PUBLISHING
NEW YORK • LONDON • OXFORD • NEW DELHI • SYDNEY

For my brother, Alfie

BLOOMSBURY PUBLISHING
Bloomsbury Publishing Inc.
1359 Broadway, New York, NY 10018, USA
50 Bedford Square, London, WC1B 3DP, UK
Bloomsbury Publishing Ireland Limited, 29 Earlsfort Terrace,
Dublin 2, DO2 AY28, Ireland

BLOOMSBURY, BLOOMSBURY PUBLISHING and the Diana logo
are trademarks of Bloomsbury Publishing Plc

First published in 2025 in Great Britain
First published in the United States 2025

Copyright © Samantha Shannon-Jones, 2025
Illustrations © Rovina Cai, 2025
Maps and chapter heading illustrations © Emily Faccini, 2025

ISBN: HB: 978-1-63973-601-0; DELUXE EDITION: 978-1-63973-876-2;
SIGNED DELUXE EDITION: 978-1-63973-877-9;
BARNES & NOBLE SIGNED DELUXE EDITION: 978-1-63973-886-1;
EBOOK: 978-1-63973-602-7

Library of Congress Cataloging-in-Publication Data is available

2 4 6 8 10 9 7 5 3 1

Typeset by Integra Software Services Pvt. Ltd.
Printed in the United States by Lakeside Book Company

To find out more about our authors and books visit www.bloomsbury.com
and sign up for our newsletters.

Bloomsbury books may be purchased for business or promotional use.
For information on bulk purchases please contact Macmillan Corporate and
Premium Sales Department at specialmarkets@macmillan.com.

For product safety–related questions contact productsafety@bloomsbury.com.

Author's note

Among the Burning Flowers is a short prequel to *The Priory of the Orange Tree*. It may be approached as either a starting point for newcomers to the Roots of Chaos series, or a deepening of the story for readers who are already familiar with this world.

You'll find a glossary and a character guide at the back of the book and two maps just ahead.

The fictional lands of this series are inspired by events and legends from various parts of the world. None is intended as a faithful representation of any one country or culture at any point in history.

The dreadful happenings of these times
have torn up by the roots Hope's noble tree,

and in the garden of the world you'd say
they've stripped the leaves as far as one can see.

— JAHĀN-MALEK KĀTUN

Contents

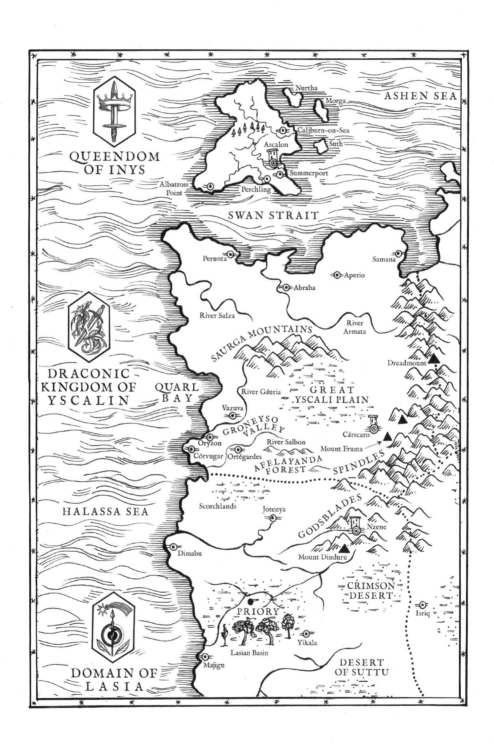

QUEENDOM
OF INYS

ASHEN SEA

Nurtha

Morga

Caliburn-on-Sea

Ascalon

Suth

Summerport

Albatross
Point

Perchling

SWAN STRAIT

DRACONIC
KINGDOM OF
YSCALIN

Perunta

Samana

Aperio

Abraba

River Salza

SAURGA MOUNTAINS

River
Armata

Dreadmount

QUARL
BAY

River Gáuria

GREAT
YSCALI PLAIN

Vazuva

GRONEYSO
VALLEY

Cárscaro

Oryzon

River Salbon

Córvugar

Ortégardes

Mount Fruma

AFELAYANDA
FOREST

SPINDLES

HALASSA SEA

Scorchlands

Jotenya

GODSBLADES

Nzene

Dimabu

Mount Dinduru

CRIMSON
DESERT

PRIORY

Isriq

DOMAIN OF
LASIA

Yikala

Lasian Basin

Majigu

DESERT
OF SUTTU

**A standalone prequel to *The Priory of the Orange Tree*, telling
the story of the Fall of Yscalin.**

A burning spring grips the Kingdom of Yscalin. Marosa
Vetalda is a prisoner in her own home, controlled by her
father, King Sigoso. Over the mountains, her betrothed,
Aubrecht Lievelyn, rules in all but name. Together, they
intend to usher in a better world.

A better world seems impossibly distant to Estina Melaugo,
who hunts the Draconic beasts that have slept across the
continent for centuries.

And now the great wyrm Fýredel seeks vengeance upon
humankind, and Yscalin will be the first to fall …

Before

Marosa

Long before it was a city, Cárscaro had been a mine.

In those days, the Gulthaganians ruled the northeast of the vast continent of Edin. Eager to conquer the rest, the Imperator of Gulthaga had sent his soldiers over the mountains west of their city, into land they did not know, to mine copper for armour and swords.

On the other side of the icy Spindles, the soldiers had scented copper and dug. But the western tribes of Edin, known as Yscals, had revered the mountains of their land. They cursed the newcomers for mining on Mount Fruma, for they saw in that peak a petrified god, the giant who had created their people.

The Yscals fought with flint and wood, the Gulthaganians with bronze. The fight had been lost from the start. Forced to work inside the mines, the Yscals had sliced their own skin to atone, fearing the displeasure of their god.

The Gulthaganians had named this outpost Karkara, meaning *birdcage*. Even when they were finally driven from

Yscalin, two centuries after they came, Karkara had remained a place of exile. Anyone who fled its walls had perished on the plain below, their bones lost to the dust.

Those days were long past, for most. The old mountain gods were forgotten, supplanted by the foreign Saint. The ancient copper mines lay buried under Cárscaro, now transformed into the splendid capital of Yscalin, and its people could come and go as they pleased.

This was not so for their future queen, the Donmata Marosa.

****

On the seventh day of spring, her eyes flew open, as if the Saint had reached down from the holy court of Halgalant to wake her. Nearby, her First Lady of the Bedchamber slept on, dark curls fanned across her pillow. Priessa had always been a deep sleeper.

Marosa listened. Half of her was in her skin, the other half elsewhere, elsewhen. Three memories flared in quick succession: a whisper at her ear, a hand tight around hers, a scream.

When nothing disturbed the silence of her room, she rose and laced a sleeveless robe over her smock. The air was thick butter around her; even the smallest movements drew sweat. She opened the doors of her apartments, hoping for a cool breeze, an iced drink.

From the bruised light in the corridor, it was daybreak. She rarely woke so early of her own accord.

'Donmata.'

The voice came from her left, where Ermendo Vuleydres stood by a window, armed with a pistol and rapier, a halberd near at hand. He must be cooking like a crab in all that gilded armour.

4

'Ermendo,' Marosa said, 'did you feel something just now?'

'A small tremor.'

'Is that not the sixth in as many days?'

'I believe so.'

His weathered face betrayed nothing. The Vardya were too disciplined to display such a base emotion as fear.

'I will take my usual turn,' Marosa said. 'If you are at liberty.'

'Of course, Your Radiance.'

There were occasional tremors in Cárscaro, but never so many, so close together. Still, Marosa was used to them. Knowing the city would shake now and then was part of being Cárscari.

They followed the path they had walked countless times, shadowed by two more guards. Here and there, Marosa glimpsed their reflections, folded into the polished walls of the Palace of Salvation. The walls that looked as if they had been painted with fresh ink.

Her prison was five hundred feet of blackstone and cinder and basalt, adorned with volcanic glass. Even on its lowest floors, with many arched windows to let a breeze through, it was always sweltering. A hundred thousand torches could not have truly lit its halls. Not only was it oppressively close, but abounding in tight stairways and trick walls to confuse intruders.

Queen Rozaria the Third had ignored her advisors when she ordered its construction. They had warned her that blackstone would hold in the heat; that only more northerly places, like Hróth, had need of such a dark fortress. Rozaria had not relented. This was her monument to Yscali strength, driven into the heart of Cárscaro. She had meant for it to look as fearsome as a wyrm, to serve as a reminder that Yscalin had risen from the ashes of the Grief.

She had succeeded, even if she had not lived to see the tower loom over the rest of the capital. It reminded the whole city of Fýredel, whose dread wings had once cast the world into shadow.

A wyrm that had never been slain.

Ermendo opened a door, and Marosa stepped on to the crescent balcony. She walked towards its balustrade and looked upon the capital of Yscalin.

Cárscaro was often called the High City. No settlement on the continent held a stronger defensive position. Built on a great cliff that shouldered out from the Spindles, it had those snow-capped mountains at its back, like a rear guard, and the Great Yscali Plain before it. The lavender there was already in bloom, mantling the land in purple all the way to the horizon.

'It looks to be a fine day,' Ermendo said. 'Queen Sahar would have wanted to spend it on the plain.'

Marosa gave the barest nod. They had both often gone to the plain with her mother, who had preferred it to the city. Some Cárscari braved the descent, usually to ride or hunt, but none held court among the flowers quite like Queen Sahar.

Along with favourites and other guests, her Ladies of the Bedchamber had often joined her outings: Sennera Yelarigas, Denarva uq-Bardant, Aryete Feyalda. They would eat in the shade – spiced red sausage, cheese and grapes – and talk over the roar of the Gloriza Falls, while Marosa played with the other children. When it was especially hot, they had waded in the shallow water from the falls. Those days had given them a respite from the dark tower.

Her father had never come with them.

Marosa had no happier memories than of those golden hours. Her mother dancing with her, making her laugh until it hurt, teaching her to ride. When Marosa was old enough to be married, Queen Sahar had used their flower days to talk with her in private, to reassure her and answer her questions.

It felt as if an age had passed since then. Now the falls were gone, and so was her mother. Marosa looked away from the lavender, to the river of fire that flowed through Cárscaro.

It had come when she was seventeen, stemming from a crack in the Spindles. The sizzling light had burned a slow but steady path. Before long, it had worked its way beneath Vatana House, and there, in a great eruption of steam, destroyed the Gloriza Falls.

Most kings would have moved their capital, but not Sigoso Vetalda. He had summoned masons and alchemists to stop the lava, sparing no expense. After failing to dam it, they had diverted it into the existing canals and dug new ones to spread the light.

They had all been confident it would crust over. Almost a decade later, it had not. Now the people crossed it through enclosed stone bridges, and its branches were named after the Six Virtues.

Her father had called it the Tundana. Its branches merged at the edge of the cliff and poured on to the Great Yscali Plain, cooling to black rubble. Many tonnes had piled up beneath Cárscaro – a stain like mud on the hem of the mountains, killing a swathe of lavender. Some years the lava would thin, allowing night to fall, but this year, it had run swift and bright since early spring. Marosa had not seen the stars for weeks, such was the reddish haze of it.

She looked at it all until her eyes hurt. The city she could see, but never touch. To her father, this palace was an eyrie, protecting the fragile egg of his legacy. He behaved as if Marosa were not already five and twenty, hatched and feathered, yearning to spread her wings.

Perhaps that was the reason she felt an overwhelming need to jump.

The need she had felt every day for nine years, since the night she was told her mother was gone.

Her palms turned clammy on the balustrade. She felt herself beginning to tip, her breath constrained by the cage of her ribs.

'Donmata?'

Ermendo came to her side. Marosa pressed her eyes shut, waiting for the feeling to pass, as it always did.

'I am well.' She straightened. 'Thank you, Ermendo. I will return to my apartments.'

****

By the time she reached her bedchamber, a bath was ready for her. The water came steaming hot from the pipes. Mount Fruma had never erupted in living memory, but it still warmed Cárscaro. Priessa allowed the water to cool before helping Marosa in, scrubbing her with olive soap, and wrapping her in linen. Once she was dry, Priessa oiled and combed her long hair.

Her apartments were the same dark stone as the rest of the palace, with vaulted ceilings, floors of black Samani marble, and windows flanked by sheer curtains. Priessa used mirrors to brighten the place and had flowers brought up every morning. Today it was poppies.

8

When Marosa was twelve, her mother had chosen three girls to be her Ladies of the Bedchamber. Priessa Yelarigas – a distant cousin – had been one of them. Four years later, when King Sigoso had dissolved Marosa's household and remodelled it to his own taste, only Priessa had survived the wind of change. Her father was the Secretary of State, one of the leading nobles at court.

Marosa trusted her above all others, except for Ermendo, her loyal guard, who had served her since she was a child. Ruzio and Yscabel Afleytan had also earned her confidence. The sisters had not tried to win her over with flattery, like most of the attendants her father had foisted upon her.

Four people, in a palace filled with hundreds, that she could rely on. If only they did not have to be trapped up here with her.

'For you.' Priessa held out a letter. 'The dove arrived yesterday morning.'

The seal was already broken. Marosa opened it to find lines of Yscali, written in a graceful hand.

From Ascalon, Queendom of Inys
High Spring, CE 1003

Lady Marosa, we pray you send us word how that you do. We have not heard from you in too long, and though King Sigoso must rely greatly upon his dutiful heir, we should be glad to read your tidings.

Ours was a short and clement winter. The snow is already thawing in Hróth, which we understand is curious for this time of year.

We hope and trust to embrace you again at your marriage to Prince Aubrecht, whensoever that may take place. Should a

religious perspective be needful, the Arch Sanctarian would be pleased to visit you in Cárscaro.

Yours in fellowship and faith,
Sabran Queen of Inys

Marosa set the letter aside, wondering how her father had reacted to it. No doubt it had wounded his pride. He had let her betrothal stagnate for so long that the head of Virtudom now felt the need to offer the aid of the royal sanctarian, who would have to travel for hundreds of miles, across sea and difficult terrain, to reach Cárscaro. It would reflect poorly on a king, who ought to be able to manage his own family matters without troubling Inys.

'I will reply anon,' she said to Priessa. 'Queen Sabran is kind to ask after my welfare.'

'Yes.'

Priessa laced her into a summer petticoat, her stays and verdugado, and a gown of tawny silk to match her eyes. A white partlet covered her neckline. In recent years, the Yscali fashion had been for gowns that sloped off the shoulders, given the rising heat, but within the palace, there was no such immodesty. Her father saw it as an insult to the Knight of Courtesy.

When Priessa stepped back, Marosa touched the golden Seiikinese pearls in her ears. A betrothal gift from Aubrecht, borne to the West from the Sundance Sea, far away from Yscalin.

'Priessa,' she said, 'is today the same?'

Her friend met her gaze in the mirror.

'Yes,' came her soft reply. 'It is the same.'

Marosa

Every hour of every day was meted out like precious oil. At eight of the clock, Marosa prayed in the Privy Sanctuary. Kneeling on a hassock, she voiced her unending love for the Saint – vanquisher of the Nameless One, saviour of the world – and the six members of his Holy Retinue, each symbolising one of the Virtues of Knighthood.

At nine, she broke her fast with Priessa and the Afleytan sisters. She never called on her other ladies, who lived in fine rooms on the floor below hers, content to enjoy their modest salaries and the prestige that came with serving a princess.

At ten, she practised the harp. Even if she could not change her life, she could vary the temper and pace of her music. She chose 'The Swan Song' – a ballad Aubrecht loved, written in praise of his ancestor.

The next hours were for studying the history and language of Mentendon, soon to be her country by marriage. Aubrecht wrote well in Yscali, and they both spoke Inysh, but to be his consort, she had to master the tongue his people had fought to preserve through centuries of Hróthi stewardship. To understand the triumphs and misfortunes of their past.

Queen Sahar, like many Ersyris, had valued education highly. Until Marosa was sixteen, she had been instructed by the finest scholars in Virtudom. They had all vanished after her mother's death, cut loose without explanation. Now she served as her own tutor. The Library of Isalarico furnished her with the books and documents she required. It also connected to other levels of the palace, allowing her to hear the courtiers on the lower floors as they went about the business of government, even if their voices were distant and distorted.

In all the accounts Marosa had read, she had never heard of a king who kept his heir sequestered from his court. When she was nineteen, she had asked her father if she could join him in council, or at one of his audiences, so she might learn the ways of ruling.

A curious request, King Sigoso had replied coolly. *Do you already seek the throne, Marosa?*

It was treason to imagine the death of the sovereign. That was the last time Marosa had asked. But out of his sight, she kept building her knowledge of history and politics, agriculture and religion, philosophy and rhetoric, poesy. She refused to be ignorant when she was crowned.

That day, she returned to her readings on the Brygstad Terror, a visitation of sweating sickness that had devastated the Mentish court – the only reason Aubrecht was to rule. Since he was the son of a secondborn prince, he had expected to be a sanctarian, not a monarch.

Marosa meant to bolster him until she was Queen of Yscalin. From what she knew, the present High Prince – his granduncle, Leovart – already delegated most of his duties to his relatives. Even before Aubrecht was crowned, he would need support. At last, she would have somewhere to practise the art of politics, and to use her knowledge gainfully, after years of isolation.

At noon, when it was hottest, she retired to her apartments. At three, she proceeded to the garden terrace, where she dined on a salmon casserole. The fish was flavoured with blood orange and saffron, the pastry thick with dried grapes, pine nuts, and blanched almonds.

A bowl of red pears sat in the middle of the table. The ancient symbol of her dynasty, matching her ruby pendant. Yscabel was eating a custard apple, while Ruzio poured glasses of iced perry and Priessa observed the balustrade, her dark brows drawn.

Her patience was rewarded. A small bird came to land, drawn to the seeds they had scattered that morning.

'Oh. How lovely,' Yscabel breathed. 'Is it a greenfinch, Essa?'

'A serin,' Priessa said. 'Most likely from Inys.'

The serin pecked the seeds. Its plumage was black and yellow, and a forked tail kept it balanced. Ever since the molten lava had appeared, it was rare for new birds to come to Cárscaro.

'A handsome bird,' Marosa observed. 'Where does it fly in the winter?'

'Lasia or the Ersyr.' Priessa raised a faint smile. 'A bird that sees much of our world.'

The serin chirruped and took wing. Marosa gazed after it.

'Donmata,' Ermendo said, 'Lord Wilstan Fynch, Duke of Temperance, Dowager Prince of Inys.'

Marosa set her glass aside. 'Thank you, Ermendo.'

Wilstan Fynch stepped on to the terrace. From the sweat on his brow, it had been a hard climb, but he was hale for his age, often going to the plain to exercise with the Hróthi ambassadors. His eyes crinkled when he saw her, banishing the austerity from that long face.

'Donmata.' He took off his bonnet and bowed. 'Good afternoon.'

'Your Grace,' Marosa said in Inysh. 'The heat is very strong today. Would you care for some iced wine?'

'No, thank you. I will take some nutmeg in milk, if I may.'

'Of course.'

Priessa went inside to fetch it. Fynch chose the seat opposite Marosa. Most Inysh nobles dressed to reflect the seasons – a recent fashion – but the Dowager Prince had worn mourning grey for as long as Marosa had known him, with no jewellery but his signet ring. Quite the contrast to his daughter, Queen Sabran of Inys, who glinted with gold whenever she moved.

'It has been far too long, Your Radiance,' Fynch said warmly. 'How do you do?'

'Very well, Your Grace,' Marosa said. 'I trust that you are still comfortable here.'

'The hospitality of Cárscaro is unrivalled. As is your generosity in inviting me to your table again.'

She wished it *were* the Knight of Generosity that moved her. The foreign ambassadors were her only means of glimpsing the world beyond Yscalin. She had long since befriended Sir Robrecht Teldan, the Mentish ambassador, who she found amiable and intelligent.

Her father had never forbidden her to extend invitations, but she sensed it was better for him not to know.

Fortunately, like Sir Robrecht, Fynch understood her preference for privacy.

'Donmata, I came to—' Fynch stopped to accept a cup from Priessa. 'Thank you, Lady Priessa. As swift as your name.'

Priessa inclined her head. 'I am aware of the Inysh liking for nutmeg in the summer, Your Grace.'

'Well, it counters the dry heat, you see, in the absence of a bloodletter.'

Marosa exchanged a glance with Priessa, whose mouth twitched. Inys was the cradle of a faith that ruled four nations, but it had also produced some of the worst physicians in history.

'Your Radiance,' Fynch said to Marosa, 'I will not impose upon you for long, but there is a delicate matter I wanted to raise.' She gave her ladies a small nod, and they left. 'King Sigoso has refused to grant me an audience since the autumn, and even that was not for long, since His Majesty had a headache that day. He and I have much to discuss. Is he well?'

'My father is a devout man, Your Grace. He spends much of his time at prayer.'

'His dedication to the Saint is admirable, but he is a sovereign, not a sanctarian.'

Fynch made her father nervous. She had noticed as soon as the Dowager Prince arrived, replacing a less attentive Inysh ambassador, who had been content to enjoy the spectacular outlooks and steam baths of Cárscaro and only ever meet with the Secretary of State.

'Yscalin was first to join Inys in worship of the Saint,' Fynch continued. 'There has been no greater friendship between realms in all of history. Let us not pain the Knight of Fellowship by allowing it to corrode.'

In her lap, out of sight, Marosa twisted the posy ring on her little finger.

'I assume there is good reason,' she said, 'but I do apologise, Your Grace. I will ask my lord father if he will meet with you as a matter of priority, but in truth, there is little more I can do.'

'Surely he listens to his own daughter.'

'Not as often as you might suppose.'

The words scraped out against her will, like a cough that had burned in her throat for too long. Fynch considered her with small brown eyes, reminding her of his inquisitive namesake.

'Donmata,' he said, 'may I ask when you last left the Palace of Salvation?'

'When I attended the celebration to mark the thousandth year of Berethnet rule.'

'That was three years ago.'

'Indeed.'

Her father had sent her with a heavy contingent of guards. All the way down the mountain, Marosa had thought he would change his mind. And yet the coach had trundled on, out into the lavender.

After a tiring journey, she had been escorted on to a royal galleon, the *Prince Therico*. Her first sight of the sea, the stormy coast of Inys – and then its fabled capital, Ascalon. The seat of Virtudom.

Queen Sabran had been a generous host. Her elegance and wit had dazzled Marosa. They were close in age, and had both lost their mothers young. Perhaps that was why Sabran had paid such careful attention to her comfort, introducing her to as many people as she could. Perhaps it was also why Sabran had refrained from ruling on whether Queen Sahar had forfeited her place in Halgalant, instead leaving the decision to the Principal Sanctarian of Yscalin.

Throughout the twelve days of celebrations, Marosa had dined with Mentish courtiers, all wanting to pay their respects to their future High Princess. She had danced with lords and chieftains, played cards with the Ladies of the Bedchamber, hunted in Chesten Forest. She had even been able to see the Ersyri ambassador, Chassar uq-Ispad, who had not set foot in Cárscaro since her mother was pronounced dead. All diplomacy between Yscalin and the South had ended that day, but Inys maintained a cordial relationship with the Ersyr, and Chassar – a charming giant of a man – had wanted to assure himself of her wellbeing.

Donmata, he had said, keeping his voice low, *if ever you wished to visit the Ersyr, your uncle and aunt would be over-joyed to receive you in Rauca.*

You are very kind, Your Excellency, but I do not think that will be possible.

Not yet.

'It seems a long time,' Fynch said, jolting Marosa back to the present. 'Do you not wish to see more of Yscalin?'

She wanted to tell him that her father had deliberated for months before permitting her to go to Inys. That he would not have let her leave, except that he had no desire to go, and the heir was the only acceptable proxy. That his grip on her had tightened ever since.

'Of course,' she said, 'but His Majesty has no other children. I believe he worries for my safety.'

Fynch did not reply at once, but she knew what he was thinking. Her premature death would cause a succession crisis, but even the unwed and heirless Queen Sabran did not spend her days confined to a single palace, and *her* bloodline kept the Nameless One bound.

'I understand,' Fynch said. 'Have you any word on your marriage to Prince Aubrecht?'

'His Majesty will set a date in due course.'

Again, Fynch was too polite to comment, and again, Marosa read his thoughts. She was some way into her child-bearing years and had no obvious reason not to marry at once.

Perhaps this sudden interest from Inys would finally spur her father to action. The thought lifted her spirits.

'I sail for Ascalon next week,' Fynch said. 'This heat is proving too much for my constitution.' He finished his drink. 'I will return to Cárscaro in time for the Feast of Temperance.'

'I doubt the heat will have eased by then,' Marosa said, 'but I understand the need for a reprieve, my lord.'

'You are most gracious.'

Inys was a cold and rainy isle, battered by the rough winds of the Ashen Sea. It was a wonder Fynch could endure Yscalin at all, but he only sailed back to see his daughter once or twice a year.

Marosa could see why. She lived in a place that was haunted by absence, and if she had been free to choose, she would not have stayed for long.

'I trust that you received a letter from Her Majesty today.' Fynch rose. 'Queen Sabran would be very glad to see you again, if you ever wished to visit. Good afternoon, Your Radiance.'

'And to you, Your Grace.'

****

That night, Marosa knelt in the Privy Sanctuary again, her gaze fixed on a relief carving of Glorian Hartbane, tenth Queen of Inys. Her name had been inscribed beneath her, for every Berethnet queen in history had looked exactly the same as the last.

Marosa was never sure if she would care for it. While she looked a great deal like her mother, she was also herself; surely any stronger resemblance would be painful. But each Berethnet only bore one daughter, who grew into her mirror image – a line of identical women, stretching back over a thousand years. A sign of their divinity.

It had been six centuries since Isalarico the Benevolent, a former King of Yscalin, had seen that sign with his own eyes when Glorian was shipwrecked on his shores. Overcome by her beauty, he had forsaken the old mountain gods to marry her, forming the Chainmail of Virtudom. Because of love, from that day forth, Yscalin had been pledged to the Saint.

Marosa looked down at her posy ring, thinking of Aubrecht. The man who would be her companion for all eternity, even unto Halgalant.

They had only spent twelve days together, always chaperoned by the Privy Council or her ladies. The first time, Aubrecht had come to court her. It had surprised her that her father was considering the match. Mentendon was the strange bird of Virtudom, and its trade with Seiiki – an island that revered sea wyrms – was a constant bone of contention. She had always expected to marry an Inysh lord or a Hróthi chieftain.

Aubrecht had been the soul of courtesy. She recalled his dark eyes and thick copper hair, his smile at the first sight of her. Unsure of how to act, she had found herself turning stiff and reticent. Fortunately, Aubrecht was a Ment, and even quiet Ments were insatiably curious. At supper, he was full of questions about her life, her interests, her ambitions for Yscalin. And when she answered, Aubrecht had listened as if there was no one else in the room.

He was not only thoughtful and well read, but a gifted storyteller. Ments were known for their oil paintings; Aubrecht painted with his words. They took her all the way across Mentendon, so she might imagine herself as its High Princess. In the world he described, they watched ships from the windswept docks of Ostendeur, walked the cobbled streets of Brygstad, rode across the Bridal Forest. She could hear the rushing waters of the Hundert and feel the heavy furs she would need when the winter set in.

By the end of the week, his every look had made her smile. And when he had ridden away from Cárscaro, she felt as if she had lost an old friend.

Aubrecht had returned six months later, once their betrothal was legally binding. She had been afraid that their mutual warmth might have faded, but Aubrecht had seemed delighted to see her again, and Marosa had returned the sentiment. They had toasted the alliance with the finest wines of the Groneyso Valley. There had been a feast, and then a dance.

After, they had sat on a terrace, looking over Cárscaro, and he had taken her gently by the hand, placing the ring on to her finger. *This is a token of troth. A promise that I will cherish you always.*

Marosa was no fool. She knew that two meetings were not enough for an abiding love to bloom, even if she bore his absence like a broken rib. She knew that men could hide their true selves; that Aubrecht might wear a mask, like her father, whose smiles were only a sheath for a blade.

But she wanted to trust Aubrecht. Even if he had been old and unkind, she would have needed him.

Once they were married, she would have duties as his consort in Mentendon. Her father would have to let her go. As soon as she got with child, she would tell him that the fumes of Cárscaro were too dangerous. Then she would tell him the lava was too great a risk to her newborn.

She would not be caged in this palace again.

Even as she imagined escape, the feeling of suffocation returned. The sanctuary had no windows. To distract herself, she slid off the posy ring and read the words engraved along the inner band.

TIME • A FRIEND • UNTO THE END

To Aubrecht, patience was the seventh virtue. Even if they had to wait, their friendship would only grow firmer with time, forming a strong foundation for their marriage.

A strong foundation for her plan.

Her dream, kept out of sight like wine, to ripen with each passing year.

She returned the posy ring to her finger. Glancing over her shoulder, she eased up a loose floor-tile. Hidden underneath it was a mirror on a silver chain, along with a miniature of her mother.

Queen Sahar wore a confident smile. The court painter had been one of her ladies, and had captured her well. Her black hair, drawn back to show a pair of gold Ersyri earrings, and her striking brown eyes, framed by thick lashes. Marosa traced the frame, her chest aching.

Why did you have to leave me?

Now she carefully lifted the necklace, not wanting to smear the glass. The oval pendant was exquisite, a mirror bordered with filigree silver. Her mother had worn it under her partlet. A symbol of the Faith of Dwyn, which even most Southerners no longer followed.

A symbol forbidden in Virtudom.

See yourself in others. Treat them as you would treat yourself, her mother had said, *and hope that they offer you the same grace. That is the way of Dwyn.*

It still hurt to see the necklace and the miniature. Marosa polished the silver to keep it from tarnishing, then used the mirror to look into her own eyes, an amber so bright they were almost orange. The eyes of Oderica the Smith – a prisoner in ancient Cárscaro, and later, the first Queen of Yscalin. She, too, had been trapped in the dark for nine years.

Marosa returned the mirror to its nook and covered it.

Her plan might take her nine years or longer. Perhaps it would cost the rest of her life.

She meant to make Yscalin as safe as Lasia, where those who rejected the dominant faith did not face execution; where people like her mother did not have to convert; where she could embrace her Southern uncle and not have it be seen as a betrayal of the Saint; where people gave each other the grace they gave themselves.

Her marriage to Aubrecht was the first step, granting her the key to her cage. She hoped that he would be her ally, once she worked up the courage to tell him. Unlike the other countries in Virtudom, Mentendon did not kill unbelievers; it even allowed scholars to question the Six Virtues. The House of Lievelyn had affirmed its loyalty to the Saint, but the Ments had initially been converted by force. Surely he would understand the need for tolerance.

She would be patient. By the Saint and the Holy Retinue, for the sake of her kingdom and her sanity, she would cleave to the Red Prince of Mentendon with all her might.

Saint, you offered your mercy and compassion to the Damsel, a woman who did not share your faith. She touched her patron brooch, a shield, the symbol of the Knight of Courage. *Help me return that mercy to Yscalin.*

Melaugo

AFELAYANDA FOREST

KINGDOM OF YSCALIN

CE 1003

'You're certain it's a lindworm?'

Estina Melaugo folded her arms, trying to show the pitiful sliver of muscle that remained to her. She carried her fine Ersyri dagger, which the woodcutter had clearly noticed. His gaze kept darting towards it, and then back to her grimy red hair, her scabbed and hollow face.

'I ask,' Melaugo continued, 'because I do not cull basilisks. Their venom is too dangerous.'

'I've never read a bestiary,' the woodcutter said, 'so I couldn't say for sure.' *You've never read a thing in your life*, Melaugo thought darkly. *Nobody in this backwater can read.* 'My sister happened on its trails and followed them to a cave. It's been slithering out to kill deer, from the bones.'

If it had been a basilisk, there would have been no bones to find. Melaugo loosed a breath.

Are you really doing this again?

'Very well.' She lifted her chin. 'I would usually charge ten gelvas for a lindworm.'

'A heavy price even for nobles,' the woodcutter remarked, 'but we don't deal in coin out here, gold or no.'

'I am well aware. What can you offer me if I slay it?'

'We've a ram for you. A wether.'

Melaugo huffed. 'I will try to ignore that insult. Do you know how dangerous it is to confront a sleeper?'

'He's a good ram.'

'I don't care if your ram is the most virtuous creature since the Saint himself. I am not risking a gruesome death – the worst death in all of recorded history – for the sake of a fucking sheep.'

'You'll need its wool in the cold months.'

'And you will need my blade all year.' Melaugo squared up to him. 'There must be many sleepers in these mountains. This one will not be the last to threaten you. They have slumbered for five centuries. All of them will be hungry when they wake, and sooner or later, deer will not sate them.'

At least she was nearly as tall as the woodcutter, even if her body had turned as thin as a reed. The corners of his mouth pinched.

She had chosen him with care. All of the villagers had been murmuring about the creature, but this man was among their elders, someone who could make decisions. He had reached for his axe when he saw her, intending to chase her back to the trees, before she said the words.

I will slay it.

'I thought you were trading a single kill. That you were planning to move on from here soon,' he said. 'But you want to be one of us.' Melaugo said nothing. 'So be it. If you agree to kill any sleepers that wake in this region, you'll have two meals a day. And the ram as well.'

For a moment, Melaugo could only stare at him.

'You are one word away from a broken jaw,' she bit out. 'What makes you think I would agree to that?'

'Because it would put some fat on your ribs,' he said, his face as hard as granite. 'We've seen you trying to hunt and forage, outsider. And to steal from us. You're lucky we've let you stay in that tree.'

She had never wanted to kill someone as intensely as she did in that moment.

'The meals are a start,' he said. 'Win our trust, earn your keep, and we won't drive you off. There's an empty house in the village, if you want it. But first you'll need to slay that lindworm.'

Melaugo pictured a fire, a warm bed. *Yes,* she thought. *Apparently, you really are doing this again.*

'The ram,' she gritted out. 'And the food.'

'If you survive, you'll need to keep away from the village for a few more days, so we can be sure you don't have the plague.'

'I've survived this long without you.'

The woodcutter narrowed his eyes. 'The lair is about two miles north,' he said. 'Follow the stream to the Haytha Tree, then turn east and walk for about a hundred more steps.'

'What the fuck is the Haytha Tree?'

'It's a yew. You'll know it when you see it.' His smile was grim. 'No doubt you'll smell the sleeper when you're close.'

****

All children of Virtudom knew the old tales – taught in every sanctuary and every household, rich or poor. How the Nameless One – a vile red wyrm – had emerged from the

Dreadmount to conquer the world, only to be vanquished by an Inysh knight, known to history as the Saint.

Five hundred years later, the Dreadmount had erupted again, and from its mouth had soared five more wyrms, the High Westerns, led by Fýredel. All made in the image of the Nameless One. All bent, for no discernible reason, on the utter destruction of humankind.

They had brought a flock of wyverns from the Dreadmount – smaller and more agile wyrms, no less terrible. On the orders of Fýredel, the wyverns had flown across the world, using its animals to breed vicious servants: basilisks, cockatrices, ophiotaurs, and many others.

For over a year, the Draconic Army – the wyrms, the wyverns, and the beasts they had spawned – had laid waste to the continents in a time known as the Grief of Ages. They had razed cities, burned crops, and spread a plague that made the victim feel as if their blood was burning. At last, the Saint's Comet had ended the violence, stripping the creatures of their fire. The creatures had crawled into every cave and mine and pit they could find, laying down to sleep like stone.

There were thought to be many thousands of sleepers, lurking in the deep forgotten places of the world. For centuries, they had not stirred unless they were disturbed.

But now the Draconic Army was waking of its own accord.

Melaugo hiked uphill, past firs, stone pines, and cork oaks. She still had no idea if the problem extended beyond Yscalin, how long it had been going on, or if King Sigoso knew of it. The beasts were stirring unpredictably, and so far, no wyverns or wyrms had been sighted.

But even one Draconic brute could devastate a settlement. And where there was fear, there was always profit.

That or a bowl of gruel and a sheep.

'What did you *think* he was going to offer you?' she muttered to herself. 'A banquet and a milk bath?'

She flexed her right hand, then her left, committing the feel of her fingers to memory. One did not confront a sleeper and not expect to lose a limb. Culling was a crime of opportunity, like housebreaking. The creature might be on the hunt, wide awake, or lying still as a boulder.

Even in a drought, this forest remained green and shaded, nourished by mountain streams, but the ground was unyielding. Though Melaugo was in her early twenties, she felt as stiff and weary as a woman thrice her age.

At noon, she came upon an enormous old yew, marked with the same runes she had seen when she first arrived in this region. This must be the Haytha Tree. She sat beside the stream to eat the pine nuts she had gathered.

During her time in Perunta, she had loved to dance in alehouses and climb the cliffs for sport. Now less than a mile on foot was exhausting.

She splashed her face, filled her waterskin, then checked her compass and turned east. After a hundred steps, she noticed a trail of animal bones and followed it away from the stream.

Before long, she reached the mouth of a cave. She leaned inside, only to grimace and withdraw. It was filthy, redolent of brimstone, and she could see the telltale yellowing on the walls.

The evidence of a sleeper.

Melaugo took a deep breath. It had been more than three months since she had last done this.

She knelt to unpack her supplies. A tunic went over her mail, made of waxed leather to keep out blood and spittle. The way the Draconic plague spread was a mystery – some were more likely to catch it than others – but all of the monsters were thought to carry it, and Melaugo took no chances. Best to treat it like the pestilence and cover up.

A hood came next, then gauntlets and steel greaves, a thick cloth for her mouth and nose, and a pair of rivet spectacles. All bought in Aperio, when she was flush with coin. Other than the bridge of her nose and a sliver of her brow, not an inch of her skin was on show.

Now she prepared her weapons: crossbow, rapier, billhook, splitting maul. Even the most unsavoury cullers never used rifles; it was perilous enough to risk an open flame inside a lair, let alone gunpowder, even though it wounded sleepers.

No, Melaugo could make do without powder, even if it took more sweat. She used the rusty hook on her belt to span her crossbow.

Next, she took out her firesteel, lit the candle in her mining lantern, and latched it shut. It might not be enough. Each time she entered a lair, there was a chance the sulphurous air would ignite, or that her light would go out altogether, stranding her in the dark with a monster. Few cullers lasted beyond their first or second kill. She was already on borrowed time.

Her palms sweated as she grasped her shield and lantern. She had lost her bear spear – her best weapon – during her last cull; her chances were even lower than usual.

Still, she did not ask the Saint for protection. She took his name in vain now and then, but had not prayed since her parents had been taken from her.

A few spiders darted away from her light. Her throat burned as she inched along the first passage, stopping to listen every so often. She edged around a corner, avoiding bones and smears of blood. It was thought that wyverns fed on lava, but their offspring relished flesh.

As Melaugo crawled on, waiting for her lantern to blow up in her face, she thought back to the bestiaries she had read, considering her opponent. The lindworm was an engorged serpent. It could suffocate her with its coils, but at least it didn't spit a venom that melted flesh and bone, like the basilisk.

Around her lantern, all was black. It was best to lure sleepers outside for the fight, but this cave was too deep and narrow for that.

At the end of another tunnel, she negotiated a small opening and slid into a crouch on the other side. Thanks to the cloth she had tied to her soles, her landing was almost silent. She held up her lantern and waited for her eyes to adjust. This cavern was larger, the air dry and hot.

And there was the lindworm, surrounded by chewed bones.

Once it must have been an adder or a slowworm or some other legless animal, minding its own business, only for a wyvern to transfigure it. Now it was at least twenty feet long and encased in Draconic armour, as coarse and tough as volcanic rock.

It was also, mercifully, asleep.

Melaugo hung up her lantern. If the lindworm destroyed her only light source, she would die.

Her heart was beating harder than she liked. As she put her shield down, she remembered her first kill. A foul cave in Aperio, so tight that it had trapped her twice. The chilling sight of the culebreya – a winged serpent, curled in a hollow. The stony rasping of its breath.

And the realisation, terrible in its magnitude, that all the stories of the past were true.

That monsters *did* lurk in the dark.

She locked a bolt into her crossbow. According to rumour, meteoric iron was best for killing Draconic things, but nobody knew where to find it. This bolt, tipped with common steel, would only work if she hit a weak point. In absolute silence, she took aim, blinking hard as her sight blurred again. Even here, staring at a creature that might eat her alive, her own hunger felt more urgent. She waited for the beast to move, to open its accursed eyes.

'Wake up,' she ordered.

The lindworm remained still.

It was coiled in a way that might conceal gaps in its hide. If it was going to keep its eyes shut, she would have to get closer. Assuming its slumber was as deep as it seemed, she could use her bill-hook to pry off a scale, but that was a last resort. She took a few steps forward.

The lindworm raised its head. Each of its fangs was as long as her face.

'Well met, serpent.' Melaugo bared her own teeth in a nervous grin. 'Did I wake you?'

A rattle stemmed from its maw, raising the hairs on her nape.

'No.' Her smile faded. 'Saint, you were ... waiting. You sensed me, so you set a trap.'

Before the implications could sink in, the lindworm began to uncoil, its hiss echoing around the chamber. Long ago, its eyes would have blazed with the fire of the wyvern that had created it. Now they were like dying embers. More than likely, then, the sire was still asleep.

Melaugo stood within striking range. As the lindworm moved towards her, she glimpsed the vulnerability she needed – a missing scale over its heart, where some brave soul had tried to kill it in the Grief.

All at once, the lindworm attacked. She let the bolt spring from her crossbow, missing its eye by an inch.

Then she ran.

The cave was larger than she had anticipated, giving her room to avoid the lindworm. Fortunate, because the bastard thing was clearly in the mood for a chase. It followed her around a limestone column, its breath hot on her back, reeking of blood. She tossed the crossbow, snatched up her shield, and drew her rapier.

Her lantern guttered by the entrance, casting bizarre shadows. Even though she was slow and weak, Melaugo let her instincts take over, trusting herself to avoid every strike. She spun with her shield, just in time to block a lunge that might have finished her. Wherever she turned, the lindworm was in close pursuit, its huge body rasping in her wake, threatening to trip and squeeze her. Those coils seemed to be everywhere, all over the ground.

With a growl, she dashed after the weak spot. It was only about as wide as her fist, but that was plenty of room for a rapier. When another coil blocked her way, she took a risk and scrambled over it, feeling its inner heat as she rolled off its back. Its hide was not slick, like that of a snake, but rough enough to cut bare skin. Only her gloves and greaves kept her safe.

Her body was already protesting. When she had faced other sleepers, there had always been a surge of strength, an icy rush of clarity. This time, it refused to come. The food she had forced down – the dried fish, the berries, the nuts – had not been enough for a fight like this. She stabbed, but the tip of her rapier only scraped along thick armour, making her curse.

Her shield was snatched from her grasp. Somehow she slipped away once more, but her primal instincts were failing. If she did not flee now, she would have crawled into her own grave. But she was so tired, and so hungry, the weakness slowing her. Fatally slowing her.

Out of nowhere, a tail whipped into her ribs, slamming her against the cavern wall. Her spectacles broke and fell off her face. She hit the ground, still clutching her rapier, head spinning.

The creature loomed above her, its eyes illuminating its face. For one dreadful moment, Melaugo wanted to give up and let it drag her away. She wanted to stop fighting and sleep.

As she stared into its gullet, she wondered how long she would last in its belly. The thought knocked her apathy loose. Her parents' faces flashed before her. Liyat appeared like a waking dream, shouting at her to get up, as the lindworm prepared for the kill. That loathsome mouth yawned open, ready to eat Melaugo whole. She waited for it to unhinge its jaw—

—and thrust her blade into the roof of its mouth.

A deafening screech. A shudder of sinew. Thick dark blood splattered her front and seeped along her sleeve. In one desperate movement, Melaugo wrenched her sword back and dived out of reach. A pair of iron fangs clanged down an inch from where her boots had been.

Melaugo smelled victory. More importantly, she smelled food. With the last of her agility, she plunged her rapier into the weak spot. The lindworm thrashed as gouts of its blood spurted out. With a heaving chest, Melaugo took her maul and hacked off its appalling head.

Her lantern flickered out.

She blindly groped out of the cave. Outside, in the daylight, she took off her left vambrace and shoved up her sleeve to check her arm. No sign of a scratch or graze. With a laugh, she dropped to her knees, and then vomited.

****

It took a long time to get back from the lair. Longer still to find the woodcutter. Seeing her alive, he gaped at her as if she were the Saint reborn. He kept his distance, but pointed to her first payment.

By the time Melaugo reached her oak, irritable ram in tow, the sun had almost set.

'I swear to the Saint,' she said, 'you had better be as good as gold, or I *will* eat you, Lord Gastaldo.'

The ram bleated.

'Yes, that's your name.' She lashed the rope around a birch. 'He's a miserable old ram, too.'

Leaving the animal to sulk, she ducked into her tree. The hollow was larger than one might think from the outside, with room enough for her weapons and the crude tools she had carved from wood.

The day she found this shelter, she had not eaten for over a week. Though dark and dirty, it had given her protection from the wind and rain.

She set down her mail, which she had already cleaned in the stream. Now to wait and see if she did have the plague.

In Perunta, she had been strong as a packhorse. Now her hip bones pushed out like knuckles on a fist, and she could see all of her ribs. They were bruising from the fight. All that work for the promise of food, which would likely amount to no more than a bowl of stew and a hunk of bread. She sat down to eat the two small fish she had dried the week before.

Out of nowhere, her stomach turned. She barely made it outside before coughing up a gush of bile. A good thing she *had* struck this deal, even if it killed her. She was already on the brink of death.

As a child on the streets of Oryzon, she had feared she would always be alone. She should have hoped for that outcome.

It would have prepared her to die alone, too.

****

Melaugo had not always been a killer of Draconic things; neither had she always been a vagrant. She had been raised on a vineyard near Vazuva, where her parents had made wine, like many in the Groneyso Valley, where the breeze was always clement and the River Gáuria kept the land green.

As soon as she could walk, Melaugo had learned to pick grapes. Her parents had been poor – they were smallholders, carrying out the hard labour of winemaking alone – but even if the work had been endless, Melaugo remembered their love, both for her and for each other.

And then King Sigoso had introduced the temperance duty, apparently to curb overindulgence across Yscalin. When the nobles were exempted from it, her parents had grown bitter. And after a poor harvest, leaving them all with empty bellies, they had grown angry.

At last, they had started to smuggle their wine.

They had been caught and jailed within a year, but Melaugo had only been nine, young enough to be deemed innocent. Wrestled into an orphanage, she had spat upon a statue of the Saint, demanding he return her family to her. A sanctarian had beaten her with a knotted belt, one knot for each of the Six Virtues. That same night, she had climbed out of a window and limped away, determined to find her parents.

Some children might have curled up and died. Melaugo was too stubborn. By the time she was eleven, she was a cutpurse in the Port of Oryzon, preying on mariners and drunks, drinking rain and stealing food, sleeping in any rathole she could find.

Thirteen years later, little had changed. The hollow of a tree was only one step from the cobblestones.

****

The fight had pushed her starving body to the limit. Part of her thought she would die in her sleep. Instead, she woke in the smothering heat of midday, bruised and tender, parched and sticky.

Melaugo brushed an oak spider from her forehead. She peered at her fingers, checking for the redness that heralded the plague. They remained the same deep olive as always, with the same tiny scars from fishhooks and fights.

With a dry mouth, she heaved on a tunic, tasting blood. Her gums were raw again.

Once dressed, she walked to her traps, head throbbing. Finding no fresh catches, she returned to her tree, too weak to hunt or fish.

A round dark loaf waited outside.

She collapsed by the oak and picked up the bread. Still warm. With a watering mouth, she sank her teeth into it, breaking the crust. It was coarse and gritty and the best thing she had ever tasted.

When she had first arrived, she had thought her crossbow would be enough to keep her fed, but hares and birds were faster than Draconic things. She had spied on the villagers as they foraged, to see which mushrooms and berries they chose, but that had only ever quelled the hunger for so long.

She ate every crumb of the bread and washed it down with a mouthful of water from the stream. Lying on the hard earth in the hollow, she imagined herself back to the coast, waking up with Liyat in her room above the shop. Meeting her on the warm sands of Lovers' Cove, where the smugglers hid their cargo. That first kiss on a starlit wharf in Perunta.

Your pride will kill you, Estina. Her voice drifted from the memory. *Just this once, I will swallow mine first.*

****

Each day, another loaf of dark bread came, sometimes with a smudge of butter or a wedge of grainy cheese. Melaugo had eaten six of them by the time one of the villagers came to her oak.

She stood up a little too fast. Once the faintness had subsided, she emerged from the hollow, blinking in the daylight.

A sinewy woman in her winter years waited outside, furrowed as a baked walnut, with callused hands from split-ting wood and long hair in a braid. Melaugo recognised her from the day she arrived.

Unless you can offer something we need, you are on your own, outsider.

'Have you decided I'm not catching?' Melaugo said icily. 'Or do you already want another beast slaughtered?'

'Neither.' She eyed Melaugo. 'If you'd told us you're a culler, we'd have taken you into the village at once. You even have your own weapons. Why hide it until you were starving?'

'I hoped you might take pity, you heartless—'

'We've not survived this long by giving alms to outsiders. We've enough sick and frail of our own to support,' was the curt reply. 'I'd have liked to leave you here for another week or two, to make sure you're not tainted, but you're wanted at the alehouse. There's a man.'

'A man?'

Her stomach turned cold. Any new arrival could be an agent of the king.

'An outsider. A rich one, from the looks of him,' the woman said. Melaugo tensed. 'Don't trouble yourself. He's no outlaw hunter. But he *is* searching for a young woman with red hair and eyes like honey. Thought it sounded like you, culler.'

Melaugo absorbed the words.

'This man,' she said. 'Does he have scars on his face, from the pox?'

'He does.' The woman looked her up and down. 'You should come and claim a meal.'

She returned to the trees. Melaugo leaned against the oak, clutching her sore ribs, and sighed.

The Knights Defendant had not found her, but somehow, Harlowe had.

Melaugo

AFELAYANDA FOREST
KINGDOM OF YSCALIN
CE 1003

Triyenas lay in the depths of Afelayanda Forest. It was home to seventy people, who lived beyond the law of the Saint. Now and then, it harboured outsiders, who sought it for distance from the authorities.

No map showed Triyenas. Few knew it existed. Liyat had told Melaugo about it, having learned the story from a friend in the region. A young man had been caught with an idol of Fruma, that old metalworking god of the mountains. Eluding the pyre, he had fled into the vast forest, where he had noticed strange runes on the trees and followed them to a tiny village. He had hidden there for twenty years, until his face and name were forgotten.

A legend passed between lawbreakers. A place that would turn a blind eye to them, where they could escape the constraints of society. Melaugo had not been sure it existed until she laid eyes on it, weeks after leaving Aperio.

She dripped with sweat as she approached the wooden alehouse, thatched with rye straw, at the edge of the village.

A few people gave her nods as she passed. A week ago, they would have forced her back into the trees without pity, but now she was their culler. She was useful.

Inside the alehouse, she looked around slowly, counting fifteen villagers, all talking in low voices as they ate. It had been months since she had been this close to so many people.

And there was Captain Gian Harlowe, sitting among them.

He sat in a dark corner, holding an earthen cup. As usual, he wore silver cufflinks and a jerkin of silk brocade. It was a wonder nobody had robbed him on the mountain roads that wound into the forest, but the icy stare and raw-boned face must have kept the thieves at bay. The woman serving drinks was clearly fascinated. She had probably never seen real brocade.

When Melaugo stepped into his line of sight, Harlowe scoured her with his gaze. She wore the best of her three wrinkled shirts, and boots so worn the soles were peeling off with every step.

'Estina,' he said. 'Dare I ask how you are?'

'First,' Melaugo said, 'you will tell me how the fuck you found me.'

'Liyat.'

Damn her.

'Sit down,' Harlowe said in Yscali. 'From the looks of you, I'm amazed you can stand.'

Melaugo obeyed, noting the trencher of food on the table. She imagined the faults he was counting: her brittle hair, her dull and sunken eyes, the number of times she had darned her own clothes.

'Liyat is a day or two behind me,' Harlowe said.

Melaugo looked up. 'She's coming?'

'She needed to find another horse first.' He gave the villagers a scathing look. 'I had to give these churls a quarter of my food, just so they would do me the great honour of fetching you.'

'There is always a price here.'

'Aye.' He interlocked his fingers, showing a sapphire ring. 'Not quite the haven from the tales, is it?'

Melaugo pursed her lips.

'Drink this,' Harlowe said. 'You sound parched.' He slid a cup towards her, full of the pine milk she had seen the villagers making. 'I've never known Yscalin so hot. Not in the spring.'

'Loosen just one fastening on your shirt. You'll feel better.'

'Don't sauce me, Estina. What do you think you're doing in Afelayanda Forest?'

'I am surviving, Harlowe, and I will thank you to leave me to it.'

'How long have you been here?'

'Three months.' She wrenched her gaze from his meal, back to his stony face. 'I assume Liyat told you what happened in Perunta.'

'Suylos did. Liyat told me she took you to Aperio.'

'I would have gone to the cove, but Suylos cut me loose. He didn't want me near him.'

'Yes, because the comptroller wants you locked in a gibbet. You were a liability to Suylos,' Harlowe said, 'but you could have blended into another city, even with that hair of yours.' He leaned towards her across the table. 'So why draw attention to yourself by culling, Estina?'

'You know?'

'Of course I know. You flouted one of the Grief Laws,' he said. 'The heralds are still roaring your description in the north. It didn't take us long to work out who the Venger of Vazuva was.' He shook his head. 'What sort of cocksure numbskull gives herself a name like that?'

She slouched into her seat. Even at her lowest point, she had never wanted to disappoint him.

'The Comptroller of Perunta is one enemy to have,' Harlowe said, 'but the Secretary of State, quite another.' A muscle feathered in his square jaw. 'For the love of the Saint, stop slavering over that poor chicken and eat it. You're making me uncomfortable.'

'I've already eaten.'

'A large mouthful of air, was it?'

Melaugo gritted her teeth. Harlowe pushed the trencher towards her, and at last, hunger overpowered her pride. She ripped into a chicken leg and wolfed a slice of hard white cheese.

'Tell me about Perunta first,' Harlowe said, watching her. 'Then we'll get on to the culling.'

'You know about Perunta,' she said through her mouthful.

'In your own words, Estina.'

Melaugo swallowed painfully. She had to remember to chew.

'The comptroller seized the *Windstorm* and hanged the entire crew, along with the landing party. The cargo included valuable Eastern goods from Mentendon,' she said. 'Suylos was furious. He rallied every moon-curser and knave he knows to help break into the Customs House. Not only to recover the cargo, but to show King Sigoso who rules the coast.'

'Suylos is a dependable ally when he blows cold,' Harlowe said grimly, 'but when he blows hot, he's a beef-witted fool.' His mouth thinned. 'I should never have left you with him.'

'No. I'm glad you did,' Melaugo admitted. 'I loved working for the Greenshanks. Lovers' Cove felt like a home to me. Even when it was hard and bloody, it … felt like having a family again.'

Harlowe narrowed his eyes.

'Well,' he said. 'I'm glad to hear it.'

Melaugo took a sip of pine milk. For all her smarting pride, she was glad to see Harlowe again. A person who knew her better than she knew herself, after so much torturous solitude.

'Half of us kept the guards and preventers busy,' she went on. 'The rest meant to steal into the Customs House and run the plunder to the smuggling tunnels. Liyat was in the latter party.'

'Liyat didn't say she was involved.' Harlowe frowned. 'It isn't like her to indulge Suylos in nonsense. Why risk being spotted with a band of rioting smugglers in Perunta?'

'There were some Mentish relics in the shipment. She couldn't let them be destroyed in the fray, so she agreed to help.' Melaugo dropped her gaze. 'The officers cornered her. Liyat will maim if she must, but she would never kill. Not even to save her own life.'

'So you did it for her.'

She nodded, seeing it again. The utter chaos of the clash. The customs officers, with their swords and rifles, eager to destroy the smugglers that plagued their coast – and then Liyat in the grip of a city guard, hauled from the Customs House, bound for prison, where they would find her Pardic pendant, marking her as an unbeliever. She would be on a pyre in days.

And so Estina Melaugo had drawn her pistol and fired. She had only meant to wound the officer, but the bullet had struck his neck. The comptroller himself had seen, and the red hair had made her stand out like a jester. She had fled to the east, turned culler, turned outlaw.

And now she was a starveling in the wilderness.

'She wasn't seen,' Melaugo said. 'They didn't have a chance to remove her mask.'

'So she took you to Aperio to lie low,' Harlowe said. 'I'll ask you again. Why start culling?'

'Because I can't do anything else, Harlowe,' she snapped. 'I squandered my apprenticeship. I have no useful skills.' She tore the other leg off the chicken. 'I did try to find work, but there was nothing that paid like culling. If you can secure a noble patron, it can change your destiny.'

'There are *nobles* getting involved in this business?'

'Only when the beasts hurt their interests. My old patron has a valuable mine on her land, but it was infested with lindworms. All that red gold, untouched for centuries.'

'Red gold.' Harlowe cocked his head. 'Was your patron Princess Viterica, by any chance?'

'Indeed it was. She paid *very* well,' Melaugo admitted. 'Even without the lindworms, it would have been danger-ous to enter a mine that old.' She shoved another scrap of chicken into her mouth. 'The other cullers died in that hole. Viterica gave me all of their coin, but it still wasn't enough. I didn't just want a bribe for the comptroller. I wanted some money for me.'

'The curse of one who knows what it is to be truly poor,' Harlowe said. 'To be for ever shadowed by the memory and fear of need.' He took a spill from his jerkin. 'What then?'

'An anonymous patron offered me a contract,' Melaugo said, 'but the meeting was an ambush. I escaped by the skin of my teeth. The Mayor of Aperio informed Lord Gastaldo

Yelarigas, who ordered the Knights Defendant to hunt me down like a hound, so I could be thrown on a pyre. Liyat had told me about Triyenas, but … I didn't really expect to find it, desperate though I was. I had nothing to offer or trade, so the villagers drove me into the trees to starve.'

'Seems they almost succeeded.' Harlowe looked around. 'So why are you allowed here now?'

'I offered them the one thing I can do. If I cull, they'll give me food.'

'Suylos would have shot you if you'd struck a deal that bad for him.'

That was true.

'I can stay here now,' Melaugo said mulishly. 'I killed my first the other day. I can survive outside the law.'

'If you don't die in some vile lair.' Harlowe held the spill over the candle on the table, so the end caught fire, and used it to light his pipe. 'You'll have your hands full very soon, Estina. I've heard of more and more sleepers coming out to hunt. There have even been wyverlings on the wing.'

'Where?'

'Lasia and Inys, so far.' He puffed on his pipe. 'A second Grief is inevitable. If the creatures are stirring… so are the wyverns. And so, in turn, are *their* masters.'

Melaugo searched his face. 'You really think the High Westerns are waking?'

'Aye,' he said, 'and the highborn will soon need someone to accuse.'

'What do you mean?'

'Sigoso Vetalda already blames the cullers, and the commons in general, for the stirrings. He claims people are disturbing the beasts for sport, and that's why they're coming out of their lairs.'

'Sometimes that *is* the case, but not always.'

'He's armouring himself against any implication of fault. He knows that some would hold the monarch personally responsible, claiming he'd angered the Saint, or some such blether. Better to accuse the commons, so we only ever turn upon ourselves.'

'Queen Sabran and King Raunus both allow culling. I assume the Ments do as well.'

'Sigoso has his own ideas about justice and truth.' He blew out smoke. 'Such a pious man.'

His face hardened when he spoke of the king. It had interested Melaugo since she first noticed. For years, Harlowe had abetted the knaves of Yscalin. He had used his ship to transport smuggled goods, and even found new runners, like her. It was a great risk for a wealthy Inysh naval officer, trusted by the Queen of Inys, who called Sigoso her friend and ally.

If she found out that Harlowe was depriving him of taxes, she would not be pleased, yet he persisted. A perseverance that spoke of a grudge.

But what grudge could a smuggler have against a king?

'You will have already realised,' Harlowe said, 'that Liyat and I are not leaving you here to be killed by a beast. I didn't trudge up these mountains to walk down empty-handed. And I didn't pull you from the cobblestones to see you reduced to this state again.'

'I never asked you to save me.'

'Don't start, Estina.'

'I am four and twenty, Harlowe. My decisions are my own,' Melaugo said, 'and I am staying here.'

'Among people who almost let you starve, risking life and limb for your supper?' Harlowe kept her pinned with those cold orbs of his, stripping away her defences. It was irritating. 'No. I'm going to make you a better offer, and you are going to accept it.'

'Go on.'

'I need a new boatswain.'

She blinked. 'What?'

'You heard me. If you can slay a sleeper, you have the nerves I need.'

'Wait.' She sat up a little. 'You want me to live on your ship?'

'You say it like I've asked you to be the local ratcatcher.' He blew his smoke towards the villagers. 'I don't just want you to live on my ship, Estina. I want you to be the voice of my crew.'

'The voice of your—' She had to laugh. 'Why would your crew ever listen to some orphaned nobody?'

'Because you're the sort of orphaned nobody who shoots a customs officer, damning herself to the gibbet, to protect a crewmate. And seafarers, above all people, respect that sort of loyalty.'

Suylos had rebuked her for saving Liyat, calling her a lovesick fool. The idea that anyone could respect it was news to her.

'I don't like this,' she informed Harlowe. 'What happened to the last boatswain?'

'Rogue wave.' Harlowe sucked on his pipe. 'I won't lie to you. There are risks. But the *Rose* is a fine ship, a good home. You'd have food and drink and new sights each morning. You could see the sky lights dancing in the North. I'd even take you as far as the East.'

'Harlowe, I'm no seafarer. You know this very well. Doesn't a boatswain need years of experience?'

'You'd have to work for the position. I'd start you off as an ordinary,' he said, 'but I've told my crew about you, and they're willing to let you prove yourself. Knowing you're a culler will only warm them to you. In any case, you know enough to work your way around a ship. I made sure of that when I passed you to Suylos. I told him to put you in a few sea parties.'

'You've been *planning* this?'

'In case of a catastrophe.' His gaze was cool and steady. 'You've been fighting to survive Yscalin since the day you were born. Even before you washed up in Oryzon, your parents were struggling, because the Six Virtues only apply to certain people. There's no generosity for the poor, no temperance or courage among the robber knights. No justice for cullers like you, who've kept people safe and been vilified for it. Your parents saw that. It's why they defied the king.'

'And I thought it was simple greed.'

'No. The temperance duty opened their eyes to the damned hypocrisy of it all. They died in a debtors' prison, racked by the bloody flux. Do you want to go the same way?'

'Obviously not.'

He had found out for her, when she told him their names. She tried not to imagine their deaths.

'I would have left you with the Greenshanks,' Harlowe said, 'but now you're an outlaw, you'll always be hunted. Leave the land of the Saint – all this sanctimonious nonsense – and join my crew.'

'I would bring down the wrath of the comptroller on your heads, not to mention King Sigoso.'

'The high seas are not subject to Yscali law.'

She could almost see it. A life on the waves, and new lands ahead, never having to beg for her supper. The idea filled her with a sudden, painful longing – a hunger for escape, for *more*.

And then she closed her eyes to the vision, like a tortoise withdrawing into its shell.

'I can't leave,' she said. 'This is my home, Harlowe.'

'You only say that because you've never known anything else.'

'No. I love Yscalin,' she insisted. 'I loved my life on the coast. I loved running circles around the preventers. I love good wine and crisp red pears, summers so hot you feel like Fýredel is—'

'Don't speak that name.' His voice was soft. 'The right wing hears all, wherever he sleeps.'

Harlowe might think himself enlightened, but in the end, he was as superstitious as any other sailor. Then again, so was Melaugo. Like many lowborn winemakers, her parents had carried out all sorts of rituals to ensure a good harvest, like planting corn dolls in the ground. It was probably against some law, but when you were as poor as dregs, survival came first.

'I *can't* leave,' she said again. 'Liyat is here.'

'Liyat will not settle with a partner. You're chasing a pipe dream with that one, Estina.'

'You don't know her well enough to say that.'

'I've known her longer than you,' Harlowe reminded her, 'and I know that she is married to her work. She also has a thicker hull than my ship. Not even a cannon would get through.'

The fear that had circled in her mind for months, silent and sinister, and Harlowe had pulled it from her skull, slammed it on to the table, and sliced its guts out, forcing her to confront it.

'You can still visit,' he said. She looked away. 'Half my crew have lovers waiting on the shore.'

'Do you?' she retorted.

'No.'

His face turned so cold, she dared not hit back.

'I've business in Oryzon,' he said, 'but perhaps Liyat can talk sense into you. If you change your mind, I'll be staying at my lodgings there until the Feast of High Spring. You might love Yscalin, but from what I can tell, it will never love you, Estina. Sooner or later, you'll be too slow and weak to slaughter beasts, and the law of the Saint will finally catch up to you.'

'Then I'll cut wood. I'll learn to hunt,' Melaugo growled. 'I'll find another way to survive.'

'You were meant for more than that.'

Melaugo sank into a morose silence. Harlowe watched her pick at the last of the chicken.

'Don't come after me again, Gian,' she said gruffly. 'I was never your burden.'

'Try not to be your own burden, Estina.'

****

Liyat arrived at the oak the next evening. Melaugo watched her approach from the hollow. She saw her low surroundings as if for the first time, and a fresh wave of excruciating shame went through her.

It had been over a year since Liyat had last seen her. Melaugo knew she was no great beauty, but at least she had owned a comb on the coast, and possessed enough coin to afford lemon soap. Perhaps out of fear of any more change, she had not been able to bring herself to cut her waist-length hair, but now it was dull and dishevelled, and her teeth, already crooked, felt loose.

At last, she emerged from the hollow. Liyat took half a step towards her, holding up a saddle lantern.

'Estina,' she breathed. 'Is that really you?'

'It's me.' Melaugo forced a smile. 'Don't I make a dashing outlaw?'

Liyat closed the distance between them and embraced her, tight enough that it stoked her bruises. It had been so long since anyone had touched her, Melaugo had almost forgotten how it felt to be held. She was as starved of human touch as she had been of food.

'You're so thin,' Liyat said into her shoulder. 'I feel every bone in your body.'

'I'm all right, Liyat.'

'Do not deceive me a second time. You said you would stay in Aperio.' Liyat drew back, her gaze hard and accusatory. 'I can't believe you turned culler. That's why Gastaldo Yelarigas is hunting you.'

'Liyat, I had no—'

'Do *not* tell me you had no other choice. You had *no* other choice than to start killing sleepers?'

'I did it for us,' Melaugo said hotly. 'I thought I could earn enough coin to bribe the comptroller to clear my name, so I could return to Perunta. Or find somewhere else for us to stay.' Her shoulders wilted. 'And then it all just fell apart. I didn't know what to do but come here.'

Liyat now had a strange look on her face.

'I should never have told you about this place,' she said. 'Better you left Yscalin altogether.' She breathed in, collecting herself. 'I didn't want to lose my temper. May I come in?'

Melaugo reluctantly showed her into the hollow. Liyat stooped to get inside. She observed the earthen floor, the spiders, the filthy sack Melaugo had been using as a make-shift pallet.

'Estina,' she said, 'how long have you lived this way?'

'I have managed.'

'Harlowe told me about your deal. These people have lived off the land since the Grief of Ages, and they have each other to rely on. How long did you think you could last on your own?'

'I've lasted three months. Not so bad for a city woman.'

'And now you look an inch from death. If culling is all these people will accept from you—'

Liyat took off her thin summer cloak. Even travelworn, she looked too presentable for the wilderness.

'The shop,' Melaugo said. 'Is it all right?'

'Yes. The guards never saw my face, thanks to you. I can remain in Perunta.' Liyat removed her bandolier, which held a pistol and knives. 'Harlowe went to Lovers' Cove to see you. Suylos sent him to me, and he asked me to take him to Aperio. That's where we read your note.'

'I do not appreciate you telling Harlowe where I am. He already thinks I'm an abject failure.'

'He cares about you. And you *must* take him up on his offer.'

'I can't.'

'You would prefer to live here, wanted for high treason for the rest of your life?' Liyat said, frustration sharpening her voice. 'Harlowe offers you more than escape. He offers you the entire world. What more could you ask?'

Melaugo sank on to the hard earth. Liyat knelt in front of her, seeking her gaze.

'What is it?' she asked. 'Why would you rather stay than leave?'

Even as she spoke, Melaugo could only drink her in. The dark curls, drawn back loosely, that framed deep grey eyes and sharp cheekbones. The tiny mole above the corner of her lip.

Is it not obvious, she wanted to ask, *why I don't want to leave?*

'I can't … let them win,' she said stiffly. Liyat watched her face. 'I was born in Yscalin. I have lived and worked and fought to survive this fucking country. Why should I leave my own home because I am poor and orphaned? Because I am not enough for the Saint?'

'Estina.' Liyat cupped her elbows. 'You have known what it is to be hungry and scared. I understand why Lovers' Cove meant so much to you. I truly do. But we cannot get it back.'

'We could. If we just wait—' Her voice cracked. 'The Donmata might be kind, like her mother. The stance on culling might change. Sooner or later, Yscalin will repeal the Act of Restraint, to reflect attitudes in the rest of Virtudom. Maybe I could earn a pardon.'

'I hear too many *mights* and *maybes*,' Liyat said, her tone forbearing. 'No one knows the Donmata Marosa. Even if she *is* more sympathetic than King Sigoso, it could be decades before she reigns. Don't live in denial.' She firmed her grip. 'We cannot turn back time, but we can keep on living. If you won't follow Harlowe, then you are coming with me to Ortégardes.'

'I can't go to a city.'

'I know an innkeeper who will shelter you. After you've regained your strength, if you are *still* set against joining

Harlowe, I'll get you to Lasia. The law of the Saint cannot touch you there.'

'Liyat, I don't know anyone in Lasia. I will be just as poor and friendless as I am in Triyenas.'

'Don't be a fool. I know people there. You can live in my house in Nzene,' Liyat said, 'and whenever I come back to see my lady patron, I will visit. I will find you work at a forge.'

The mysterious patron. In Perunta, Liyat was known as a dealer of curiosities. In secret, she collected forbidden books, relics of lost faiths, and other artefacts that would be seen as evidence of heresy. An anonymous Easterner, based in Nzene, paid her to recover them.

For three years, Liyat had formed a web of associates to hunt down the objects, get them to Perunta, and smuggle them on to Nzene. The work, for all its dangers, was her calling. That passion was precisely why Melaugo had first been drawn to her, the night they met, when Liyat had made it clear that she would brook no disrespect from the new criminal in Perunta.

Melaugo had dallied with a girl or two in Oryzon, but Liyat was an iron-willed and independent woman, unimpressed by artless flattery. In fact, nobody had ever succeeded in charming her. She was an ally of Suylos, part of his consortium on the coast, but she answered to no one in Yscalin. And as soon as she pointed that pistol, Estina Melaugo was in love.

She had shoved down the feeling with all her might, trying not to let it show. And yet Liyat had kissed her first. It was the only time in her life that a foolish hope had come to fruition.

'No,' she said. 'I can't accept your offer, Liyat.'

'You saved my life. Let me save yours.'

'You did that by getting me out of Perunta, by taking me to—'

'No, Estina. I owe you a life,' Liyat cut in. 'And this is not living.'

Melaugo ran a hand over her knotted hair, battling tears of frustration.

'Do not die alone and afraid in the dark,' Liyat said softly. 'Leave the culling in the past. Come with me, and we will face the next fork in the path.'

The collar of her shirt had fallen open, revealing a small pewter medallion engraved with Pardic, a language older than Yscalin. The pendant that would have been a death sentence.

'Ortégardes,' Melaugo said, defeated. 'For now.'

Liyat took her by the chin and kissed her. Her lips were softer than anything in the forest. Melaugo drew her close, wishing they had never left Lovers' Cove, where Suylos landed goods. The warm and firelit cave; the secluded inlet with its white sand.

'Collect your weapons. We'll tell the villagers you're leaving,' Liyat said, 'and stay in the room they offered me for the night. It has been too long since I slept by your side.'

Marosa

When Marosa was a child, many of her relatives had lived in Cárscaro. And then the lava had arrived, and Princess Viterica, her paternal aunt, had claimed the House of Vetalda should not ignore the omen. If Mount Fruma erupted, it would kill them all, ending their dynasty in a day.

King Sigoso had disagreed. *You have no faith in the Saint,* he had told his sister. *The Knight of Courage spits on you, Viterica.*

Impervious to even the holiest expectorate, Viterica had taken her children north, but often wrote to Marosa, asking her to visit. Over the years, those invitations had become a comfort, even if Marosa had no choice but to decline.

Her other relatives had gone to their own castles, mostly in the Groneyso Valley. Now she and her father were the last two in Cárscaro, and never did she feel more tense than when he called her to his side.

Ermendo escorted her to the royal apartments, which occupied the highest floors of the Palace of Salvation. She kept her hands clasped at her waist. They no longer shook when her father called, for she knew how to survive him. All she had to do was play the clay-brained fool.

King Sigoso was hard at work in his Privy Chamber. His thick chestnut hair was shot with grey, as was his beard, which tapered to a point under his chin. A ruby pear hung from his livery collar.

As a young man, he had been known for his sharp wit, studious nature, and devotion to the Six Virtues. Later, he was praised for emulating the Saint by marrying a Southern convert.

A convert who had gone on to betray him.

Now he almost never smiled; his ring finger was unadorned. Marosa often wondered why he had never found another consort. The Arch Sanctarian would have allowed it.

Ermendo closed the door behind Marosa. She knew better than to wait for acknowledgement.

'Your Majesty,' she said with a curtsey.

'Marosa.'

King Sigoso did not look up from his writing. He rarely looked at Marosa at all, for he would see his faithless queen. The resemblance was strong – Marosa had the same curved nose and lofty cheekbones, the same rich black hair – but her eyes were the proof that she was trueborn.

'Your uncle has written to me,' he informed her.

'Do you speak of Lord Ussindo, Father?'

'Your Southern uncle, Marosa. That shameless unbeliever who calls himself the King of Kings.'

That was unusual. To her knowledge, King Jantar had not written to her father in nine years.

'I see,' she said, feigning cool disinterest. 'What does he want?'

'His letter pertains to your mother.'

Her chest tightened.

'Jantar does not believe his beloved sister died by her own hand. He seems to think I have her chained in my dungeons,' her father said. 'What use she would be to me down there, I have no idea, but the fool has spent nearly a decade in denial. Rather than accept what happened, he blames me for her choices. To that end, he also demands evidence of your wellbeing.'

She forced herself to feel nothing, think nothing, reveal nothing.

'Such intemperance is insulting. Only an evildoer could imagine such things,' she said. 'What could have moved him to make such wild accusations now, so many years after the fact?'

'I would not know. The mind of a heretic is a strange and twisted place.' King Sigoso spared her an impassive glance. 'You will answer his letter. You will assure him of your personal safety and convince him, in as many words, to cease his raving and leave Yscalin well alone, or I will send my entire army to fight him back. Do you understand, Marosa?'

'Yes, Father.'

'Good.' He dipped his quill and continued writing. 'How is your betrothed?'

He knew very well. Every messenger dove that came to the palace was trained to fly to a bartizan near his quarters, where the Secretary of State would read the letters they carried.

'Prince Aubrecht seems well,' Marosa said, 'though when last he wrote, he told me that Clan Vatten has been provoking the House of Lievelyn. He suspects they still want Mentendon back.'

Let him see that she had nothing to hide. Let him think that she did not mind him reading her letters, or had failed to realise he was doing it.

'That is one of the reasons I made this betrothal,' King Sigoso said. 'The House of Lievelyn is young and intemperate. You will ensure they keep peace with the Hróthi. That none of this old grudge touches Yscalin.'

Yscalin had vocally opposed the Mentish Defiance, which had won the Ments their independence from Hróth. Marosa knew it would take some time for her Mentish subjects to trust her. That meant ensuring that the Hróthi did not try to claim back the land they had lost.

'Of course.' Marosa paused, realising. 'Is ... a time for our marriage decided, then?'

'Yes. You will marry Prince Aubrecht on the first new moon in autumn. Preparations are underway as we speak. A wedding to demonstrate our prosperity.'

The tidings set her heart alight. The letter from Queen Sabran really must have impelled him to set the arrangements in stone.

At last, she knew when she would leave.

'I am yours to command,' she said, careful not to show her relief. 'Where will it be held?'

'The Great Sanctuary of Ortégardes. It is the oldest and grandest in Yscalin, befitting its Donmata.' He returned his quill to its stand. 'After the marriage, you will join Prince Aubrecht on progress in Mentendon. The Lievelyns intend to send you to eleven cities.'

'I will endeavour to be a credit to Yscalin.'

'I do hope so.'

In one movement, her father rose from his desk. She held still when he took her by the chin.

'The Red Prince,' he said, 'is useful to us. But you are not a Ment. Once you are with child, you will return here, so I can ensure that you raise a virtuous heir for Yscalin. Your firstborn will not be tainted by a realm that trades with the wyrm lovers of the East.' His grip tightened a little, nails pressing into her skin. 'You won't disappoint me, will you, Marosa?'

'No, Father.'

'And you won't try to run away, like your mother?'

'I am heir to this kingdom. I would never abandon it.'

'Good.'

Marosa stared back at him, refusing to blink. Let him see his own eyes, the eyes of Oderica.

'Write to your uncle. Give the letter to Lord Gastaldo by tomorrow eve,' her father said, breaking the silent battle of wills. 'And if you see Lord Wilstan Fynch, tell him to leave me in peace.'

****

She dreamed that night, as she often did, of her mother being hauled away.

Some Ersyris thought that roses soothed an unquiet dream. Queen Sahar had grown them on the terrace and stitched their petals into satin pouches for Marosa, tucking them under her pillow before she went to bed.

Now there were no roses, and so the nightmares came.

Marosa, wake up. A whisper in her ear, sharpened by dread. *Listen to me. You must be very quiet.*

What is it, Mother?

We are going to your uncle in Rauca. I will explain once we are safe.

She was sixteen again, in her old bedchamber, and her mother and Denarva were braiding her long hair into a cap, refusing to answer her questions, faces pinched in the dim light. Soon they all wore linen smocks and aprons, like the launderess, and carried heavy cloaks and packs disguised under bedsheets.

Now they were stealing through the palace with Denarva uq-Bardant, the Ersyri handmaiden, and they could only risk one candle, so Marosa could hardly see where they were going. Her mother kept a firm hold of her, and they had to be quick, there was no time to lose—

And there were the guards, waiting for them.

Marosa snapped awake, soaked in sweat, Priessa fast asleep beside her. Slowly, she sat up and drank from the cup of sleepwater by her bed.

It had been nine years, but the memories were as sharp as ever. Shaking the locked doors of her room, screaming for an explanation. She had no idea why they had been sneaking through their own home in the dead of night, or why her mother had believed that none of them were safe. After three days of fear, a guard had slipped a note under her door, written in Ersyri.

I did it to protect you. Do not anger or defy your father. If he asks you to deny me, obey him, but know that you are my world and my heart. Stand firm, like a desert rose, and you will yet be queen. My dreams for you could sow the whole of Edin with undying roses.

Marosa still had that faded note, tucked into the alcove where she kept the pendant. It was the last time she had ever heard from her mother.

A week later, Lady Sennera Yelarigas had released Marosa from her room, sat her down, and told her why her mother was gone. Queen Sahar had fallen in love with a servant. She had planned to elope to the Ersyr with him, forsaking her duties as queen consort of Yscalin. And when caught in the act, she had ended her own life, too ashamed to face her court.

Much later, Marosa had learned that Aryete Feyalda, Third Lady of the Bedchamber, had been the one to betray the plan. Sahar had confided in her, and she had gone to the king, to stop her from taking Marosa. For her loyalty, Aryete had been given a small castle.

But Marosa remembered no secret lover. There had only been the three of them. Perhaps her mother had planned to meet him at the Gate of Niunda.

Sometimes, in her fevered dreams, Marosa was sure Denarva had fought. She thought there had been smokeless fire; that she had smelled burnt hair and flesh; that the oily black walls had glistened with red. But that had surely been a figment of a mind deranged by fear.

Denarva – kind, bold Denarva, a consummate hunter, always quick to laugh – had been executed for abetting treason. After a trial, Sahar would likely have been exiled, had she not ended her own life. Under normal circumstances, Marosa would have been permitted to see the body, but her father had forbidden it, claiming the sight of the corpse would disturb her.

There was not much ground to be spared in Cárscaro. Most of its dead were buried on the Great Yscali Plain, in hallowed ground where rosemary grew. But royal bones were not interred beneath the flowers. Instead, they rested in black tombs in the Palace of Salvation.

Queen Sahar had not been given that honour. She was an adulterous traitor, whose conversion to the Six Virtues had clearly been either lax or dishonest. Perhaps she had even been a spy.

Marosa had never learned what happened to her body. Better not to ask. Denarva's had been hurled into the lava, leaving her soul to roam for ever, with no way to enter the heavenly court.

The sleepwater worked quickly. As Marosa drifted off, one last picture crossed her mind. Not something she had witnessed, but a scene she had fashioned herself, in her nightmares. Sahar knotting her bedsheets together, then writing the note by the light of a candle.

Hanging from the ceiling like a leaf upon a tree.

****

Marosa woke again, slower. At first, she thought the trembling of her bed stemmed from her own body, racked by one of her shaking fits. They came from time to time, when she had nightmares.

But no, it was the Palace of Salvation that was quaking.

Marosa rose and unlatched a window. Across the city, the torches in the streets were aflicker. The Cárscari shouted as the Tundana glowed and spat. Even from high above, she could hear them.

'Marosa—'

Priessa had woken. She tried to draw Marosa away from the window, but Marosa resisted, her gaze soldered to the city, as a rumble stemmed from the Spindles. It echoed in her very bones.

'It's so loud,' Priessa murmured. 'Is Mount Fruma erupting?'

'We are doomed if it is.' Marosa spoke with a strange calm. 'We will not get away in time.'

Far below, people were rushing towards the Gate of Niunda, the ancient door to Cárscaro. The stone arch marked the beginning of the only paved and safe path to the ground.

'Fear not,' Marosa said. 'The Palace of Salvation has never fallen. It will hold.'

'I would not stake your life on it.' Priessa made for the doors. 'They must ready a coach for you.'

Marosa continued to watch the city, feeling its incessant shivering beneath her palms.

When Queen Rozaria had decided to raise the Palace of Salvation – a tower house like nothing the world had ever seen – she had hired the finest Hróthi masons to realise her plans. Those Northern builders knew what it was like to live on sleepless ground, for theirs was a land ruled by fire mountains, smoking with hot springs. They had carefully mapped the city, ensuring the foundations were built on solid rock, away from the abandoned mines that webbed Cárscaro. The tower had been made to stand the test of time, and so it had for centuries.

When Priessa returned, she was breathless and flushed, curls spilling out of her braiding cap. 'His Majesty has ordered that we stay here,' she said. 'We are to wait out the earthquake.'

'Then we shall,' Marosa said. 'Sit down, Essa.'

Priessa sank on to the bed. Marosa knelt before her and grasped her trembling hands.

'My friend,' she said, 'it will be all right. We are safe.'

She had told herself the same tale for years; she knew how to make a lie sound convincing. Priessa mirrored her nods. She had comforted Marosa many times when she was frightened.

Cárscaro did not cease its shaking. Marosa and Priessa lay abed together, not wanting to lose their balance by standing, trying to sleep through the quivers and jolts. Marosa gazed up at her canopy, remembering every other small quake, all the way back to her childhood. Her mother must have been afraid, the first time she had felt one after her marriage.

At last, around two of the clock, Cárscaro fell silent.

A knock startled them both upright. Priessa unlocked the doors to admit Ermendo.

'What news?' Marosa asked him.

'There is some minor damage to the city,' he said, 'but not to the Palace of Salvation.'

'Thank the Saint.' Priessa pressed a hand to her middle. 'Is everyone all right?'

'Yes, my lady. Some of the merchants have already taken their coaches and left, but I suspect they'll be the laughing stock of Cárscaro once they've returned. True paragons of courage,' Ermendo said drily. Marosa smiled. 'Would you care for some wine, Donmata?'

'Yes.' Marosa rubbed her eyes. 'Thank you, Ermendo.'

Priessa returned to her side, a little paler than usual. Marosa nudged her.

'You see?' she said. 'It was nothing.'

'I am not sure of that. First the Tundana, and now this,' Priessa said, her tone clipped. 'When you are crowned, you must choose a new capital, for all our sakes.'

'Hush.' Marosa laid a warning hand on her arm. 'Do not imagine his death.'

Priessa glanced away, composing herself.

Ruzio soon came upstairs with honey wine, stuffed olives, and white cheese. Yscabel came after her with bread, following her older sister, as usual. There was more than a decade between them.

'Yscabel, you should go back to sleep,' Priessa said. 'Your night duties begin next year.'

'I didn't want to be alone.' Yscabel curtseyed. 'I know I must disappoint the Knight of Courage, but … the tremors frighten me, Lady Priessa. I would stay, if it please the Donmata.'

Yscabel had turned fourteen only the month before. When Marosa nodded, Priessa beckoned her to the table.

'Very well,' Priessa said. 'Let us honour him with bravery now.'

By then, it was almost dawn. They ate and drank and spoke of gentle things. As they grew tired and made to recover lost sleep, a roll of thunder came, making the city shudder again.

Marosa returned to her window. Her ladies came to join her, pressing close on either side. She heard the rattle of tiles on the rooftops, then a rumble as deep as the mines beneath Cárscaro, making her lift her gaze to Mount Fruma. Before her stricken eyes, several large slabs came loose and tumbled down the slopes.

'Saint be with us,' Ruzio whispered. 'What it this?'

'A rockslide.' Priessa kept a protective hold on Marosa. 'The tremors must have caused it.'

Marosa could not rip her gaze from the mountain. There were occasional rockfalls in Cárscaro, where a boulder would suddenly drop, but this was different.

'It's all right,' Priessa said. 'The palace is safe.'

'But what of the stonecutters, the water tower?'

Now the sound changed to an ominous crack. As Marosa watched, transfixed by fear, a sheet of stone crumbled away from the mountain. Ruzio gasped as it shattered and crashed down the steep incline, chased by smaller fragments, grey dust billowing around. The debris rushed into the eastern outskirts of Cárscaro, overwhelming the houses there.

It took some time for the dark haze to clear. When it did, Marosa could only stare in disbelief. Where the colossal sheet had fallen, there was now a yawning break in the mountainside.

A cave had been revealed.

'Fruma,' Yscabel said in the barest whisper. 'He seeks vengeance upon the children of Isalarico.'

Marosa looked at her, lips parting in question. Yscabel clapped a hand over her mouth.

'Donmata,' she said, 'I beg your forgiveness. It's only kitchen gossip. I didn't mean—'

What Yscabel did or did not mean, Marosa never established, for then a mighty clamour filled the night.

A sinister light stemmed from the cleft, rivalling the river of fire. Marosa gripped the balustrade, her knuckles turning pale, as the opening abounded with movement, violent in its intensity.

A thundercloud seemed to emerge from the cave. Marosa could not understand what she was seeing, even as it spilled forth in a rush, solid and molten at once, and swept towards the Palace of Salvation. A twisting mass of shadow, which moved like nothing she had ever laid eyes on. Before it could reach them, Priessa and Ruzio pulled her away from the window.

'No, no.' She tried to fight them off. 'I have to—'

'Donmata, we must get out of sight,' Ruzio insisted. 'Yscabel, away from the windows!'

Marosa was not especially strong, but she did have the element of surprise. No one expected nobles to make sudden movements. With one sharp wrench, she broke free of Priessa and Ruzio, who was already distracted by her care for Yscabel. Before they could stop her, she burst from her apartments and rushed along the corridors, chased by her protesting guards.

She ran until she reached the balcony. Just as she shoved through its doors, the cloud passed over the lava, and she could see it, all of it. The bat wings and serpentine tails, ripped from a bestiary.

Wyverns.

The word tolled in her mind, paralysing her. She did not want to accept the evidence of her own eyes. For the first time in five hundred years, a flock of wyverns was soaring over Cárscaro.

It splintered at the edge of the cliff, leaving the Cárscari screaming in its wake. With piercing calls, the wyverns dived over the precipice, following the lava falls towards the Great Yscali Plain.

And then, by the distant light of dawn, Marosa beheld a sight that sent a knife into her soul.

Since she was sixteen, she had dreamed of death. None of her nightmares touched what she saw now. As she watched, red lights flared across the Great Yscali Plain, as far as the eye could see. At first, they were isolated bonfires, small and glimmering. One by one, those fires grew.

They have their flames.

The realisation stole the feeling from her skin. The Saint's Comet had quenched their fire when it put them to sleep.

Like some terrible murmuration of starlings, the wyverns spread out across the Great Yscali Plain, sowing that unnatural red fire, the light of the Dreadmount itself. For a short time, there was utter stillness, the Cárscari stunned into silence, as they watched the flowers burn. All Marosa could hear was her own heart, and the uneven breaths of the people behind her.

Then half of the flock returned; the screams began again. The wyverns swooped upon the Great Aviary, which stood on a bluff above Vatana House, and brought it crashing to the ground. Marosa was too high to see her people; she only heard them crying out in terror.

More fire sprang in the corner of her eye. A small wyvern flew along the Tundana, its wings skimming the lava, before it blew a jet of flame, burning the archers that guarded the Gate of Niunda. More of the beasts fell upon the unattended catapults and bolt throwers on the cliff, weapons made for a second Grief of Ages. Marosa watched them crumble to embers.

'They know what to destroy,' Priessa said hoarsely. 'They remember.'

Marosa Vetalda was used to nightmares, but now she felt as though she had been pulled into a folk tale. All the heroes of the Grief were in her body in that moment. She stayed at her post, like a soldier at war, and watched a hundred wyverns landing on the rooftops.

During the Grief of Ages, the Cárscari had descended to the old mines to wait out the destruction. Now, in this softer time, most of those mines were sealed for their safety. A bitter twist of fate.

'Please,' Ermendo said. 'Come inside, Donmata.'

At last, Marosa let him guide her away. The doors to the balcony clanged in their wake.

In less than an hour, the Great Yscali Plain was on fire to the horizon. The flowers Isalarico the Benevolent had planted to celebrate his marriage, all gone. By noon, there was so much smoke in Cárscaro, Marosa could no longer see a foot beyond her window.

So when the voice came – a voice like stone grinding on stone – it seemed to stem from nowhere.

'KING OF YSCALIN,' it said. 'COME FORTH, OR YOUR CITY BURNS.'

****

In Inys, the Virtues Council was led by the Dukes Spiritual – scions of the Holy Retinue, the six knights who had served the Saint. The monarchs of Yscalin were guided by the Grandees, the heads of the six families who held the highest titles and controlled the most land in the kingdom.

Marosa followed Ermendo down the Grand Stair, shadowed by her other guards. She could already hear the disarray in the Council Chamber.

Since his own family had quit the capital, King Sigoso had kept his Privy Council small. In total, they numbered eighteen, prized for their ability to flatter and obey. Most of them had assembled by the time Marosa reached the Council Chamber, a great round hall on the twelfth floor of the Palace of Salvation. Portraits of her ancestors hung on the sleek black walls. The heavy scarlet curtains had been drawn, so no one could see in or out.

The crowd was not only composed of the inner Privy Council. She recognised the Grandees – the pillars of government – but also several knights and ambassadors and other residents of court, all gathered around her father, who sat alone at the head of the table, his expression impenetrable, observing his advisors. He was arrayed as if for a banquet, wearing a crown of red gold. The Captain General of the Vardya stood close beside him.

When it came to religious matters, the Yscals submitted to the Queen of Inys, the voice of the Saint. In every other way, the king was lord and master. He was a riveting presence, keeping his subjects on tenterhooks. No one spoke without his permission. No one contradicted him. All eyes were usually pinned to his face, watching for any hint of displeasure.

Now it was only chaos that reigned. All courtly protocol had evaporated.

Marosa met his gaze across the room. Not once had she set foot here, in the heart of governance, where Yscalin was shaped. Her father had always stopped her. This time, he gave her a nod.

It took his nobles some time to notice her. 'There *must* be another way,' Lord Alvo Sánctogan was saying, his large face turning puce. 'We cannot send His Majesty into the jaws of a wyrm!'

'If we do not, the entire city falls,' argued Sir Robrecht Teldan. 'His Majesty and the Donmata with it.'

'You low serpent of a Ment. Do you mean for your Red Prince to supplant His Majesty?'

'Don't be absurd.'

Marosa surveyed the chamber. If her father was allowing this degree of disorder, it had to be for a reason. He was letting them all talk over each other, so their panic would strip away their decorum, exposing their true selves. Of course he would use their fear to his gain.

Perhaps she would follow his lead. Already she could make an intriguing observation of her own. Yscalin presently had four ambassadors in residence, but only three were present.

Wilstan Fynch was nowhere to be seen.

'Donmata.' The Duchess of Ortégardes was the first to address her. 'Thank the Saint you are all right.'

She was loud enough to quieten the others. Slowly, they turned to look at Marosa.

Marosa knew them all by sight. Priessa had shown her their miniatures, but only a few had accepted her invitations to meals. From their expressions, some of them had not even realised how old she was. It had been many years since she had walked among them.

'It is a High Western,' she said. 'Is it not?'

Despite her fear, her voice held strong.

'So we fear, Donmata,' a young man said. 'No mere wyvern ever spoke a human tongue.'

Marosa regarded him, taking in his striking face. Lord Bartian Feyalda, the Count of Oryzon. She had played with Bartian as a child, but had only seen him from a distance for nearly a decade. He had grown tall, his features had sharpened, and he sported a fashionable beard.

He and most of the others were in their lavish bedgowns and slippers. They had clearly been here since the wyverns appeared.

'Two were slain during the Grief,' she said to the chamber at large. 'Which of the other three do we face?'

There was a long and deep silence.

'Only one would be so bold as to threaten a king,' her father said. He spoke quietly, but everyone heard. 'One whose first act, when he revealed himself to our ancestors, was to burn a scion of the Saint. The right wing of the Nameless One has woken from his sleep.'

Nobody dared to breathe. Bartian glanced away from the king, towards Marosa.

'Fýredel,' Marosa said.

The profane name was like poison on her lips. A shiver passed through the whole chamber.

'All that time,' the Duke of Aperio said. 'All that time, he was slumbering upon our doorstep?'

'He was never slain,' the Counsellor of War pointed out. 'The Spindles hide many caves, few of which have been explored.'

'Are we certain the Gulthaganian mines do not hold any wyverns or Draconic creatures?' Marosa asked him. 'Are more about to burst up from beneath our feet?'

'Not in my opinion, Your Radiance. King Alarico sealed the mines well. There is no way in or out.'

'Then we cannot move our subjects down there to protect them, as was done in the Grief?'

'No.'

Marosa glanced at her father. He remained at the head of the table, unmoving.

'Can Yscalin withstand another Grief?' she asked the nobles. 'Are we ready for this fight?'

She found that it was easy to speak before a crowd, even with her father watching. All she had wanted, for nine long years, was to be able to address her future advisors without restraint.

'We Northerners certainly are,' one of the tall Hróthi ambassadors said, eyeing her. 'I trust you Yscals have prepared.'

'His Majesty has taken all reasonable precautions, as did his ancestors,' Lord Gastaldo said. Even in this calamity, he was finely dressed, down to his livery collar and lace cuffs. 'We have invested in many siege engines and weapons since the Grief.'

'The wyverns burned the artillery,' Marosa said. 'I saw it.'

'Cárscaro is well placed to repel an attack from the Great Yscali Plain, but not from winged enemies, coming from so close,' the Counsellor of War said. 'They may have been observing our defences for some time.'

'We should never have stayed here. It was foolish and arrogant,' Marosa said, the words spilling out before she could stop them. 'Aunt Erica was right to leave.'

'Be silent, Marosa,' King Sigoso said. 'You know nothing of this matter.'

Some of the counsellors averted their eyes. Once Marosa might have quailed, but now she returned his icy gaze.

'Here is our situation,' the Counsellor of War said, breaking the silence. 'All of the artillery has been destroyed, and there are clearly too many wyverns to be felled by bows and rifles.' He paced as he spoke. 'Until the Great Yscali Plain stops burning, there is no way out of the city, nor for our allies to reach us. Cárscaro commands an unparalleled view of its surroundings; now that very advantage will be turned against us. Even if we called for aid, the wyverns would kill any soldiers that answered.'

King Sigoso ground his jaw. His eyes were circled by shadow, and a vein ran like a river from his hairline to the side of his nose. Marosa found his silence more chilling than his words.

'What do you propose?' she asked the Counsellor of War, daring to speak up again. 'Is there any precedent from the Grief?'

'The wyrms burned cities without remorse or warning, but there were times when they withheld the killing blow.'

'Indeed,' the Principal Sanctarian said. 'This summons puts me in mind of the last great Inysh battle against Fýredel, when he laid siege to Hollow Crag. He demanded that Glorian Shieldheart emerge to face him. It was only the arrival of the Saint's Comet that saved her life.'

Marosa could not stand to look at the man, with his green robes and placid face, his cheeks hollowed by fasting. Though generosity was one of the virtues he preached, he had not shown mercy when asked to decide whether Queen Sahar would be allowed to enter Halgalant. Instead, he had formally relinquished her seat there, leaving her to wander for eternity.

'When will it come next?' she asked the Council Chamber. 'Does anyone know?'

'No one knows for certain, Your Radiance. Many comets were observed in antiquity,' Sir Robrecht Teldan said. 'But as far as the astronomers of Mentendon know, no comet will be seen in our skies for at least four years. Our Seiikinese trading partners say the same.'

'Do not speak of the heretic Easterners,' the Principal Sanctarian said coldly. 'The Saint was the one who sent the comet, to save his beloved descendant. He will do the same for Yscalin.'

Sir Robrecht looked away, his jaw clenching beneath his silver beard.

'High Westerns *can* be slain. We know this,' Marosa said, her conviction rising. 'Dedalugun was felled in Lasia, and Taugran in Seiiki. We may not know how it was done, but—'

'COME FORTH, KING ON THE MOUNTAIN.'

Marosa flinched at the sound of that voice, which seemed to grind through the very foundations of Cárscaro. If the

Dreadmount could speak, she was sure that it would have sounded like Fýredel.

'Why is this happening?' came a whisper. 'Why have they woken now?'

'The commons are full of vice,' the Duke of Groneyso said, his face tight with disgust. 'Not all of them follow the Six Virtues as we do in His Majesty's court. Perhaps the Saint has chosen to relinquish his protection.'

'It's the Saint-forsaken cullers,' Lord Gastaldo sneered. 'Low and greedy criminals, profiting off the commons' fear. They have been prodding the sleepers for years, for no reason other than moneymaking. I sent the Knights Defendant to cull *them*, but they persist.'

As Marosa watched them, she realised that none of them had any idea why this was happening. Not even the Principal Sanctarian.

'Enough,' she called. 'Peace. We must decide what to do.'

'Well said, Donmata.' Lord Gastaldo collected himself. 'Majesty, we are at your command. What say you?'

King Sigoso gripped the arm of his chair. She could see his mind turning, like the cogs inside a pocket watch. If he answered the summons, Fýredel would likely burn him. If not, he failed the Knight of Courage.

'Summon my decoy,' he said to Lord Gastaldo. 'Array him richly and give him the Grey Crown.'

The least valuable. Lord Gastaldo bowed and quit the Council Chamber.

'No one is to leave the Palace of Salvation. No quake nor wyrm can fell this tower,' King Sigoso went on, ignoring the stares. 'Whatever Fýredel wants of us, my decoy will soon learn it.'

The Duchess of Ortégardes cleared her throat. 'Who is the decoy, Your Majesty?'

'Orentico Feyalda. He bears a passing resemblance.'

Bartian looked away. The Feyalda were a cadet branch of the House of Vetalda, and had always been loyal, but Marosa could not imagine that any of them would take on this risk by choice.

'We have enough grain to last up to four years,' the Counsellor of War said, 'but that will be of little use if Fýredel burns us all. I have not read of any wyrms besieging a city for long.'

'That means nothing,' the Duchess of Samana said roughly. 'During the Grief, the wyrms had only just emerged from the Dreadmount. We do not know how they will behave in this new era.'

For a long spell, there was silence, as if no one dared to draw attention to themselves, even with several feet of rock to shield and hide them from the wyrms. After a time, Marosa moved to stand beside Bartian, who was peering through a gap between the curtains.

'Donmata.' He glanced at her. 'I wish we had reunited under different circumstances.'

'Indeed. I am glad to see you, Bartian.'

He found a joyless smile for her before he returned his gaze to the window. 'Why has he not already killed us?' he said under his breath. 'He has burned the fields. Why not destroy the city, too?'

'Perhaps he means to watch us starve. For revenge,' Marosa murmured. 'Do wyrms understand that concept?'

'I believe so.'

'What have we done, in their minds, to deserve so much violence?'

'A wyrm has no mind. It is evil incarnate. We worship the Saint, who vanquished his master. Is that not enough?' Seeing her face, Bartian softened his tone. 'The comet will come again. I am sure of it.'

'But not today.'

'No, indeed.' He glanced over his shoulder. 'Where are your ladies?'

'In my apartments.' She looked at him. 'Orentico is my second cousin, I think, but we have not met.'

'His Majesty has no love for bastards.'

'Is the resemblance strong?'

'Very, but Orentico is younger. Fýredel may see through the deception.'

'Surely he cannot know what my father looks like.'

'Either way, Orentico is doomed.'

'Glorian Shieldheart survived Fýredel twice. It *is* possible.' Marosa laid a consoling hand on his arm. 'Orentico is doing his country a great service. The Knight of Courage will reward him, whether here or in Halgalant.'

Bartian nodded, and pressed her hand in return.

'Do not touch my daughter,' King Sigoso called, sharp as a cutlass. 'She is betrothed.'

Marosa stepped away, her face burning.

'Forgive me, Your Majesty.' Bartian bowed. 'The Donmata was only—'

'I trust you do not mean to argue with your sovereign, Lord Bartian.'

Bartian closed his mouth.

Marosa moved to a different part of the Council Chamber, finding her own viewpoint. Soon the other nobles were looking out as well, straining to see through the smoke that choked the streets. Past her drawn reflection, Marosa could just see a pair of wyverns on the rooftops, watching the city.

She estimated each was fifty to seventy feet in length, from their snouts to the ends of their serpentine tails. Just as the bestiaries described, they had only two hind legs, but their leathery wings acted somewhat like arms when they landed, allowing them to crawl along the ground. Their talons were appalling, as were the twin horns that stemmed from their skulls. They were thought to possess hollow bones – there was surely no other way they could fly – but she had still not expected their wings to be quite so immense, with savage hooks at the tips.

Beside them was a wyverling, half the size. Unlike its kin, it stood upright, like a bird, with its wings folded against its sides. All three creatures looked battle-scarred, with missing scales.

The scars of the Grief of Ages, left by warriors long dead.

Marosa tore her gaze away, cold sweat on her nape. Far below, hundreds of Cárscari had gathered at the defensive wall that surrounded the lower floors of the Palace of Salvation. They must be seeking the protection of its thick volcanic walls, but she knew her father. He would not let the commons into his own home. She willed them to give up and get to shelter. Thanks to the Act of Preservation, the entire city was made of stone or brick, with no wood or thatched roofs to be seen. Their homes would shield them from any more fire.

At last, the gates to the palace opened. When a figure emerged from inside, the crowd parted.

The decoy. Marosa could not see his face from this high up, through so much smoke. Accompanied by city guards, Orentico Feyalda climbed into a horse-drawn coach.

As the coach rolled along the river of fire, the Cárscari made way for it. Bartian watched, his face tight, as his cousin made the slow journey towards the break in the mountainside.

After a time, they lost sight of Orentico. At some point, when the road ended, he would have to continue on foot.

'Donmata,' Ermendo said, 'perhaps you should come away from the windows.'

His eyes were on a wyvern that had turned its fiery gaze towards her. Marosa retreated slowly.

Day turned to dusk, and dusk to night. A full moon rose, casting silver light into the smoke, allowing more wyverns to be seen. At last, Bartian risked cracking a window open, so everyone could hear and smell the city. It was quieter than Marosa had expected – a hush broken only by occasional hisses from the intruders, and the distant, frantic sobs of the Cárscari.

It seemed all the louder, then, when a weight fell on the balcony outside the Council Chamber.

Bartian flung open the doors. 'Lord Bartian,' the Captain General barked, but he was already outside, and smoke was rushing into the chamber, sending half the nobles into coughing fits. Marosa went as far as the threshold and saw Bartian crouched beside a thing with limbs.

She had never seen a corpse before. It was so charred she could not see its face. Only its teeth. All she could do was stare at it. Not an hour ago, this had been a man. A living man.

'THE MOUNTAIN KING SEEKS TO DECEIVE ME,' Fýredel said. His stentorian voice reached through the city, rattling the glasses on the table. 'NOW YOUR PEOPLE KNOW YOU WELL.'

Even at sixteen, on the darkest night of her life, Marosa had never held so much fear in her body.

'YOU CANNOT HIDE,' the wyrm proclaimed. 'COME FORTH, CRAVEN KING, IMPRECATION TO HIS SUBJECTS.'

One by one, they all looked to King Sigoso.

'There is no choice, then,' the Duchess of Ortégardes said.

King Sigoso looked at her, and his eyes were that of a wolf, a hunter.

'Tell me, Your Grace,' he said, 'do you imagine the death of your sovereign?'

She turned pale as a cloud. King Sigoso rose from his chair, watched by the terrified nobles. Marosa wondered if he would refuse to go. If he would stay inside his fort, choosing his own life over the rest.

'I will not be called a coward by a wyrm,' he said. 'The Saint shall protect me, as he protected Glorian Shieldheart.'

Marosa watched him stand, and their eyes met. If he did not return, she would be queen by morning.

Do I say goodbye, or let him go with nothing more of me?

In the end, she decided not to speak. After all, he had ordered her to be silent. His gaze sharpened, and she knew that he, her own father, was wishing he could send her in his stead. And when he left to face his end, the trepidation in her chest warred against a sense of grim triumph.

Now it is your turn to disappear.

****

All night, the Privy Council watched and waited. All night, the flowers burned. Every minute stretched into an agonising hour.

More choking smoke blew up to Cárscaro, forcing its people to keep to their homes, even as they prayed for their king. Those who had fled earlier from the earthquake began to return through the Gate of Niunda, coughing and wheezing, only to find their city invaded. The wyverns let them pass unscathed, watching them in unnerving silence from the rooftops.

'I cannot stand this,' a noble said. 'What are they doing?'

'Waiting for orders, perhaps.'

'From the High Western?'

Bartian said nothing. He was sitting on the floor, staring vacantly at the wall.

At three of the clock, a guard descended to speak to the city watch. They reported that most of those who had left had succumbed to burns, or perished from breathing in too much smoke.

Marosa sat at the end of the table, watched by the nobles. There was little change in the light outside; the reeking smoke had benighted the city. It could have been midnight or dawn.

At last, the Captain General came to the doors, looking shaken.

'His Majesty has returned,' he rasped. 'He lives.'

The Principal Sanctarian made the sign of the sword, while the Counsellor of Finance slid to the floor in a faint. Marosa left the Council Chamber and rushed down the winding steps.

'Fetch the Royal Physician,' she called to the nearest servants.

Most of the Privy Council followed her. Only a few remained behind, rooted in place.

The whole palace had long since woken. Marosa soon reached the lower floors, where the corridors were high and wide, with balconies where one could look between several levels at once. Here, she saw more and more courtiers and servants, staring at her with surprise and dread. Only when she reached the entrance hall did she stop, her skin filmed with sweat. Lord Gastaldo and the others soon caught up with her.

'Be calm,' Lord Gastaldo ordered the nearest courtiers. 'The Saint is with us.'

Marosa swallowed. She ought to have been the one to say it, but her voice had deserted her.

The ebony doors, banded with iron, were almost twenty feet in height. When they swung open, a familiar man entered, stooped and alone. Marosa started towards him.

'Stay back.' Her father thrust out a hand. 'Marosa. Stay back.'

Marosa stopped. In her stead, several of the guards surrounded their sovereign.

'Father,' she said faintly. 'What happened?'

Even from several feet away, she could smell his clothes. He reeked of iron and smoke.

'Fýredel spoke to me. Now I see,' King Sigoso said. 'We have … been deceived, all these centuries.'

'I don't understand—'

'Send out word across the world. Send every surviving bird in Cárscaro. Tell them all – every city and land – that this is no longer a kingdom chained to the legacy of Galian Berethnet, the false and wicked Saint. This is the Draconic Kingdom of Yscalin, bound in worship to the Nameless One.'

He raised his head, and Marosa took a step away, almost falling into Ermendo, who steadied her.

Sigoso Vetalda, King of Yscalin, no longer had the eyes of Oderica.

They were grey as cold ash, all the way through.

Melaugo

ORTÉGARDES
KINGDOM OF YSCALIN
CE 1003

Ortégardes was one of the six regional capitals of Yscalin, collectively known as the holy cities. Circled by orange and lemon groves, it lay along the Pilgrims' Way on the banks of the River Salbon. This was where Oderica the Smith, the first Vetalda queen, had been crowned.

No place in Yscalin was more devoted to the Knight of Courtesy. Here, scribes could be hired to write eloquent letters; gifts for all occasions could be found; artists and their patrons flourished. A famous olive soap was made; pomanders were shaped and filled with scent. Entry to the public baths was cheap, for cleaning oneself was a kindness to all. At its hundreds of shrines to Dame Medwin Combe, Yscals prayed for mercy, love, and inspiration.

Melaugo was just hoping for a cup of wine, a proper bed, and no lindworms within a hundred leagues.

It had been a hard ride, leaving her more irritable by the day. When they had first reached the Salbon, she had used her last few coins from Aperio to buy a wide-brimmed hat, both to protect her scalp from the sun and conceal her face on the road. Her parents had worn the same kind of hat while they laboured in the vineyard, though made of straw instead of cloth.

They rode past orchards of pomegranate trees in flower. Melaugo wished the fruit were on the branch. She had often indulged in pomegranate in Aperio, when she had the coin to afford it.

As they neared Ortégardes, Liyat said, 'Harlowe never told me how you met.'

'He's a man of few words when he isn't angry.'

'Yes. In truth, he is a mystery to me, even though I have known him for some time.'

'He sounds like someone else I know,' Melaugo said. Liyat did not reply, and Melaugo tried to ignore the sting of guilt for her bluntness. 'Harlowe found me in Oryzon when I was thirteen. He caught me picking his pocket. I thought he would take me to the magistrate – that I would be flogged – but instead, he paid a blacksmith to take me on as her apprentice.'

'An apprentice fee is no small price to pay.'

'He's rich as a lord, as far as I can tell. Queen Rosarian liked him.' Melaugo drank from her waterskin. 'The blacksmith tried her best with me, but I was hard to teach. I hated the Oryzoni for their hypocrisy, their cruelty towards urchins. After several years of shirking, I lost my temper and insulted one of her best patrons, a knight. She cut me loose then, though I stayed with her until Harlowe returned. He came back every so often.'

'Was he wroth with you?'

'Of course. He rarely isn't.' She stowed the waterskin to guide her steed around a rut. 'During my time with the blacksmith, Harlowe had discovered what happened to my parents. I told him I wanted to be a smuggler, like them.

I'd met a few over my years in Oryzon – some had even paid me to act as a lookout. Harlowe could see that I wasn't made for honest work.'

'So he brought you to the Greenshanks.'

'Yes.'

Liyat nodded. They had shared a bed many times, but they still knew too little about one another.

This far south, the spring wind blew hot as wyrmfire, making them both sweat. Liyat spurred her mare towards the city wall, and Melaugo followed.

They stabled their horses near the gate and slipped down to the moat, sinking up to their ankles in mud. Melaugo had tucked her plaited hair away, leaving no red strands to betray her. Once she was settled at the inn, she meant to use oak gall to darken it, so she could venture outside for short walks. They sidled through a storm drain, which smugglers used to trade in the city, and moved a grate aside, emerging in a cobbled alley.

Melaugo had visited Ortégardes before, but only at night, and not for long. By day, washed in sunlight, the City of Courtesy was a sight to behold. She had never absorbed the majesty of it – the limewashed houses, the cascades of flowers, the cypress and palm trees lining the streets. Some of its older buildings looked Southern, for they hailed from an era when there was a shared culture spanning the continent of Edin, which now survived only in the Ersyr. Liyat had told her that, one night while they lay abed, admiring one of her relics.

The crowning jewel was the Great Sanctuary of Ortégardes, the first to be raised in Yscalin. Its rainbow windows were hundreds of years old. Made of pale Vazuvan marble, with twisting white pillars flanking its doors, it was a monument to beauty, like everything in this city.

'The Donmata is to be married there,' Liyat said. 'I hope she will be happy.'

'I hear she could do worse than the Red Prince of Mentendon,' Melaugo replied, 'but I can't feel too sorry for her, either way. She lives in obscene luxury without having to lift a finger.'

'I would not trade places with her. Not for all the world. Imagine it,' she said. 'You and I could not be together. Not until one of us bore a child, and even then, it might be forbidden.'

Melaugo had been ready to argue her case, but that reply stopped her.

Liyat led her along an elegant colonnade, where daylight gleamed through archways, reflecting off the Salbon. Pleasure boats lazed through the clear water, surrounded by darting orange fish. Many people wore bright yellow, apricot, or pomegranate red – a sunset of fine silk and linen. Melaugo took the splendour in with mingled wonder and dislike, thirsting for her own hoard of gold, which Lord Gastaldo must have confiscated from her lodgings in Aperio.

They crossed a bridge into the Cloth Quarter and entered an inn called the Golden Pear, where Liyat spoke to a woman in Lasian. Next Melaugo knew, she was in a modest bedchamber with a tiled floor and a door leading to a court-yard, where she could soak up the sun.

'Thank you,' Melaugo said. 'Truly, Liyat.'

'We will speak about where you go next,' Liyat said, 'but for now, you should regain your strength.'

Melaugo nodded. She sat on the bed and breathed in the clean scent of the rushes on the floor.

Liyat came to lie beside her and slid an arm across her waist. The sun fell on to her cheek through the window.

Melaugo stroked her windswept curls back with one hand. They both needed to eat, but the ride had been long and hot, and before she could move again, she was sleeping.

****

For days, Melaugo tried to rest. There was a small bathing chamber and a chest for her to store her weapons. She ate in the kitchen at noon every day and stayed out of the other guests' sight. It hurt to eat too much, even though she was hungry.

On their sixth morning in Ortégardes, she worked her way through a casserole of white cheese, hard-boiled egg and greens, trying not to overstuff her belly, and sipped a black Ersyri drink that made her feel awake. The shutters were ajar, so she could glimpse people going about their business, hear their laughter and the clang of sanctuary bells.

Melaugo took it all in. Even if she could not go outside with the fear of death hanging over her, she could listen to others' lives unfolding. Surely that was better than Triyenas.

You were meant for more than that.

Get out of my head, she told Harlowe. *Out with you, salt-worn bastard.*

Liyat returned from her walk to the bakery. By then, Melaugo was lying in her room with the windows screened against the burning sun, as most Yscals did at midday in the hot months.

'Here.' Liyat presented her with a small package. 'Your favourite.'

Melaugo sat up and opened it. Inside was a pastry shaped like a cowry shell, the one she had loved to eat in Perunta.

'Thank you,' she said, with a tired smile. 'I missed these.'

'I'll get you *my* favourite tomorrow. Orange cake,' Liyat said. 'A speciality of Ortégardes.' She set down two loaves of fresh white bread. 'It will ruin all other sweet things for you.'

'I look forward to it.' Melaugo tore the pastry in half and tasted the almond filling. 'Any news?'

'The heralds are still calling your description, even here.' Liyat walked past her to crack the doors open, letting in a breeze. 'I see no choice. You must go to Lasia.'

'I'd sooner risk staying in Ortégardes.'

'How can you?'

'I'll dye my hair and keep my hat on.'

'That will not be enough.'

'It has to be.' Melaugo shifted on the bed. 'Liyat, think about this. I don't speak Lasian.'

'You could learn.' Liyat hung up her cloak, then started to remove her bandolier. 'In a few days, you can join a caravan across the marchlands. In the meantime, I will send a dove to my friends and get you a new apprenticeship. Nzene rewards promising smiths.'

'I don't want to smith.'

'Then what *do* you want?'

'I want to be with you,' Melaugo said, 'yet I feel as if you are trying to be rid of me.' Liyat looked towards her sharply. 'Saint above, will you not even come with me across the marchlands, Liyat?'

Liyat looked as if Melaugo had struck her.

'I came for you,' she said. 'I came to Triyenas.'

'You might never have done that if not for Harlowe. Three months and you didn't even notice I had left Aperio.' Melaugo was suddenly boiling over. 'Did you even care that I was gone, or did my shot in Perunta give you convenient grounds to cast me aside, like Suylos did?'

'Estina, you are not being fair. You know I can't just abandon my work,' Liyat said, a flush on her cheeks, 'but I had
every intention of returning to Aperio to see you.'

'This sounds like an excuse, Liyat.'

'Do you think me so cold?'

'No. I believe you are proud and guarded – impressively, even
more so than I am – and that you are terrified to have a weakness, because you have been wounded so many times before.'

Liyat looked as tense as a hunted deer. Melaugo could see
her fighting her instinct to run for the hills, to escape this
confrontation.

'Don't leave,' Melaugo said, softer. 'Hear me out.' After a
pause, Liyat nodded. 'In Oryzon, I never let a girl too close,
in case they spurned my affections. Sooner or later, I would
start avoiding them, even if it caused them pain. Even if it
caused the very thing I feared.'

She dared not look Liyat in the eye as she spoke. It would
make her feel as if she was dying.

'I had long thought of myself as a burden, a millstone,'
she said to the floor. 'In the eyes of the law, that had been
true. An urchin forever asking for a coin. A mouth nobody
cared to feed. The very sight of me unsettled the Oryzoni,
because it showed them the Saint could forsake a child, but
none of them wanted to bring me into their own perfect
households. I was too low. I knew that, in their hearts, they
wished I would just … disappear.'

At this, Liyat stepped towards her. 'Estina.'

'Wait. Let me confess this, or I never will,' Melaugo
said, stopping her. 'I have borne witness to how deeply you
care about the world, about people. I have also seen your
humour and warmth, and how quickly you hide all of this
– all of you – when you feel that you have shown too much.

I understand, because I was the same. I have spent years defending my dignity as if my life depended on it, afraid to let anyone crush it any more than it has already been crushed. But you made me want to let my guard down. To be vulnerable. I let myself dream of trust and affection. But I fear you cannot do the same.'

Liyat kept her distance, her face wary.

'I thought you were content with what we had in Perunta,' she said. 'That we could be a comfort to each other.'

'Yes, you wanted someone to warm your bed. I wanted the same,' Melaugo said, 'but every time I slept at your shop, I wished you would ask me to stay.'

Liyat remained as stiff as a manikin, but her gaze was the opposite, tender and molten.

'I know you must carry great pain. You speak to the dead in your sleep,' Melaugo said. 'I hoped that we could help each other heal from our pasts. I formed this notion without consulting you, and that was a selfish mistake. I'm sorry.' Her voice strained. 'But I must know, once and for all, for the sake of my own sanity: is there any chance that you could want to build a life with me, or am I chasing a pipe dream, as Harlowe believes?'

'Harlowe said this?' Liyat whispered.

'He claims you're married to your work. But I would never seek to take that from you.' Melaugo went to her, so they stood a few inches apart. 'I see how much discomfort I am causing you, merely by forcing you to confront this. It pains me to do it. But I need to understand, so I can judge how much to give to this affair. I am a winemakers' child – I will not waste the fruits of my labour by tipping them on to the ground. So tell me, can you offer me a cup?'

Liyat blinked in clear surprise, for which Melaugo could not blame her. She had taken even herself by surprise with that burst of poesy.

Before Liyat could answer, a knock drew their gazes towards the door. Melaugo slipped behind it, while Liyat cracked it open.

'Yes?'

'The Knights Defendant summon the people of Ortégardes,' an unfamiliar voice said. 'No exceptions.'

'Very well.' Liyat kept her composure. 'Where do we go?'

'Everyone in this quarter is to proceed to the Plaza Oderica.'

He went to knock on other doors. Liyat shut theirs and looked at Melaugo, who reached for her new hat, her mouth thin.

****

They joined hundreds of people leaving their shops and homes. Liyat led, knowing the city well. Melaugo tried to ignore the foreboding. She pulled the brim of her hat down as the crowd washed them towards the Plaza Oderica, where the Great Sanctuary of Ortégardes stood.

She could have killed the city guard for interrupting their conversation, but even though it was long overdue, perhaps Liyat needed a little more time.

Her cheeks were still burning from her final outburst. Perhaps she really ought to leave Yscalin and become some kind of wandering bard. Most likely, Liyat would close herself off and withdraw, and she would have destroyed one of the few joys she had ever known.

The people of Ortégardes were filing out of their lodgings and villas, some of them none too pleased to be summoned. Melaugo had never seen so many unlaced shirts or bare shoulders. In the warm half of the year, the city guards in the south of Yscalin tended to overlook any contravention of the sartorial laws, even in the city devoted to the Knight of Courtesy.

The Knights Defendant waited in a crescent formation at the top of the steps to the Great Sanctuary. There were forty of them, all on white stallions, wearing armour and masks that evoked a crueller period of Yscali history.

Liyat looked at them with quiet contempt. They were the last remnant of the Order of Ederico, which had spurred the Yscali conversion to the Six Virtues after the death of Isalarico the Benevolent. They had killed or banished anyone who refused to accept the new faith entirely. Now they visited the settlements of Yscalin at random, punishing vice and heresy, destroying the exact sorts of objects that Liyat fought so hard to protect.

Melaugo squinted at them from beneath the brim of her hat. They were flying a banner showing the red pear of Yscalin, but *without* the True Sword, which appeared in the heraldry of all four countries in Virtudom.

'The banner,' she said to Liyat. 'Do you see?'

'Yes, but … why?'

'I have no idea.'

Ortégardes was such a large city – far larger than the capital – that it took some time even for one district to be gathered. In the end, silence descended as one of the knights kicked her steed forward. Beneath her engraved steel helm, she looked gaunt, with a hollow gaze.

'People of Ortégardes,' she bellowed, 'I am Donma Lusua Vuleydres, a sworn member of the Knights Defendant.'

As was the custom, the knight paused so that people could pass her words from the front of the crowd to the back. Fortunately, her voice carried, and Melaugo had the ears of a barn owl.

'Long have you been loyal to Galian Berethnet, he who called himself the Saint,' Donma Lusua continued. 'Long have my fellow knights made sure to keep his law throughout this land. But I have come to tell you, here and now, that his time is over in Yscalin.'

Melaugo arched an eyebrow. All around the vast square, there were mutters of confusion and anger as the words reached each part of the crowd. Liyat lifted a hand to her neckline.

'I can't hear a word,' the man beside her grumbled, straining to see. 'What's she saying?'

'Five centuries after the conversion, His Majesty, King Sigoso of the House of Vetalda, has seen the light of the Dreadmount,' Donma Lusua shouted over the clamour. 'He has sworn allegiance to the Nameless One, and to Fýredel, the Iron King, Lord of the Mountain!'

Now the mutters turned into sharp cries, full of outrage. Melaugo could not believe what she was hearing. The woman was not only condemning the Saint, but praising the wyrm that had almost destroyed the world. She might as well have chopped some wood and built her own pyre.

'What sort of jape is this?'

'A test from King Sigoso, surely,' someone murmured. 'A test of our loyalty to the Saint.'

'Are you absolutely sure that's what she said?'

'Hear me,' Donma Lusua called. 'The Nameless One seeks only to cleanse the world of corruption.' Her voice cracked. 'We fought the mighty Fýredel during the Grief of Ages, but this time, we must not resist his coming. Until this kingdom has been scoured of the unholy Saint—'

'Blasphemer,' a man bellowed, and his accusation set everyone off, like a flame put to a keg of gunpowder.

'Heretic!'

'What do you mean by this?'

'Do not resist,' Donma Lusua ordered again, but Melaugo could have sworn there was fear on her face. 'Please, do not resist—'

Liyat reached for Melaugo, her breath coming short.

'Whatever this is,' she said, 'I want no part in it.' She started to shoulder through the crowd, which was now surging forward, towards the Knights Defendant. 'That man over there was right. This must be some perverse test of faith. We should leave.'

Melaugo nodded. 'We can wait in the storm drain,' she said. 'Just until—'

A chilling scream cut her off.

The entire crowd stopped moving and fell silent. All eyes were on the sky, from whence the scream had come. No human could make such a sound, but Melaugo had heard something like it before. In the dank caves and abandoned mines where only sleepers dwelled.

So when it landed on the dome of the Great Sanctuary of Ortégardes, she was among the first to accept it.

She had seen Draconic creatures, but nothing of this cruelty or magnitude. Even longer than the lindworm in Triyenas, the horned monster was covered with scales, and its wings, torn and brindle, were like those of some immense bat. A bullwhip of a tail lashed behind it.

A fucking *wyvern*, in broad daylight.

For five centuries, the people of Virtudom had been weaned on tales of the Grief of Ages. They knew what they were looking at – the foes that stalked their prayer books and their bedtime tales. Melaugo looked speechlessly at Liyat, whose terrified gaze was fixed on the wyvern.

And then the wyvern let out a roar, and it was as if a cannon had gone off.

Melaugo kept hold of Liyat. The icy calm of a culler kicked in, even as fear sparked in her breast and the streets erupted into chaos.

That roar had made the wyvern real.

They were standing at the edge of the crowd, else they would have been lost in the fray at once, unable to get clear. By instinct, they rushed the same way they had come. Just as they pulled free of the horde, a man slammed into Melaugo, and she hit the cobbles, tasting blood as she bit her own tongue.

'Bastard,' she spat. He was already gone.

'Estina.' Liyat was shouting with all her might, yet Melaugo could barely hear: 'Everyone will be heading for the gates. The stables will be plundered. We have to use the drain to get there first!'

Melaugo allowed herself to be hauled to her feet. On the dome, the wyvern roared again. She looked up to see five more winging over the square, monstrous in size and aspect. Some of the city guards were loading their crossbows, while others had drawn their swords.

'Where are the springalds, the cannons?' Melaugo snarled. 'What was the *point* of building them?'

Liyat did not reply. Her gaze was darting around them, assessing their surroundings, coming up with a rational plan. In silent agreement, they started to run, buffeting past other Yscals.

Ortégardes was surrounded by a crenelated wall, built when the Yscali monarchs had been courting war with Lasia. It was lined with springalds, mangonels and cannons – weapons proven to kill wyrms – but none of them were being used. Though the wall had sixty round towers, it was far lower on gates, with only two wide enough for large crowds. A crush was forming on Cypress Street as thousands of people made for the nearest.

Melaugo stopped as another wyvern shot overhead. Next she knew, the crowd was covered in red fire.

The screams were deafening. She pushed Liyat into a doorway before a second eruption of fire, impossibly hot, rained down on another part of the crowd. Melaugo could hardly breathe, and not just because the air scorched in her throat. The implications of this were appalling. If the wyverns had their flames, then a High Western was either awake, or close to it.

A second Grief of Ages might be about to begin.

'Open the gates,' came the agonised shouts from the crowd. 'For the love of the Saint, open the gates!'

'They're closed?' Melaugo croaked. 'Why the fuck would they be closed?'

'You heard that disgrace of a knight,' Liyat bit out. 'King Sigoso is complicit in this madness.'

'That is not possible. No wyrm has *ever* treated with—'

'Estina, we'll question it later. We have to get out of here now.' Liyat leaned past her to look at the street, hair clinging to the sweat on her face. 'The other gates will be locked, too.

The storm drain isn't far. This time, we do not stop until we reach the stables. Are we agreed?'

Melaugo nodded. Together, they left the shelter of the doorway and took a narrow backstreet towards the city wall.

Liyat ducked into the drain first. Melaugo left its cover open, so a few lucky others could find their way out before the Knights Defendant sealed it. They barrelled down the smugglers' tunnel, and soon they were back above ground, wading through the moat, almost falling.

On the other side of the city wall, they could see more wyverns approaching from the north. As Melaugo smelled burnt hair and flesh, she saw that the gates had not only been shut, but chained together. If she had been harbouring any doubts about human complicity, that sight banished them. There were no guards to be seen; no one from whom a key might be wrung.

On one of the towers that flanked the gate, a mangonel was mounted, with no obvious way to reach it from this side. Before Melaugo could improvise, a wyvern shattered the war engine with one blow of its tail, showering the moat with shards of wood and metal.

They kept running towards the stables. Inside, more panic-stricken people were claiming horses at random. Liyat went for her own mare, but a desperate man already had it by the reins. Seeing Liyat, he reached for his sword.

Before he could use it, Liyat shot him in the shoulder. The mare reared up. While the man writhed in pain and cursed Liyat, she stowed the gun and calmed the horse as best she could.

'Where should we go?' Melaugo asked her, heaving for breath. 'The Lasian border?'

'No. There is no cover in the marchlands,' Liyat said. 'But Harlowe and his ship will still be in Oryzon.'

'What use is a fucking ship?' Melaugo almost screamed. 'It's wood!'

'It's a way out,' Liyat shot back. 'We need to leave Yscalin, and the *Rose Eternal* is heavily armed. It's our best chance.' She reached for her saddle. 'Unless you have another plan?'

Melaugo did not have another plan. Her mind was a white roar of dread, barely contained by her skull. Her mare had already been taken, so she wrestled a sleek black palfrey from its stall. It resisted her with some force, whinnying in alarm.

'Trust me,' Melaugo growled, 'you don't want to be near a wyvern. I don't know how they turn you into war beasts, but I doubt you'll like it.'

The palfrey snorted. While Liyat held off the other thieves from the back of her mare, Melaugo buckled on a saddle and swung her leg across it. Together, they joined the rest of the Yscals who had been outside when the gates closed. Some were trying to get in, hollering the names of their loved ones, but most were fleeing in droves, either on horseback or foot.

Not daring to look back, Melaugo sent her palfrey galloping after Liyat, on to the wine road that led to the coast. In their wake, the people of Ortégardes cried for mercy, trapped by their own defensive wall.

****

The screams from Ortégardes took hours to fade. When they did, the silence was thunderous. Melaugo hoped it was because she and Liyat were too far away to hear them, and not because there had been no survivors. The wyrms had been known to raze entire cities, leaving the streets littered with bones.

For almost a day, Melaugo rode after Liyat, who barely uttered a word. The other absconders stayed away from them, and from each other. Perhaps they were all convinced they had shamed the Knight of Courage with their flight, but Melaugo was a realist. Other than leaving the storm drain open, there was nothing she could have done without her weapons. Perhaps some fortunate soul would come upon them in the Golden Pear. Now she had only a single blade.

If Harlowe had already left Oryzon, that blade was another way out.

They soon ran into others on the wine road – a river of Yscals, all bearing what they could, making for the western ports of Córvugar and Oryzon. Some rode on carts and horses, while others were on foot. Melaugo glimpsed appalling burns on some of them; others were covered in ash and soot, coughing.

This assault had been going on for hours or days. Hard to tell the precise amount of time. At every turn, the wyverns had overtaken the messengers, making it hard for word to spread.

It seemed they had come from the Spindles, perhaps even from Cárscaro. Now they were making their way between the largest settlements of Yscalin, often announced by the Knights Defendant, and it seemed the artillery had been sabotaged. King Sigoso had sent letters to all of the city officials and castellans, commanding them to ensure his subjects' compliance.

'I swear to the Saint, it was in his own hand,' one man was saying, his face red and sweating. 'His Majesty *told* us to destroy the war engines! He ordered us not to resist the wyverns!'

'That's the Grand Chancellor of Abraba. He used to punish any word against the king with public floggings.' Liyat watched him. 'If even *he* is condemning Sigoso, this story can only be true.'

Abraba was the City of Temperance. Small wonder that they had crumbled, with instincts like theirs. They had probably been afraid to use too many arrows. But farther down the road, Melaugo overheard some hopeful news about Samana, the City of Courage, where many guards and soldiers had defied their sovereign. Refusing to dismantle the artillery, they were using it to drive off the wyverns. Their grand chancellor had apparently joined the rebellion.

Samana was one thing. It was a garrison city, the stronghold of Yscali military power, where most Western artillery and firearms were made – but Melaugo had little hope for the rest of Yscalin. Even though it had the largest standing army in the West, expanded by King Sigoso after the sudden death of Queen Sahar, none of its soldiers had ever faced wyverns.

During the Grief, everyone had either hid or fought. As far as Melaugo knew, there had never been a formal surrender to the wyrms. It was a unique tactic; she would grant Sigoso that.

At last, they reached the crossway between the wine and salt roads, where some people had collapsed in exhaustion. Not all of them had steeds, and many were carrying packs or children. Melaugo looked back, sweat on her brow. In the distance, the sky was dark with smoke.

'We can't rest for long.' Liyat led her tired horse towards the river. 'King Sigoso must be held to ransom. There can be no other reason he would try to stop us mounting a defence.'

'A good king would still urge his people to fight to save themselves,' Melaugo said bitterly. 'Yscalin has artillery and—'

'Not enough. Half of the war engines are in a state of disrepair,' Liyat said. 'Nobody wanted to spend the coin to maintain them. Every generation has believed that it would not be their burden.'

'Who told you this?'

'You know I have friends all over Yscalin.'

Melaugo glanced over her shoulder again, swallowing the metallic tang of her own fear. 'If all of the sleepers on this continent have woken,' she said, 'it will be overrun in a matter of days.'

'And the Draconic plague will return.' Liyat climbed back into her saddle. 'We have no choice but to leave. It will spread like wildfire.'

'What about your work?'

'I will see to it later. Harlowe once offered me a place on the *Rose*. For now, I will accept.'

'A ship is nothing to a wyrm.'

'Our ships are not like any they have ever faced. If Harlowe can keep the plague off the *Rose*, there will be no safer place.'

'And what if he's already gone?'

'He won't go without you, Estina. In all these years, has he ever given up?'

Melaugo drew a deep breath without answering. Liyat gave her a last unreadable look before she turned her mare towards the salt road.

Melaugo

Liyat rode like a windstorm, with Melaugo behind, weary to her bones. She never had much cause to ride, but Liyat sought relics all over Yscalin, and was used to the trials of horseback.

They kept to as much cover as they could, riding under trees and through fields of wheat, covering the most distance at night. Every so often, a wyvern soared overhead, forcing them off the road. The sound of their wings betrayed their approach.

At a certain point, Melaugo took the lead. She knew the way to Oryzon as well as she knew anything.

At the western end of the Groneyso Valley, they passed the remains of the ancient Rose Sanctuary. A sanctarian wandered in the rubble, her robe charred, wringing blistered hands.

Harlowe might well have already sailed, if the same chaos was descending on Oryzon. If so, they would have to ride to Nzene, which could take weeks or months. That was if the wyverns had not already reached the South. For all Melaugo knew, they could be appearing everywhere.

During the Grief, all they had craved was mindless violence. Even with the king's surrender, she could not imagine how it would be any different now.

When they approached the Port of Oryzon, where Melaugo had eked out her formative years, the flock was not far behind. All day, the wyverns had been calling to each other in their wake. Melaugo wondered if the Knights Defendant had reached the coast first, to herald their arrival, or if these people were unaware that King Sigoso had surrendered to the Nameless One – but as soon as they grew close, the sounds of terror could be heard.

They rode to Halassa Street, to the house with the yellow door, where Harlowe lived whenever he stayed on the western coast. Melaugo pounded on the door, but there was no answer.

'He's gone.' She almost laughed. 'The bastard has left. Just as I was about to accept his offer—'

'He could still be in the harbour,' Liyat said.

She led her mare onward, and Melaugo followed, pulling the nervous palfrey past the imposing walls of the Customs House of Oryzon and down to where thousands of Yscals lined the docks.

The people swamped the small fishing boats, several of which had overturned, and climbed aboard any ship they could see by whatever means they could. The crews either helped them over or used rifles and harpoons to deter them. Melaugo caught sight of an urchin and tensed, seeing herself as that little girl, defenceless and alone. The girl looked her right in the eyes.

Before she could act, the crowd had engulfed the child.

Holding on to the brim of her new hat, she looked at the ships, many of which she knew well by sight. The *Red*

Moon, a caravel belonging to the Comptroller of Oryzon, was already some way out of the harbour. She must have been among the first to receive the warning.

Most of the others were merchant carracks. The Halassa Sea lapped at the nearest hulls, the greenish waves clouded by silt. As Melaugo watched, a woman used a loose rope to scale a Mentish flyboat, only for a gunshot to send her crashing down. Another corpse already floated nearby, circled by stained water. Someone began to pray aloud.

'We can't risk boarding those,' Liyat shouted over the din. 'We'll be at the mercy of their crews.'

'Better than wyverns!'

'I would choose a wyvern over certain seafarers. At least it would be quick,' Liyat said. 'Did Suylos never tell you about keelhauling?' She turned, shielding her eyes from the sun. 'I told Harlowe that I meant to take you to Ortégardes if you refused his offer. He knows how long it would take us to get here.'

Melaugo could not reply, even as Liyat pulled her along the harbour, searching for a gap in the crowd. She knew this port like she knew her own freckles, and the *Rose Eternal* was nowhere to be seen.

Harlowe was gone. At last, he understood. The weight of her would sink the whole ship.

'Estina.' Liyat grasped her arm, fingers biting into her skin. 'There.'

She pointed. Melaugo followed her line of sight, squinting against the glare of the low sun. In the distance, about two and a half miles away, was the outline of an Inysh man-of-war.

A ship of that size was hard to miss. And not many of them came to Yscalin.

'Shit,' Melaugo breathed. 'Is that the *Rose*, for certain?'

Without replying, Liyat took off her bandolier, then unlaced her jerkin and tossed it aside. Melaugo stared at her.

'I would usually not protest you undressing,' she said, 'but why the fuck are you doing it now?'

'Where there are wyverns, the plague follows. Every chronicle agrees on that,' Liyat reminded her. 'I don't know about you, but I would rather die by drowning than by cooking from within.'

She knelt to remove her riding boots. Without looking back, she sprinted to the end of the wharf, past the shallows and the people, and dove into the water. Melaugo hesitated, unsure if she was impressed or appalled, then cursed and stripped down to her shirt and breeches.

At the end of the wharf, she stopped, heart pounding. Liyat waited for her in the water.

'Liyat,' Melaugo gritted out, 'I may not know about keel-hauling, but I do know that I am a terrible swimmer. The *Rose* is too far. We'll be dead before we—'

'No. I have an idea.' Liyat kicked away from the wharf. 'Hurry, before the wyverns reach us!'

Melaugo swore again and plunged in after her.

There was blissful silence, then salt in her eyes. Her fellow smugglers had taught her to swim, but she had not tried since leaving Perunta, and a few days of hearty food had failed to restore her wrecked body. By the time she caught up to Liyat, every joint and limb was sore.

'Saint's shrivelling codpiece,' she stammered. 'Harlowe really wants me to be a seafarer?'

'Just swim, Estina!'

They forged past the merchant ships and the old hulk that served as a gambling den, towards the distant *Rose*. Melaugo stopped to sputter, the balls of her arms screaming in their sockets. The sea was calm, but trying to stay above the surface was exhausting her.

'Estina.' Seeing her stop, Liyat came back. 'Come on!'

'Just leave me.' Melaugo coughed up seawater. 'Liyat, please, go without me. I can't—'

'Yes, you can.' Liyat wrapped a strong arm around her waist. 'Hold on to me.'

Melaugo gripped her shoulders. They bobbed on the surface like a pair of bottles, treading water. Behind them, red fire and screams filled Oryzon. Beside Melaugo, Liyat watched the sky.

'What are you waiting for?' Melaugo said, shivering.

As though it had been summoned, the sun broke through the clouds. Liyat thrust up a hand, and the small mirror in her grasp caught the light. She tilted it back and forth, so it flashed.

'You're signalling.' Melaugo laughed so hard she coughed again. 'You're *signalling*, Liyat!'

'It might not work. We need to keep moving.' Liyat pulled her on. 'Stay with me, Estina.'

There was no choice now. Most of the harbour was ablaze, the wyverns circling the ships, setting fire to all of them, from the cogs to the ornate galleons. A few other people were swimming for their lives as well.

The *Queen Idreiga*, a royal warship, was berthed on the northern end of the harbour. As Melaugo swam backwards, unable to take her eyes off the destruction, three wyverns converged on it, and the gunpowder inside was kindled. It ripped the ship apart with a force that blew the wyverns back. She dived underwater before the heat could reach her. When she broke the surface, the *Queen Idreiga* was a smoking wreck, and bodies scattered the churning waves around it.

Liyat came up beside Melaugo. With all their strength, they forged onward, though Melaugo was already floundering again. She kept hold of Liyat, who supported her as much as she could while keeping them moving.

The sun was setting now, and with it, their hope of being saved. Liyat held up the mirror once more, catching the last few rays. They had gone too far to turn back. When Melaugo started to sink, she knew she was too exhausted to kick back to the surface. Liyat suddenly let out a laugh.

'Estina,' she gasped out, 'look!'

Melaugo looked. A rowboat was riding the waves, closing in.

When it reached them, a scarred Hróthi woman offered a hand. Liyat grasped it and was pulled, sodden and breathless, into the care of a dozen people. She reached back for Melaugo. Their fingers slipped apart, and Melaugo thought she would be washed away, but then they were both in the boat, wrapped in mantles, and there was a warm hipflask in her grasp.

'Estina Melaugo?' the Hróthi woman said. Melaugo nodded. 'Good. Back to the ship, now!'

'What about the others?' Melaugo croaked. 'There were people in the water, they were swimming—'

'I see none.'

Melaugo slowly looked. She was right.

Several oars swashed through the waves. For a time, Melaugo could do nothing but hold on to a shivering Liyat. To her faint surprise, Liyat grasped her just as tightly, even brushing a kiss against her temple. Melaugo leaned against her and let her eyes drift shut. A man gave them both knitted work caps to keep the chill at bay, placing them on top of their wet hair.

By the time they reached the *Rose Eternal*, it was almost dusk. The harbour blazed in their wake, though the rest of the city was darker, only its greenery burning. The Act of Preservation was protecting it from the fire – but while the law might save the buildings, it would not help the people inside. Not for long. All she could hear in the distance was screaming.

The *Rose Eternal* was anchored in deep water, where the Halassa Sea was rough. Its lanterns had been dowsed, so it could no longer be seen from the shore. Melaugo climbed on to its deck, still drenched to the bone, with Liyat just behind. Harlowe waited on the quarterdeck, his pipe in hand.

'Estina,' he said.

'Harlowe,' she rasped.

'I see you've accepted my offer. Only took the end of the world.'

Melaugo wheezed something that might charitably be described as a laugh.

'Liyat. Good to see you.' Harlowe gave her a nod as she reached the deck. 'I knew Sigoso was a hypocrite, but I didn't quite expect this. I imagine you'll want to go to Nzene, but for now—'

'Yes. I accept the offer, if it stands,' Liyat said. 'Both of us will join the crew.'

'Good. I could use someone with your knowledge.'

'Captain,' came a cry from behind him.

Melaugo turned. A single wyvern was flying in their direction, just visible in the dying light.

Harlowe watched it approach with a stony look. It was coming towards them quickly, its vast wingspan eating up the distance. As it drew closer, he signalled to one of his crew.

'Harlowe?' Melaugo said, her voice higher than usual. 'Harlowe, I hope you're planning to fire at—'

'I see you're already taking to the job,' Harlowe said drily. She glowered at him. 'Ready the harpoon gun. Plume, fire on the upward roll!'

'Fire on the upward roll,' the quartermaster echoed, his voice loud and clear.

Melaugo reached for the mast of the ship, while Liyat gripped the wale. As the Halassa Sea raised the *Rose Eternal*, their boots slipped on the deck, and Melaugo wondered if this was how she would die, like Sabran the Ambitious and King Bardholt, burned alive on a wooden bier.

By now the wyvern was close enough for her to see its eyes, its maw. Melaugo turned numb. The guns boomed – a sound so colossal it rattled her teeth – before cannonballs and chainshot went soaring. One chain ensnared the wyvern by its foot, while a ball struck it hard in the breast and a harpoon missed it by an inch.

The wyvern screamed and beat its wings, wrenching itself back. The downwind was strong enough to knock most of the crew off their feet, and Melaugo went right down with them, smashing her elbow against the deck. She forced down the pain and stared up at the wyvern, at its horns and teeth. It had to be sixty feet long, with a wingspan at least twice that length.

Liyat had been right. During the Grief of Ages, ships would have seemed like toys to a wyvern. Now it was confronted with a man-of-war, with more than a hundred guns on the broadsides alone.

'Fire,' Plume roared again, and the cannons released another volley. The wyvern spat embers, which rained on the deck, before it banked away and flew back towards Oryzon.

'Get us out of here,' Harlowe said to his quartermaster. 'Before the damned thing returns with its friends.'

His deckhands were already smothering the small red fires. Melaugo caught her breath and stood. When Harlowe turned to her, she folded her arms with some difficulty, dripping salt water.

'Listen to me,' he said. 'I'm heading for Ascalon, to warn Queen Sabran of what has befallen this place. If we reach

Perchling and you still don't want to be my boatswain, I'll let you disembark there, and you can go wheresoever in this world you will. But give me this one voyage to convince you. Have we a deal, Estina Melaugo?'

He held out a weathered hand, unsmiling. Melaugo glanced at Liyat, who gave her a nod.

'You win,' Melaugo said, and shook.

****

They made decent pace under cover of night. Despite its bulk, the *Rose Eternal* was swift. Most of the crew stayed awake, but a few rested in hammocks, Liyat and Melaugo among them. Liyat seemed to drift off, but Melaugo could not, despite her exhaustion.

For the first time in her life, she was not in Yscalin.

Before they descended, a gunner had shown them both around the ship by the light of a single lantern. They had been provided with bread and beef stew, though neither of them had the stomach for it.

In the small hours, Melaugo gave up and made her way to the deck, too sore of limb and soul to rest. The scarred Hróthi woman, whose name was Bara, brought her a cup of hot mead. Melaugo decided to ignore the obvious risks of a stove on a wooden ship. It was a trifling danger compared to wyverns. Nursing the mead, she took a slow walk along the deck, taking in the iron capstan, the rigging and cannons, the harpoon gun that had helped save their lives.

She had never realised how many people were needed to keep a man-of-war moving. Harlowe commanded a crew of hundreds. At least a quarter of them were Northerners, like Bara, one of several carpenters. The Hróthi had a long history of seafaring. The others seemed to come from all over, including the East, which had startled the wits out of Melaugo. Most people of Virtudom would never meet or see an Easterner.

Harlowe wanted her to be the voice of this entire crew. To secure their respect, she would have to learn quickly and find her sea legs. It all looked complex, but perhaps that was what she needed. A distraction to keep her from losing her mind.

The *Rose Eternal* creaked as she cut through the waves, sails billowing in the wind. They made a sound like a drumbeat. To her own surprise, Melaugo found it soothing. So was the motion underfoot. If not for her aching body, and her fear, she might have slept very well in the hammock.

In silence, she went to the right side of the ship. They had been sailing for hours, and there seemed to be no end to the destruction on the western coast. The wyverns had torched almost every harbour.

Her breath came in a fog. Before long, she wished she had brought the bedding from the hammock. She had never been this cold, even on the worst nights in Triyenas, but she could not rip her gaze away. There was a dreadful beauty in that fire. The stars twinkled overhead, blurring every time she blinked, bright and piercing even with the red haze far below.

Liyat came to stand beside her, wrapped in a heavy woollen blanket. 'Could you not sleep?'

Melaugo shook her head. 'Could you?'

'Not well.' Liyat sipped from her own cup. 'Long ago, my people lived beyond the great salt desert. A group of them followed Suttu the Dreamer, knowing they might never return. I often wonder how they felt when they looked back for the last time.'

She rarely opened up like this. Melaugo had no wish to interrupt her.

'I imagine my shop has already burned.' Liyat paused. 'But perhaps it is for the best.'

'How so?' Melaugo asked. 'You loved the shop.'

Liyat looked at the blazing coastline.

'A few years ago, an ancient compass came into my keeping. At some point in time, its needle had rusted in place,' she said. 'I was like that compass when you found me. I had finally established a safe place, a home, in Perunta. But the longer you remain still, the more rust starts to cover you, and underneath, you become fragile. And soon it hurts to move at all.'

'You never stopped moving. How many times did you leave Perunta to find relics?'

'Yes, but it was always there, waiting for me to return. My work could be dangerous, but it was what I knew, and even the risks were predictable. Perhaps that was why you frightened me so much. Because you were different. I wanted to make space for you in my life, but I fought, because it hurt.'

Melaugo kept listening.

'For me, change is difficult. It is paralysing. It makes me feel vulnerable,' Liyat said quietly. 'I live in fear of making the wrong choice, because I have seen how badly that can go.'

'And you ... thought I might be the wrong choice.'

'I would have felt the same about anyone who made me feel the way you do.' She drank again. 'But now the burden of choice has been taken from me. All of our lives have been shattered this day. The rust has been stripped. I am free to chart a different course. To start anew.'

'What about your work?'

'Harlowe will help me continue with it, but he will also train me as a cartographer.' Liyat looked her in the eyes. 'Estina, if I have ever made you feel unwanted or burdensome, I apologise. You are neither. You brought laughter and joy to my life, which lacked both for too long.'

Melaugo returned her gaze, a lump rising in her throat.

'I cannot promise I will heal. Perhaps it is in my nature to rust,' Liyat said. 'But life on the *Rose* will be different, I think. Always on the move, yet always home. And whatever happens next, I want us to face it together. Before, I think that I could only ever have held out a cup for your wine, and a small one, at that. Now look what we have. The depths of an ocean.'

To demonstrate her point, she threw her tankard overboard. Melaugo looked after it with a small huff of laughter, and Liyat smiled in a way Melaugo had never seen her smile before.

'But perhaps an ocean is too big,' she said. 'Perhaps this ship will be enough to hold both of our wine, so it can grow finer each year.' She looked Melaugo in the eyes. 'Do you agree?'

Before Melaugo could stop it, a tear had slid down her cheek, tasting of the sea. She was the winemakers' daughter and the urchin, the smuggler and the culler, and Liyat was accepting them all.

'Yes,' she said. 'I will happily rust in place with you, Liyat of Nzene.'

Liyat kissed her on the lips, lingering for some time, and wrapped the blanket around her shoulders. A fortress that shut out the wind. And Estina Melaugo realised she had never felt as safe or wanted or settled anywhere, while everything else she had ever known crumbled.

All night they stood that way, beneath the stars, and watched Yscalin burn.

AFTER

Aubrecht

BRYGSTAD

FREE STATE OF MENTENDON

CE 1003

The Free State of Mentendon often changed its clothes, but it favoured grey, no matter the season. One day it wore a cap of clouds; the next, a cloak of fog, a veil of rain. Still, when the sun did shine, Aubrecht Lievelyn fancied there was no finer place in the West than Brygstad.

His writing desk faced a bow window. From that vantage point, he could see the whole of Lievelyn Square, where his people were enjoying the warm spell. They ate cherries and strawberries, cooled themselves by the Fountain of Ebanth, let their children run wild on the cobblestones.

Not for the first time, Aubrecht wished he could join them. When he was only a young count, he often had, despite his parents' concern for his safety.

And then the Brygstad Terror had changed everything. Now here he was, the future High Prince, ever discouraged from leaving the palace. And when he read the letter, he knew why.

To Leovart Lievelyn, Grey Prince of Mentendon, wishing you well upon the occasion of your eightieth birthday. May you not suffer a feather death, for that would be a shame for all the ages to behold.

The message was in Low Hróthi, a dialect Aubrecht had not seen or heard in many years, but the hand was familiar, as was the wax seal. It showed the breaking wheel of Clan Vatten.

Aubrecht looked up from the page, beholding his own reflection in the forest glass. No wonder his granduncle was ignoring these letters.

Brygstad was a Hróthi name. There was some debate over whether it should be changed to a Mentish one – Thisunath, after the lost capital, or the simpler Brudstath – but for now, it remained as it had been for centuries. A constant reminder of the Hróthi occupation.

He glanced back at the people in the square. For centuries, the Ments had been unwanted guests in their own country, ruled and exploited by the Hróthi. Now they were independent once more, but Clan Vatten still saw fit to send these petty threats.

Not for much longer. Soon Marosa would be here, and the Vatten would never dare to threaten the House of Lievelyn again. Not with the Donmata of Yscalin knit into the family.

The thought of Marosa eased the tension from his jaw. Only a few weeks to go, and they would be married in Ortégardes. At last, she would be his companion, and he would be hers.

He wondered how she would feel when she realised his situation.

Taking a deep breath, Aubrecht gathered up the letters that required the attention of the High Prince himself. He left the peace of his Privy Chamber and prepared to face his granduncle.

The sweating sickness had killed more than half of his family. Since Edvart and Lesken – the ruler and the heir – had both succumbed, it was deemed that Aubrecht, at two and twenty, should rule next.

And then Leovart had convinced everyone that *he* really ought to be on the throne, given that poor Aubrecht was clearly numb with grief. It would be cruel to crown him at such a tender age. Mentendon did not have to be like other monarchies, burdening the young. The Hróthi prized age and wisdom in their leaders – why could the House of Lievelyn not follow suit?

And that was how Aubrecht found himself here, a decade later, watching as Leovart squatted on his throne, and the Council of State remained too paralysed by courtesy to comment.

He found Leovart dozing in the Privy Library, where he must have been pretending to do something of use. Above him, like a judge, was a painting of a better ruler. Kathel Lievelyn, the first High Princess of Mentendon, who had led the Mentish Defiance against Hróth.

Her portrait showed her with a head of magnificent red curls. According to legend, that hair was the reason their early ancestors had been driven from the North, accused of being agents of a fire god named Mentun. Aubrecht knew he was called the Red Prince across the West – apparently to distinguish him from the Grey Prince, a moniker that had been kept out of the palace with as much force as if it were the pestilence. Leovart did not like to be reminded of his age.

If only anyone else could forget it. Aubrecht looked with pity and frustration at the old man, sound asleep in his chair. The last batch of letters was piled on a shelf behind him, clearly unread.

'Your Royal Highness.' Aubrecht approached the desk. 'Granduncle. It's Aubrecht.'

Leovart kept snoring.

'Granduncle,' Aubrecht bellowed, and Leovart startled awake with a snort. 'Good morrow.'

'Saint above, boy, what is it?'

'Skuldir Vatten has written again.'

'What does he want?'

'He offers you belated wishes for your birthday, but he also ... raised the subject of death. We ought to ensure the coastal defences are—'

'Bah, let Skuldir rot. Queen Sabran will not brook any more carping from Hróth.' Leovart squinted at Aubrecht. 'For the life of me, I can't remember why we didn't offer you up to *her*, rather than plight you to the Donmata. Now I've squandered my only eligible relative.'

You were too busy trying to court Queen Sabran yourself, Aubrecht thought.

'I am very happy to marry the Donmata,' he said. 'And grateful that a time has finally been set.'

'You can blame Sigoso the Cold for the tarrying. He must have lost his faith in marriage after what tha—' Leovart paused to cough, 'what that wretched Southerner did to him. He's lucky we're taking the girl, frankly. Our future princess consort, and he wants her back within the year.'

'King Sigoso is not old, Granduncle. Marosa will have many years in Mentendon before she is crowned.'

'No.' Leovart coughed again, harder. 'No. He wants her back as soon as she's with child.'

Aubrecht was sure no one had told him that.

'I see,' he said, after a pause. He would digest the knowledge later. 'How are you feeling, Granduncle?'

'Very well, thank you.'

'What have you been doing today?'

'Oh, the … accounts.' Leovart dabbed his mouth. 'I'm very busy, Aubrecht. Come back later.'

Aubrecht might once have stayed, to coax and wheedle until he was blue in the face, but he had long since learned that Leovart would feign a headache, or some other ailment, to avoid the matter of Hróth. By the time he reached the doorway, Leovart was asleep again.

In spite of his better judgement, Aubrecht still loved him. Lievelyns had to stick together, through thick and thin. There were too many circling wolves for swans to turn upon themselves. He went back to his study, rubbed his temples, and picked up the next letter.

At the time, Leovart had made a fair point about the succession. Aubrecht had been newly orphaned, left to care for his three younger sisters, including a weakened Betriese, who had barely survived the sweat. He had also been trained to enter the faith, despite living at court. His uncle had wanted him to be Principal Sanctarian of Mentendon, to raise Mentish standing with the Berethnets.

Crippled by grief, with no knowledge of politics, Aubrecht would not have been able to rule a country. Now that he *was* ready, Leovart seemed resolved to die on the throne. The wind that fought the barge of progress Mentendon had otherwise become.

'Aubrecht?'

Suddenly he had sympathy for Leovart never getting anything done. He glanced up to see his twin sisters at his threshold. 'Perhaps we could speak later,' he started, but they had already marched in. 'I have a great deal to do today.'

'You sound like Granduncle.' Betriese leaned over his shoulder. 'What is it you're doing?'

'I am attending to the needs of Mentendon.'

'Do stop pretending to write letters every time we step into your eyeline.' Bedona snatched one up and raked her gaze over the crabbed writing. 'This looks dull. Saint, is this about *sewers*, Brecht?'

Both of them followed the Inysh manner of dress, like many of the younger courtiers. At this time of year, they wore apricot and spring green, paired with rose-gold jewellery. The latter clashed with their scarlet hair, but Aubrecht knew better than to point this out.

'Even dull letters need answering. Especially the ones about sewers,' he said patiently, 'unless you would like Brygstad to be overrun with night soil.' He slid the letter from the Vatten out of sight. 'Nonetheless, I am at your disposal. How may I help you this morning, Bedona?'

'We'd like to write to the Donmata Marosa,' Betriese said in her delicate voice. 'Does she speak Mentish?'

'She is learning.' Aubrecht touched her rosy cheek, making her smile. 'I am sure she would appreciate a letter in Mentish, Bette. Let me know when it is done, and I will send it for you.'

'At least we'll have something to do,' Bedona drawled.

'Be grateful for your empty days. Ermuna will take on a great burden when she becomes my heir apparent.'

'While we stand around looking beautiful until you marry one of us off?'

'Bedona, I told you. You will marry who you please on my watch.'

'Oh, good.' She lounged on the edge of his desk. 'I always thought the stable lad was handsome.'

'Within reason.' Aubrecht attempted a stern look. 'Begone, both of you, please. I am working.'

'Stop working and get ready for your wedding.'

'I agree.' Betriese sat on the arm of his chair and wrapped her arms around his shoulders. 'The Donmata hasn't seen you for *years*, Brecht. You'll need to work terribly hard to impress her.'

'You *are* boring,' Bedona remarked.

'Bedona.' Aubrecht could not help but smile again. 'You shame the Knight of Courtesy.'

'Leave Aubrecht be,' a welcome voice said. 'Bedona, your dancing master is looking for you.'

'Oh, hang the dancing master.' Bedona sighed. 'Why in Halgalant do I need to dance?'

'To save you from idleness,' Ermuna said crisply. 'Go, before I call your manners tutor to assist him.'

In perfect unison, the twins flanked Aubrecht and kissed his cheeks. He embraced them both. His mother had died to give them both life, but he could not have done without them. They left the room, arm in arm, whispering in the language they had invented as children.

'Thank you,' Aubrecht said to Ermuna.

His eldest sister gave him a nod. Unlike the twins, Ermuna was dressed like a Mentish courtier, in contrasting ebony and ivory, with a blackwork partlet. It made her long red curls stand out. She looked so much like Kathel Lievelyn, she might have been her living ghost.

'Bette *does* make a sound point,' she told him. 'You ought to write to the Donmata.'

'How do you know I have not?'

'Because I have seen the number of other letters you have to answer.' She eyed the pile. 'Does she write often?'

'Every few weeks.' Aubrecht stood. 'Leovart claims Sigoso wants her back as soon as she is with child.'

'That will not happen.'

'It was agreed that our first heir would be for Yscalin.'

'Yes, and the second for Mentendon. We need both before the Donmata leaves.'

'We may not be able to conceive at all.'

'Ever the pessimist.' Ermuna studied his face. 'What else is troubling you, Brecht?' When he passed her the letter from Skuldir Vatten, she opened it and read, gaze darting across the page. 'They are shaking their fists. Let them wear themselves out, like children in a strop.'

'It has been over a century since the Mentish Defiance. Are they not already tired?'

'A century is not long to the Hróthi. They are proud,' Ermuna said. 'But King Raunus is a virtuous man. He and Queen Sabran will keep the Vatten on their leash.' She put the letter down. 'Without Mentendon, they are not the great power they were, even on the sea.'

'That makes us more of a temptation. Mentendon is richer than it ever was under their rule.'

'The Hróthi intermarried with too many Ments during the last decades of the stewardship. Half of our nobility has Vatten blood,' she reminded him. 'They still respect the old way of peaceweaving. Unless they have no other choice, they will not attack kin.'

'But *our* house has no Vatten blood. Granduncle refuses to see this.'

'As ever.' Ermuna turned to face him. 'To soothe your fears, when you are crowned, you ought to betroth me to one of their rivals. Clan Ókyrr, perhaps. Clothild would be pleased.'

Aubrecht regarded her. 'You would be willing, Erma?'

'If that is what we feel is best for Mentendon. When you are High Prince, I will be Archduchess of Ostendeur,' Ermuna pointed out. 'A worthy and tempting match for a chieftain.'

Her face was as hard to read as ever. Aubrecht had always had the impression that she did not care for the idea of marriage, but his eldest sister, his closest friend, remained a mystery to him.

'Would it not provoke the Vatten?' he said.

'A wolf is no threat without teeth or claws, even if you goad it.'

His queenly sister, always comporting herself with such dignity and pride. She should have been firstborn.

'We can speak of this another time,' Aubrecht said. 'It has taken Granduncle long enough to arrange my marriage to Marosa. A Hróthi match would need more care in its negotiation.'

'The sun has set on his rule now. He could abdicate with dignity and serve as your advisor.'

'He fears irrelevance. You and I may feel the same at his age.'

'I would not put myself above Mentendon.'

Aubrecht believed her.

'A happier question for you,' Ermuna said. 'Aunt Liuthe has asked me to help oversee the preparations for your progress. We have it all in hand, but I wonder if you could tell me which jewels the Donmata likes to wear, and which flowers she favours.'

'She often wore amber or sard to match her eyes. And the flowers she loves most are lavender, pear blossom, and rose.'

'I will ensure the cities are adorned with them for her.'

'Thank you.' Aubrecht let out a slow breath. 'I hope all of this will not cost too much.'

'Aubrecht, you speak as if we are still a beggared realm. I have checked the accounts. Our trade with Seiiki continues to grow. It is worth a little expense to introduce you both to the people and display our alliance with Yscalin. Another show of strength to the Vatten.'

'Very well.' Aubrecht smiled. 'You were always Mother's daughter when it comes to coins.'

'I know.'

They looked at their parents' marriage portrait. Paltar Lievelyn, the former Archduke of Ostendeur, and his companion, Fralet Dabanon utt Brudstath, from the Dabanon banking dynasty. A love match between Ments, made despite the pressing need for more foreign alliances.

'May the Saint cheer them in Halgalant.' Aubrecht made the sign of the sword. 'I wish they had been able to meet Marosa.'

'We will make her feel safe and welcome, as they would have,' Ermuna said. 'I promise.'

'Thank you, Erma.' He kissed her pale forehead. 'What would I do without you?'

'You would forget you were a prince.'

She left him to his thoughts. He scrunched up the letter from Skuldir Vatten and threw it into the fire.

****

Brygstad Palace had been built over the course of forty years. A breathtaking feat of Mentish marblework, it had long been a safe haven for the House of Lievelyn, except for when the sweat had slipped between its cracks. Now there were stoups of wine in the corridors, meant for handwashing, and the courtyards and gardens abounded with medicinal herbs, like lemon balm and lavender.

In his apartments in the North Pavilion, Aubrecht bathed and drew on a silk nightshirt. It was balmy enough that his Privy Chamberlain had opened the windows and iced his evening wine.

In a few weeks, this bedchamber would no longer be his alone. Marosa would have her own rooms, but at night, they would often be together. He took out her miniature and studied it, the smile returning to his face.

He had always thought the fabled eyes of Oderica must be a lie. The legend of a dying prisoner, taken into the mountain for nine years. The god Fruma had lit her eyes, allowing her to see in the dark, and taught her to smelt iron to defeat the invading Gulthaganians. A heathen origin for a Saint-fearing dynasty, one they had tried to reframe over time.

The court painters showed almost every Vetalda with those strange eyes, like gold or bronze. But when he met Marosa, they had robbed him of breath. He could have easily believed she held dominion over some divine forge.

He was not yet High Prince of Mentendon, but to be a companion to the Donmata of Yscalin, the great military power of the West, would be a formidable task on its own. Politically, they made a strong match, if unusual. Mentendon had a monopoly on the Eastern trade, while the House of Vetalda was old and wealthy, with the largest army in Virtudom. Marosa was also niece to King Jantar of the Ersyr, a connexion that Aubrecht meant to nurture.

They could not put religious differences ahead of progress. The history of Mentendon proved that. So did the flourishing trade with Seiiki, which had saved the Ments from ruin. Aubrecht only hoped that Marosa would understand the Mentish tolerance for heretics and freethinkers.

The friendship that had flowered between them felt as delicate and precious as a rosebud. He wanted to water it with care; to let it bloom with time and warmth. But as soon as they were married, the court would be waiting. Ideally, they would have two children, at the least.

It was usual for monarchs in their position. Aubrecht knew that, but the prospect troubled him. Marosa had been watched so closely in Cárscaro, and now she would be watched again.

He saw it then, so vivid he could smell and hear it. His beloved mother, her bedsheets soaked in blood, her copper hair darkened by sweat. A pair of babies in cradles beside her. She had never stopped bleeding, even though the physicians had tried to save her life.

Look after your sisters, Aubrecht.

And then, eight years later, the sweating sickness. The smells of vinegar and rosemary as more and more of his relatives perished. His mouth filled with a sour taste as he remembered burial after burial. Liuthe howling with grief, a sound no human ought to make. The fear that the Vatten had plotted it all.

Betriese in her sickbed, pale as death.

Aubrecht tried to remain in the present, but the memory was already worming its way through him. The sight of her small, clammy face, the sound of her uneven breaths. He had ignored the physicians' desperate pleading when he entered that room. For hours, he had prayed at her bedside, willing her to open her eyes, knowing he might be next to catch the sickness.

Please, Saint above, not her, not Bette. Mother told me to look after her. I will give you anything.

And now Marosa was joining their family. A family stalked by sorrow. And what if it was her the Saint would take in exchange for Betriese?

What if Marosa died like his mother, in childbirth, and he was the cause?

Aubrecht pressed his fingers to his forehead, where a dull pain was building. Sometimes his thoughts became so intense, they physically hurt. Only Liuthe knew of this affliction, this incontrollable fear of loss. Part of him wished he could love less acutely, so his wild imaginings would not hold so much power over him, but he knew himself too well to think that it would ever change.

He slowed and counted every breath, trying to break his plummet. Many women gave birth several times and survived. Marosa was still young. But knowing that she would be in pain – that she might lose her life – was enough to keep wrenching him back to the past.

Just as he had stayed with Betriese, he would stay with Marosa. He would pray until his voice was hoarse. He would send for the best midwives, even if he had to look for them beyond Virtudom. He would do anything to keep her alive – even if the child was lost, even if they had to try again.

On his watch, no one else he loved would die before their time.

Aubrecht

BRYGSTAD

FREE STATE OF MENTENDON

CE 1003

'Aubrecht.'

He woke at once, his fingers still wrapped around the miniature. When he cracked his eyes open, he saw Ermuna holding a lit candle, her hair in the intricate plait she wore to bed.

'Aunt Liuthe has called us,' she said, her voice low. 'You must come.'

Aubrecht rose without complaint. His Privy Chamberlain helped him into a bedgown.

In a crisis, no matter the hour, the Lievelyns gathered as a family before they summoned the Council of State. If Liuthe had woken them in the middle of the night, it must be urgent.

Liuthe Dabanon utt Brudstath, Dowager Princess of Mentendon, received them in the Swan Chamber. Aubrecht thought his aunt had never looked frailer. Though she was much younger than Leovart, the sweat had nearly killed her in her forties, leaving her thin and grey.

'Aunt.' Ermuna kissed her papery cheek. 'Where is Granduncle?'

'Another ague. His physician is tending him,' Liuthe said. 'I dare not give him these tidings.'

Aubrecht joined the two people who were already seated at the table. Clothild was his fourth cousin, while Gaspart was his third, once removed. He chose the chair beside Clothild, whose flaxen hair was nearly hidden by a stickelchen, an unmistakably Mentish headdress. She was the only person in the room who was not, and had never been, a redhead.

'Brecht,' Gaspart said. 'I hear you're finally to be married, come autumn.' He rubbed his bloodshot eyes. 'Treasure your sleep, for the love of the Saint. You'll be a father before long.'

Aubrecht grimaced. 'Is Henselt still restless?'

'He won't settle with the wet nurse.'

'Think of the poor souls who have no wet nurses to rely on,' Clothild said lightly. 'You have it easy, dear cousin.' Gaspart grunted and reached for the wine. 'Such joyful news, Aubrecht. When will the Donmata arrive?'

'By the end of summer, I hope.' Aubrecht smiled. 'I think you will love her, Clothild.'

'I have no doubt, if you do. We all look forward to meeting her, after so much anticipation.'

'I met her in Ascalon,' Gaspart reminded her. 'The first and last time she was ever seen in public, as far as I know. Do you think she'll be up to this great progress of yours, Aubrecht?'

'Of course,' Aubrecht said. 'She is a princess.'

'A princess in a tower.'

Aubrecht hardly noticed the remark, too busy watching his aunt. Liuthe was usually a woman of good humour, despite the sorrow she carried, but her face held as little mirth as a skull.

The twins were considered too young for these family meetings – they would be allowed to join when they were twenty – so the last to arrive was Aleidine Teldan utt Kantmarkt, Dowager Duchess of Zeedeur. Despite the early hour, she was dressed as well as ever.

'Liuthe,' she said. 'I planned to return to Zeedeur tomorrow. Do I need to stay?'

'I would be grateful if you did, Ally.'

Aleidine sat beside Aubrecht, who gave her a nod. While Aleidine was no Lievelyn, her late aunt had married his grandfather, and she always gave shrewd council. She had opened her home in Zeedeur to him many times.

'How are you, Aubrecht?' she asked him. 'How is the Donmata?'

Aubrecht grinned. 'Does everyone know now?'

'His Royal Highness sent word to us yesterday,' Aleidine said, the corners of her eyes crinkling. 'I so enjoyed meeting Her Radiance in Ascalon. A fine match for our clever prince.'

At last, Liuthe took her place at the end of the table, using her cane for support. They all watched her with curiosity.

'I bear strange and distressing tidings,' she said. 'I hardly know how to break them to you.'

'This family is accustomed to anguish,' Gaspart said in a dry tone. 'Let us hear it, Liuthe.'

'Yscalin has declared its allegiance to the Nameless One.'

The table was silent. She might as well have said that Yscalin had declared its allegiance to apple tarts.

'The Nameless One,' Ermuna echoed. 'Aunt, what can you mean?'

'A letter arrived from Cárscaro, informing us that Yscalin has broken from the Chainmail of Virtudom. The Saint no longer holds sway there,' Liuthe said. 'We should expect war against his followers, and if we do not pledge to serve wyrm-kind, then we shall fall.'

Aubrecht could only stare at her.

'I … feel as if I am in a dream,' Aleidine said, with a faint laugh. Clothild had twin lines between her eyebrows, a sign that she was sinking deep in thought. 'Are you in earnest, Liuthe?'

'I would not have called you here if I were not.'

Gaspart barked a laugh. 'Is Sigoso mad, or drunk?'

'Was it sent by dove?' Aubrecht asked. 'Or did a rider come?'

All he could do was pretend this was real, even if his mind rebelled against the notion.

'It came by dove, in the usual manner,' Liuthe said. 'As to *your* question, Gaspart, I know that King Sigoso does not indulge in wine or beer. You could not find a man less likely to be drunk.'

'Or to pledge allegiance to the Nameless One, presumably. And yet.' Gaspart reached for his glass. 'Well, he wouldn't be the first monarch to lose his wits.'

'It may be a forgery,' Clothild said in her reasonable manner. 'A foolish stab at a jape.'

Aubrecht frowned. 'What sort of fool would risk his own head for a jape?'

'A very committed jester,' Gaspart remarked. 'In all seriousness, *does* Cárscaro have a court jester?'

'The letter *is* from King Sigoso. I recognise his seal and hand,' Liuthe said, with conviction. 'Unless his signet ring has been stolen or forged, which I cannot imagine, these are his words.'

Aubrecht imagined his composure as a nervous steed, to be calmed with a steady hand, but he suddenly felt very cold.

'Aunt,' Ermuna said, 'I have a thought I mislike.' She looked around the chamber. 'What if a High Western has awakened in Cárscaro?'

A brief silence followed, during which Liuthe furrowed her brow.

'The High City sits on the hip of Mount Fruma,' Ermuna went on, returning all their gazes. 'If you were a wyrm as large as they were said to be, would you not choose a mountain to sleep in?'

'The alchemists of Svartal have noticed more and more tremors in the Spindles,' Aubrecht said, thinking back to the letters. 'Not only that, but ... the Draconic sleepers of Edin have been stirring for years. It is not widely known, but several officials have informed Granduncle. They ascribe it to people accidentally disturbing the creatures, but now I wonder.'

Clothild narrowed her eyes. 'Why did you not say, coz?'

'I did not want to scare anyone.'

'Aubrecht, we must *all* know everything. That is the strength of the House of Lievelyn.'

'It could be Fýredel himself,' Aleidine said, distracting them. 'Surely his awakening would rouse them all.'

'Orsul and Valeysa had their own wyverns,' Ermuna said. 'It could be any of the three.'

Aubrecht looked back at his sister, whose jaw was tight. She had studied the Grief of Ages since they were children, trying to understand the cause of the devastation. To no avail.

'Mentendon is prepared. Edvart made sure of it,' Liuthe said. 'Fýredel will not expect us to have rifles and war machines, nor ships with cannon and chainshot, nor any of the other defences we have invented since the Grief. Mentendon is even fortunate enough to have bed cross-bows, thanks to Seiiki. The wyrm anticipates easy prey, but this time, we are ready to bite back.'

'And is Granduncle ready to lead us?' Aubrecht asked the chamber. 'Is he our Glorian Shieldheart?'

There was a deafening silence.

'Well,' Gaspart said, clearing his throat, 'will gunpowder work on the wyrms, do you think?'

'It certainly works on sleepers,' Clothild said. 'Mother has used it to clear them from her land. The force of the explosion injures or destroys them.'

'The sleepers are part animal,' Aubrecht reminded her. 'The wyverns and wyrms are … pure fire, pure Dreadmount.'

'I believe the same principle will apply. Two High Westerns were slain during the Grief.'

'While we imagine ways to kill wyrms, we must declare war on Yscalin,' Ermuna said. 'It would be one thing if the Vetalda had simply renounced the Saint, but to have openly declared allegiance to the Nameless One?'

'Ermuna.' Aubrecht shook his head. 'You cannot think the Yscals would do this by choice.'

'I agree with Erma.' Gaspart stroked his auburn beard. 'Can anyone be *made* to write a letter, in that monstrosity of a tower?'

'The Yscali ambassador is on her way,' Liuthe said. 'Let us hope she can explain this.'

It had taken Aubrecht weeks to reach Cárscaro. Its defensive position was unparalleled, but it had struck him as a lonely place, and its king a cold and humourless man. Though their meetings had been civil, it was clear he believed Yscalin far superior to Mentendon.

King Sigoso had always been watching Marosa. Every glimpse of her father had clearly rattled her, even if she had tried to conceal it. And now he had turned either to madness or to evil. Aubrecht had the sense that a man like that – observant and controlling – would never hold a court so lax that someone would be able to forge a letter with his signet ring.

But it was impossible for the Vetalda family – the most loyal and committed to the House of Berethnet – to have renounced the Saint. During the Grief, they had fought to the end.

'The Resident Ambassador to Yscalin,' the Grand Steward announced, and the doors swung open to admit Lady Sennera Yelarigas. A handsome woman in her early fifties, she wore a gown that belled at the hips, fashionable in Yscalin.

She was married to Gastaldo Yelarigas, the Secretary of State, faithful servant of King Sigoso. If anyone in Mentendon could shed light on the situation, surely it was Lady Sennera.

'Your Excellency,' Liuthe said. 'I take it you have been informed about the letter.'

'Yes, but I do not claim to understand it,' Lady Sennera answered in Mentish. 'My lord companion knows the king better than anyone. His Majesty is the most pious and courageous ruler in Virtudom, save only for Queen Sabran. He must have been taken to ransom.'

Aubrecht raised his eyebrows at Liuthe, who only smiled a little at the veiled insult to Mentendon. When Liuthe had first learned that he was to marry an Yscal, she had advised him to swallow any dregs of pride as soon as possible. Marosa would have enough for them both.

His aunt had been wrong on that front.

'By whom, pray tell, Your Excellency?' Gaspart asked the ambassador. 'A forger or a fool?'

'There are heretics and evildoers in every realm, Lord Gaspart. Perhaps it was one of your Eastern trading partners,' Lady Sennera said, with disdain. 'Do any Seiikinese live here in Mentendon?'

The idea was so absurd and close-minded, it was all Aubrecht could do not to admonish her.

'The Seiikinese are forbidden to leave their island, as we are forbidden to enter,' Clothild said coolly. 'In any case, I am sure they have no interest in such chicanery, nor in your king.'

'Then perhaps your Hróthi kin have a hand in this, Lady Clothild.'

'You know full well the Hróthi have always been close allies to Yscalin. Too close, arguably.'

Aubrecht had to conceal a smile. Now and then, he saw a flash of Northern ice in Clothild.

'Enough. This bickering serves no one,' Liuthe said. 'Lady Sennera, I understand that you must be tremendously confused and shaken, but I will brook no insults to my family, nor to any of our trading partners, in my own court. Kindly be seated so we can discuss this.'

Even as Liuthe spoke, a sharp intake of breath came from Aleidine. Aubrecht frowned.

'Ally.' Liuthe narrowed her dark eyes. 'What is it?'

'Forgive me, Liuthe. I just had a thought,' Aleidine replied. Lady Sennera took the seat beside hers in frigid silence. 'Has anyone else read *A Flower in a World of Ash* by Lady Nikeya?'

Gaspart lifted a bushy eyebrow. 'The First Warlord of Seiiki?'

'Indeed.'

'She wrote a book?'

'A very fine one,' Aubrecht confirmed. 'My Seiikinese is poor, but I read the Erbevez translation.'

'I read the original,' Ermuna said. Lady Sennera looked as if she might erupt. 'Why do you ask, Aleidine?'

'*A Flower in a World of Ash* is an eyewitness account of the Great Sorrow, as the Easterners call the Grief,' Aleidine said. 'Near the end, the First Warlord describes the downfall of her father, Lord Kuposa. She believed he forged a bond with a wyrm. His eyes turned grey, his disposition changed drastically, and he spoke as if with the tongue of Taugran. His physicians believed it was some new form of the red sickness. The plague.'

'I remember,' Aubrecht said, 'but Lady Nikeya was an imaginative woman, with a poet's gift for metaphor. I always thought it was an attempt to tarnish his legacy. He had conspired against Queen Dumai, whose claim Lady Nikeya had supported.'

'Perhaps not,' Aleidine said. 'Perhaps she was being quite literal.'

'You think Sigoso the Pious has made some unholy connexion to a wyrm?' Clothild cast the ambassador a cold look. 'Surely not.'

'Certainly not,' Lady Sennera said.

'He may have been coerced,' Aleidine said in calming tones, 'but ... if I am right, I fear everyone around His Majesty is in grave danger.' She looked at Aubrecht. 'Even his family.'

Aubrecht met her gaze, remembering the next part of the book.

Marosa.

'This Eastern tale has no bearing on Yscalin,' Lady Sennera stated. 'We all know the Seiikinese revere wyrms. This man of whom you speak most likely opened his mind to its trickery.'

'Lady Sennera.' Clothild sighed. 'The Seiikinese do not worship—'

'We know precisely what they worship, thank you, Lady Clothild. But my king never would.'

'For his sake, I hope not, Your Excellency.' Aleidine put on her eyeglasses. 'May I see the letter?'

Liuthe passed it along the table. As Lady Sennera watched it change hands, her expression changed, and Aubrecht saw the worry beneath that layer of Yscali pride and arrogance.

'Your Highnesses,' she said, 'I trust that Mentendon will not move against Yscalin.'

There was a brief, tense silence.

'Chance would be a fine thing,' Gaspart said cheerfully, breaking it. 'We barely have an army.'

'Gaspart,' Clothild hissed.

'The decision lies with His Royal Highness,' Aleidine said. 'We should wake him, Liuthe.'

'Only the Queen of Inys can declare holy war,' Liuthe reminded her. 'Where she goes, Leovart must follow, but I do not know what she will make of this turn of events. If Sigoso speaks true, the blow to the Chainmail would be catastrophic – but if the wyrms have woken, they will exact revenge upon all of humankind. We must protect *our* people, as is our duty.'

'We could enter the caves, as our forebears did,' Gaspart said, sobering. 'Mentendon has many.'

Aubrecht could no longer speak. He was sliding into the past again, to the sickroom where Betriese was dying.

Ever since that night, his dominant instinct had been to protect his sisters from anything in the world that would harm them. Now he was the heir, that instinct needed to stretch much farther, to cover all of Mentendon. He had to be more courageous than Leovart.

'Perhaps we should watch and wait,' Clothild said. 'There may be more to this. We should consult with the rest of Virtudom to see if they received the same message from King Sigoso.'

Clothild was always first to call for temperance in a crisis, not wanting to show any hint of Northern recklessness. Aubrecht understood, but it would not do. They could not sit idle.

'We cannot afford to wait,' he told her. 'The Grief of Ages brought humankind to the brink of extinction. Our world has never recovered.' He looked around the table. 'I recommend we dispatch scouts to Yscalin. If Aleidine and Erma are right, the Yscals are at the mercy of a wyrm, and potentially, a monarch who does not mean to resist. We must help them.'

'What can we do?' Gaspart asked him. 'A fencing match with Fýredel?'

'Respectfully, Gaspart, what choice do we have?' Aleidine said. 'Lie down and burn?'

'That might be a little easier, yes.'

'Our ancestors fought the wyrms to the end,' Aubrecht said firmly. 'Regardless of past tensions and disagreements with Yscalin—'

'You mean when they helped Hróth to press its hulking great snowboot on our necks for centuries?'

'—its people are our fellow warriors in the Chainmail. We have a moral duty to aid our allies, as the Saint would have desired.' Aubrecht rose. 'To that end, while our intelligencers see what is happening in Yscalin, I will lead a small armed force to secure the Donmata.'

There was a brief silence, during which Gaspart huffed, as if he expected Aubrecht to laugh.

'Aubrecht.' Liuthe shook her head. 'Are you suggesting that you go yourself?'

'I would shame the Knight of Courage if I did otherwise,' Aubrecht said, soft and firm. 'If any of our theories on this matter have even touched on the truth, Marosa could be in mortal danger. Regardless of the reasons Sigoso sent this letter, I must go to her.'

'No.' Ermuna snapped up, her face turning white. 'Aubrecht. You can't.'

'Aubrecht,' Aleidine intervened, 'I really didn't mean for you to—'

'—act like a fool?' Gaspart said. 'Brecht, with the greatest respect for your mettle, you are no match for a wyrm. Only a select few royals have ever been known for that sort of thing.'

'Glorian Shieldheart would have gone,' Aubrecht said, with conviction. 'So would Lady Kathel.'

'You are *not* Glorian Shieldheart.' Liuthe planted her cane on the floor and stood, brushing off the servants who moved to support her. 'Aubrecht, I know you care for Marosa – I loved Edvart from the first day I laid eyes on him – but this is folly. Let the intelligencers go first.'

'She is not only my betrothed, Aunt Liuthe. She is your future High Princess, the future Queen of Yscalin, and heir presumptive to the Ersyr.'

'And you are *our* heir.'

'Marosa is my friend as well as my betrothed. I may not yet have formally vowed to protect her, but the Saint knows I must, to be worthy of her,' he said, passion lifting his voice. 'She has lived in that dark tower for years, unable to see beyond it. I will *not* abandon her there.'

There was another silence. Aubrecht looked between their uneasy faces, his chest tight with frustration.

His family did not believe he was capable of it. Perhaps they were right. They must still think of him as the sanctarian, the spare. But if Marosa was in danger, he wanted to be the first one she saw from any party that went to her rescue, so she would know that she was safe.

'Prince Aubrecht,' Lady Sennera said, 'Cárscaro is not lightly entered, nor escaped. If I believed it were possible, I would be returning now, to join my daughter and companion. As you know, there is but one path to the city, from the Great Yscali Plain, where there is no cover for leagues. If a wyrm *has* awakened there – Saint forbid – then you would be seen at once. Even if you were to bring the entire army of Mentendon, large or small though it may be, you would have no hope of reaching the Donmata.'

'Then we approach from behind,' Aubrecht told her. 'From the east.'

'Through the mountains?'

'Yes, Your Excellency. There is an ancient bridle path through the Spindles that leads almost directly into Cárscaro. The Gulthaganians used it to move Yscali copper to their own city, and later to send their warriors into the Ersyr, when they laid siege to Rauca.'

From the look on her face, this was news to her. Aubrecht wondered if even King Sigoso knew.

'The Pass of the Imperator is treacherous, but navigable in the warm months. I could hire a small group of mercenaries and depart with them from Svartal,' he said. 'Should we find that the Cárscari have been coerced, we will extract the Donmata Marosa, Sir Robrecht Teldan, and your daughter, Lady Priessa, with all haste. I am certain there will be a way.'

Lady Sennera seemed lost for words, while Aleidine nodded her gratitude. Sir Robrecht was her uncle, a man in his late seventies. He loved Yscalin so much that he had never wanted to retire from his position there. Now his knowledge of its court might prove invaluable.

'Thank you, Your Highness,' Lady Sennera eventually said. 'And … my companion, Lord Gastaldo?'

'If we can.' Aubrecht looked at her. 'If he is not complicit.'

Gaspart drained his glass of wine.

Ermuna was uncharacteristically silent, as if she feared the lightest sound might cause him to leave. Her entire body was rigid, her fingers tightly interlocked under her breastbone. The sight pierced him with shame. She looked as petrified as if she was fifteen again.

'Yes. Look at your sister,' Liuthe ordered him. 'Look at how afraid she is, Aubrecht. How will Bette and Bedona feel when I tell them their brother has left them to go on a fool's errand?'

'I am not—' Ermuna cut herself off, sweat on her face. 'Not afraid. I only—'

'No. I forbid this,' Liuthe told Aubrecht. 'I have lost too many relatives. The man I loved and his siblings. My daughter. I will not lose my nephew as well. I will tell the Royal Guard to confine you if I must. You are not High Prince of Mentendon just yet, Aubrecht Lievelyn.'

Aubrecht clenched his jaw. Once again, he was to be treated like a naïve boy, and not a man.

But as he locked eyes with his aunt, he saw the agony, the fear, and it shattered him. Even a peaceful animal would scratch or peck as a last resort, and his aunt was a swan to her bones.

'Very well. I will give our scouts time to establish the truth,' he said quietly. 'But I *will* organise the mercenaries and see the party off from Svartal. I must know that Marosa is alive and well.'

'Do you know any mercenaries, Brecht?' Gaspart enquired. 'I ask in absolute earnest.'

'I am the Red Prince of Mentendon. Surely I can find some.' Aubrecht offered Liuthe a bow. 'Forgive my folly, Aunt, and the distress I caused you. I ask for permission to go at once, so I might speak to the Margrave of Svartal. I believe she may be able to help.'

'Do you swear to me, upon your place in Halgalant, that you will not go to Yscalin?'

He touched the brooch of his patron, the Knight of Generosity.

'Upon my place in Halgalant,' he said, his voice soft in defeat, 'I will not.'

Aubrecht, we are overtaken. Fýredel has woken in the Spindles; he was sleeping in our midst all along. Our voices passed through the rock of Cárscaro and into his accursed ear. Rozaria built a palace from a fire mountain, and in this act of arrogance was our undoing.

They came from within; our defences were useless. Now we are under the eye of his wyverns.

I try to rebel, but I cannot be seen. I beg you, shelter any Yscals you can, if they flee as far as Mentendon. Leave me to my fate – do not imperil your own life for me – but be happy, and rule well, as you were meant to do. Know that my last thoughts will be dreams of the life we might have shared.

I will see you again in Halgalant.

Yours,
Marosa

Marosa

CÁRSCARO

DRACONIC KINGDOM OF YSCALIN

CE 1004

Before Yscalin fell, the collared doves of the Royal Aviary had carried many letters between the cities of the world. All of them could fly great distances. All of them had known their way home.

Unlike the public aviary on the cliff, the one at court had not been destroyed when the wyverns came. Safe inside the palace, it had been full of living doves when King Sigoso gave the order. Hundreds of letters had been written, stamped with his seal, and fixed to the birds. They had soared away from Cárscaro, bearing word that the House of Vetalda had renounced the Saint and pledged loyalty to the Nameless One.

None of those birds had ever returned.

The crest of the House of Taumargam was a white dove, its wings displayed, the Sarras Mountains at its back. Perhaps, one day, Queen Sahar would send a wind from wherever she was now, bringing back one bird – just one – that might be used to call for help.

Until then, Cárscaro was once more a prison.

****

Marosa did not know how a year had passed. A year with her city held to ransom.

The first rush of fear had been like molten steel. It had cut off her screams as it poured over her, sealing her lips and stopping her breath, then cooled and hardened, colder by the day, until she was laden and heavy; until she showed as little feeling as a suit of armour. She had to remain calm, to stop the servants and courtiers from succumbing to hopelessness.

Each morning, she stood on the balcony, as if nothing had changed. Beyond her mountain city, the land was black and cold. All the lavender was gone, turned to ash and blown away.

Ermendo stood close, crossbow at the ready. He was one of the few who still had one, since the Vardya had stripped the people of their weapons. Fýredel was taking no chances. The city watch had been permitted to keep their swords, but only to quell riots and ensure no one attacked the wyverns. Everyone in Cárscaro was to accept the new way of things.

Marosa looked through the spyglass Bartian had lent her. Her hands were clammy, but Ermendo had insisted upon her wearing gloves. Now the wyverns had returned, so would the Draconic plague.

At first glance, the streets looked ordinary. Most of the buildings were intact, except for the sanctuaries and armouries, which lay in ruin. Her people were still meeting their loved ones, collecting water, hanging laundry to dry in the sun. They still bought food at the market, for Cárscaro had always had full granaries, given its isolation. In that, her father had been shrewd.

But for all her people were pretending normality, they lived their lives quietly, as if they were afraid to be seen. There was almost no sound from the streets, except for chilling roars.

Marosa angled the spyglass towards the Plaza Vetalda, the largest public square in the city, where the Cárscari had once lingered to talk and trade, or to hear from the herald. Now it was wholly deserted, except for a pair of wyverns, both drinking from the Tundana. Though the creatures did not attack on sight, people tried not to go outside more often than necessary.

She had tried to establish a pattern in the wyverns' behaviour, to no avail. They came and went from Cárscaro, but there were never less than twenty in or around the city at any given time.

After a long moment, she turned the spyglass on the Gate of Niunda. Several corpses dangled from it, some with missing limbs.

The vestiges of her secret rebellion.

Marosa lowered the spyglass, sick to her stomach. After the requisition of weapons, all of the guns had been stored in the Palace of Salvation. On her orders, Ermendo had convinced some of the Vardya to smuggle matchlocks and gunpowder to a group of willing subjects, so they could make the journey for help. They had intended to slip away under cover of night and get to Lasia, but the wyverns must have caught their scent. Now they hung in chains.

She sleepwalked towards her apartments, followed by a silent Ermendo. Each plan that came to mind seemed futile with Fýredel so nearby. She was as much a captive as Oderica had been, and there was no Fruma to swallow her into the mountain. Her father had been a fool to stay here, hundreds of miles from the sea, with no escape.

Her food was served at the usual time. There were stores of grain and livestock, but the Privy Council had no idea how long this state of affairs would last, so only small amounts were served.

She pushed her food around her plate. Priessa watched her dully.

During the Grief of Ages, the wyrms had declared their presence, then burned the land without remorse or explanation. There had never been a situation like this, where a king and his court had been held to ransom, with submission as the price. As far as she knew, the doves had instructed city officials to quell the people, succour the wyrms, and destroy all trace of the Saint.

Every day, Marosa hoped the rest of Yscalin would find a way to fight back. She hoped that other countries had not already fallen. There was no longer any news from outside.

She usually spent the mornings at prayer. Now she went straight to the library, where she read every bestiary and chronicle she could find, looking for some way to defeat the creatures. Ordinary weapons could be used to slay wyverns – harpoons, javelins, even bows – but it was impossible to bring them all down at once. Only the Saint's Comet had that power.

An enormous banner had always hung between the floors of the Library of Isalarico, displaying the crest of the House of Vetalda. The new one showed the True Sword on a red field, torn in twain, flanked by wyverns. Marosa tried not to look at the blasphemous image.

'Donmata?'

The voice came from her right. Marosa looked up to see Lord Wilstan Fynch.

'Your Grace,' she said, surprised. 'I have not seen you in some time.' She closed her book. 'How are you?'

'As well as I can be. We are confined to the Vaulted Gallery,' he said. 'After what happened to Sir Robrecht, I was happy to obey.' He sat beside her. 'But I convinced the Vardya to let me take a brief turn this morning. I hoped that I might find you here.'

'I hoped that the pages of history might yield a way out. So far, they have not.' She looked him over. 'You should wear gloves, my lord. None of the creatures are inside, but my father—'

'Yes. It *is* the plague, then?'

Whatever Fýredel had done to her father in the bowels of Mount Fruma, it was eating away at his body.

Sometimes he appeared to be himself, other than his misty eyes. When Marosa had first seen them, she had thought he was blind, but from what she could tell, he saw more than ever. On lucid days, he commanded the Privy Council in person. More often, he walked the corridors like a boneless soul, with a strange fire in the grey, staring at every servant and courtier.

He seemed to understand the risk that he might spread his condition. His Grooms of the Stool made certain to cover his body, except for his face, which drooped like melting wax, gradually sinking away from the bone. From time to time, blisters appeared on his skin, as if he had been scorched. They scarred the way deep burns did, leaving raised welts in their wake.

'Some new form of it, perhaps. Otherwise he would already be dead,' Marosa said. 'I am sorry that you are trapped here with us.'

Fynch looked away.

'I came to find you,' he said, 'to make a confession, Your Radiance. I did not mean it to be so, but … I may have thwarted any chance of aid from Virtudom.'

'Your Grace?'

Fynch took some time to continue.

'A few days before Fýredel woke,' he said, 'I sent a message to my daughter, telling her a terrible suspicion I had formed. A suspicion that will have made her see your father as her enemy, and prejudiced her against the idea that his turn to evil was forced.'

'What suspicion?'

'It is better that you see for yourself.'

'Whatever it is, surely our allies in Virtudom would never think us willing servants. What would we gain from pledging allegiance to Fýredel, who burned Yscalin once before?' Marosa leaned towards him, even as he avoided her gaze. 'You told me that ours is an old and strong friendship. For more than seven hundred years, we Yscals have been loyal to the House of Berethnet.'

'Had I had foreseen what was to come, I might have chosen my words with more care. Alas, I cannot take them back. But if you wish to understand my reasons, go to the Privy Sanctuary.'

'The Privy Sanctuary has been sealed. I am forbidden to pray to the Saint.'

'Lady Priessa may be able to obtain the key. Her father has it in his possession,' Fynch said. 'When you have seen, come to visit me, if you can.'

He was gone before she could answer.

Marosa stayed where she was for some time, heart thumping behind her stays. Returning her book to the shelves, she strode back to her apartments.

Priessa sat beside the window, circles under her eyes. She closed her prayer book when Marosa arrived.

'Essa,' Marosa said, 'does your father ever let you into his study?'

'Not alone.' Her eyes were raw, curls pouring to the small of her back. 'Why do you ask?'

She wore only a black kirtle and linen shirt over her smock. With King Sigoso distracted, most of the courtiers were dressing for the heat. The Knight of Courtesy would forgive them.

'Lord Gastaldo has the key to the Privy Sanctuary,' Marosa said. 'I need it.'

'To retrieve your pendant?'

'In part.'

Priessa considered. 'My father carries his keys on his person,' she said. 'It may take me some time to liberate them.' She concealed the prayer book. 'Did you find anything of use in the library?'

Marosa shook her head and sat. They both gazed out of the window. Priessa was likely thinking of her mother, who lived at the Mentish court, where Aubrecht must be in an agony of confusion.

She had been so close to being with him, far away from her father. For an indulgent moment, she imagined herself in his arms, warm and safe and cherished, watching their children laugh and play.

And then she brushed the picture away, before it could destroy her. Aubrecht would not be able to save her from Cárscaro. She did not want him to try.

'A year of desolation,' Priessa murmured. 'Why has no one come?' When Marosa was silent, she rose. 'Let me bring your supper. I will send Ruzio and Yscabel up.'

Marosa remained on the settle. After a time, her two other handmaidens arrived.

'I saw Lord Bartian this morning,' Ruzio said. 'He says that some Cárscari have been called to the Fell Door.'

The news was like cold water soaking through her clothes, leaving her covered in goosebumps. The Fell Door was the name the people had given the crack in the mountain.

'Why?' she asked, fearing the answer. 'What does Fýredel want with them?'

'I do not wish to know.' Ruzio reached for the cosmetic box. 'You ought to sleep after supper.'

Marosa nodded. Ruzio combed rose oil through her thick hair, smoothing it with one hand as she went.

'Yscabel,' Marosa said gently, noting her wan face. Yscabel started. 'How are you this evening?'

Yscabel wore her walnut hair in a braiding cap, like many women did at court after their commendations. She could no longer hide behind it, as she often had when she was younger.

'I am well, Donmata,' she said. 'I believe the Saint will protect us in the palace.'

'I am sure that you are right.' Marosa patted the settle. 'Come. Let us try our best not to think of Fýredel tonight.' Yscabel moved to sit beside her. 'Tell me, have you ever played whist?'

'I've never taught her,' Ruzio said.

'That will not do. It is an Inysh game,' Marosa told Yscabel. 'I played it with Queen Sabran.'

Ruzio finished her combing and joined them. Yscabel managed a weak smile as Marosa dealt their cards.

Priessa soon returned with supper. By then, Yscabel looked a little better. When it was time for them to retire, she curled up on the truckle bed. Ruzio sat beside her, like a guard, while Marosa lay down and let her eyes close; sleep took her as quickly as a comet crossed the sky. She dreamed she was in the corridors, running towards Aubrecht, surrounded by candles with red flames. No matter how desperately she tried to reach him, he never came any closer.

Ruzio suddenly grasped her elbow, waking her with a jolt. Marosa opened her eyes and looked around in confusion, still mired in the dream. When she saw the disturbance, she sat up.

Her father stood in the doorway, observing them all without blinking. In the gloom of the bedchamber, his eyes were tiny embers burning in beds of ash.

His gaze snapped to Ruzio, who pulled Yscabel to her side. Priessa must be tending the candles in another room, as she often did during the night. Marosa willed her to stay away.

'Father,' she said, wary. 'Are you well?'

'Only seeing that you are here, daughter,' King Sigoso said. 'Where I can see you.' His jaw seemed to work very hard as he spoke. 'How did those weapons get to the commons?'

'I do not know.'

'Then I must ask others.'

He turned and left without a word, trailing the smell of bonfires. Yscabel was shaking.

'That was not His Majesty,' Ruzio said in a hoarse voice. 'It was Fýredel, looking at us.'

Marosa looked at her. 'How do you know this, Ruzio?'

'I have seen his eyes like that before, when he walks about the palace. He moves and speaks differently, as if his own mouth and limbs were strange to him. They say the High Westerns could see through their wyverns' eyes. I am certain this is the same connexion.'

'Then Fýredel has seen us?' Yscabel whispered. 'He knows of us?'

Ruzio drew her close.

'When His Majesty's eyes are only grey,' she said, 'I think his mind is still his own, to some degree, though the sickness must torment him. But when the light comes … yes, I think the wyrm sees through him, the better to know the workings of our court.' Yscabel let out a wordless sound, and Ruzio firmed her embrace. 'It will be all right, Yscabel. The Saint protects us.'

Marosa felt a pang of envy as they held each other. She had never wished for a sister – Priessa had always been that for her – but their closeness made her miss her mother terribly.

'Go back to sleep, both of you,' she said quietly. 'Let Fýredel see we are harmless as babes.'

****

For the next few days, Marosa followed her usual routine, not wanting to arouse suspicion. In that time, she never saw her father. To distract herself from the danger, which kept her body rigid at all times, she found out what she could about the present state of Yscalin.

From what Priessa could glean, the Privy Council had mounted no resistance. Quite the opposite. Across Yscalin, the Knights Defendant – now the wyverns' soldiers – killed or imprisoned those who rebelled. Their ranks had apparently tripled in size. The Principal Sanctarian, protesting the blasphemy, had been hung from the Gate of Niunda and left to die of thirst.

The freedom and dignity of the Yscals, sacrificed to buy the lives of everyone in Cárscaro. No one had done this in the Grief of Ages. No country had submitted to the wyrms.

Each night, when her eyes stung from reading, Marosa prayed in her bedchamber. As a child, she had been loyal to the Saint alone, never doubting his Six Virtues. It was only when she was fourteen that her mother had secretly told her about other faiths, including hers.

Now Marosa did not know whose help she ought to seek. The Faith of Dwyn was a way of life, lacking any god or figurehead, and she doubted that even the Saint could rid Cárscaro of this many wyverns. She still asked him to deliver her fellow Yscals to safety, and to set her city free.

And then, in the silence of her mind, she asked the same of Fruma, the neglected god of the mountain, who had taken Oderica into himself and taught her the art of smithing. Nine years later, she had emerged to face the Gulthaganians, meeting their bronze swords with iron.

Later, the story had changed. Now it was the Saint who taught Oderica, even though the Saint had not been born.

Fruma, hear the blood of Oderica, she whose eyes were lit by the mountain. Marosa did not know how to pray to a mountain, but she would try. *Fruma, firstborn, your body has been overtaken. I beg you, keep the beast within, so he may never fly.*

****

The next morning, the first violence broke out in the palace. Knowing they had the protection of thick walls, its hundreds of residents had not made too much of a stir, even though their king was possessed. Many of them had friends or relatives in the city, whose lives they feared to risk.

Marosa overheard the commotion from the Library of Isalarico. She rushed down the Grand Stair, Ermendo hard on her heels, halberd at the ready. They reached a wide arched corridor, where several of the Vardya stood with Bartian. He sported a long cut on his cheek.

'Donmata,' he said hoarsely.

'Bartian, what happened?'

'His Majesty was walking here. One of the scullions attacked him with a cleaver,' he replied, breathing hard. 'Your father seized him by the throat. His Majesty was not wearing gloves.'

'Where is this scullion now, my lord?' Ermendo asked.

'Confined to his room in the servants' quarters,' another guard said. 'His Majesty is safe, thanks to Lord Bartian.'

Bartian touched his wound, grimacing. His ruff was flecked with blood. Marosa passed him a silk handkerchief. 'How were you hurt?' she asked him. 'Did the scullion attack you both?'

'No. I stepped in front of your father,' he said. 'I suppose it was instinct.' He pressed the handkerchief to his cheek. 'Perhaps it would have been better if I had not.'

Marosa glanced at the guards, but they were deep in conversation. 'This will not end with his death,' she said to Bartian, keeping her voice low. 'Fýredel would only choose someone else.'

'Let us hope it is Gastaldo. He claims to speak for His Majesty. The Grandees do as he asks without question, forcing our subjects to abjure the Saint. He hangs the faithful on the Gate of Niunda, leaving them there as fearful examples. The Knight of Courage spits upon that chamber,' Bartian said under his breath. 'They should be looking to you, not Gastaldo.'

'I doubt it would improve our situation. In any case, I would sooner not draw attention from Fýredel.'

'No,' Bartian conceded. 'We need our heir.' He looked her in the eyes. 'Donmata, I do not know if you've heard, but the wyverns have been taking people to the Fell Door.'

'Yes, Lady Ruzio told me. Is there any pattern to the abductions?'

'Not to my knowledge.' The corners of his mouth tightened. 'Marosa, the wyverns' offspring were known to eat flesh in the Grief. What if there are Draconic beasts in the mountains?'

Even as he spoke, a wyvern flew past the window with a scream, making them both flinch.

'Donmata,' Ermendo said, 'you should not be here, with plague still in the air.'

'Very well.' Marosa looked up at Bartian. 'Be safe, my lord.'

'And you, Your Radiance.'

****

For days, Marosa waited for news of the scullion, reading every record she could find of the Draconic plague. During the Grief of Ages, it had started with a vivid redness in the fingers. Over weeks, it would take root and spread, betrayed only by fever and discomfort. And then, with little warning, a fire would ignite every vein in the body, leading to an agonising death.

But their eyes had always been unchanged. Not grey, nor lit by strange embers.

Her father had a different strain, sown in him by Fýredel. Perhaps the scullion would be resistant to it. But then Ermendo came to Marosa one evening, while she was leafing through an Inysh treatise called *The Wyrm Sicknesse*, written fifty years after the Grief of Ages.

'His fingers are red.'

Marosa looked up. 'And his mind?'

'Still his own, and no sign of grey eyes. He complains of aches and fever. It looks to be the old form of the plague.' Ermendo paused. 'Should we kill him now, or let it progress?'

Her stomach tightened as she considered it. Whatever her decision, the scullion was doomed.

'See how long it takes the plague to move through him,' she concluded. 'We must know our enemy, to see if it is changed from the Grief. But when he begins to feel the pain, end it.'

Ermendo bowed and left. Marosa closed *The Wyrm Sicknesse*, not wanting to see any more of the illustrations.

Three weeks later, the scullion was dead.

****

It was another two days before Priessa made good on her promise. During that time, a butcher threw a boar spear at a flying wyvern. The creatures had thick armour, but that spear had struck it under the left wing, penetrating its heart. It had fallen dead across Shamble Lane, destroying several buildings.

No sooner had it crashed down than a panic had started. Thousands of people had run in fear of the other wyverns, ending in a crush at the Gate of Niunda. Most of them had been torched alive.

Marosa had not been able to move for hours after she heard the news. She lay alone in bed, behind the drapes she rarely closed, her pillow damp with tears. There had been children among the dead, even newborns. And she, their future queen, was powerless to stop it.

Priessa came to her the next evening. She touched Marosa on the shoulder, lifting her from the dark pit, and showed her an ornate key.

'Father went to the Fell Door for an hour today,' Priessa said. 'He left all his valuables in his study.'

Marosa looked at her. 'Your father spoke to Fýredel?'

'Apparently so. When he returned, he went straight to the Privy Council. His eyes are not grey.' Priessa pressed the key into her grasp. 'We should go to the sanctuary now, before he realises this is missing.'

Marosa followed her. Ermendo let them pass without remark, as if he had not even seen them.

They descended to a lower floor, avoiding the servants as best they could. Better no one saw their crime. At last, they came to the studded door of the Privy Sanctuary.

When King Sigoso pledged to the Nameless One, he had ordered that all relics and ritual objects be destroyed. The second rib of the Saint – a gift from Inys – had been discarded with as much care as the contents of a chamber pot. But the objects of material worth, the gold and the precious jewels, had been shoved into the Privy Sanctuary before it was sealed. That was the only reason this place of worship had been spared the destruction wreaked on the others.

Marosa turned the key in the lock. As soon as she was inside, she retrieved her mother's pendant and the crumpled note. Priessa picked up a silver brooch depicting the True Sword.

'The Principal Sanctarian wore this,' she said. 'He helped to tear Queen Sahar from grace. How swiftly he fell in turn.'

'I wish I could take more pleasure in it, but no man deserves to die as he did.'

Priessa watched her pace the chamber. 'Why else have we come here, Marosa?'

'Lord Wilstan believes there is something in here I should see,' Marosa said. 'Something that … incriminates my father.'

'In what?'

'I do not quite know.'

They searched the sanctuary in silence, sifting through crates and heavy chests. Priessa came upon the green samite robes of a sanctarian, dark with dried blood at the collar, while Marosa found box upon box of patron brooches, ornate girdles, and pairs of spurs, confiscated from the courtiers. Children received all three when they reached the age of twelve, formally embracing the Six Virtues. When she looked up, a shape on the opposite wall gave her pause.

'Wait,' she said. 'What is that?'

Following her line of sight, Priessa turned to look. A large rectangular object, covered by a dusty shroud, was propped against the wall behind her. She uncovered it to reveal a portrait.

The woman in the painting had no face; it had been scoured and ripped away. The sight disturbed Marosa. Her river of black hair was still discernible, as were her pale hands, clasped in front of her. She wore a gown of blue silk in an old-fashioned Inysh style, with a square neckline, revealing a pendant shaped like a seahorse, hung from a rope of white Ersyri pearls.

'Rosarian the Fourth,' Marosa murmured. 'Mother sent her that necklace for her fortieth birthday.'

'Saint,' Priessa said. 'Why is her face like this?'

The late Queen Mother of Inys. It was blasphemy to damage her image.

'Perhaps my father did it to please Fýredel,' Marosa said. 'The wyrm must despise the Berethnet queens. They are descendants of the Saint, the knight who vanquished his master.'

Without answering, Priessa drifted away to search the dusty shelves. After a time, she found a small coffer. 'There are letters here,' she said, reading one. 'My father uses this cypher, but I do not recognise the hand.'

She took a scrap of parchment and a charcoal from her girdle. Marosa came to look over her shoulder as she converted the symbols to letters. The message was not written in Yscali, but Inysh.

Your gift has been received. It will be done on the Feast of Midwinter. Soon the sanctity of Virtudom will be restored, and a brighter age will be upon us. The Saint shall grant us places of honour at the Great Table.

Yours in courage,
Cupbearer

'Cupbearer.' Marosa read it again, unsettled. 'Queen Rosarian died on the Feast of Midwinter.'

The Regency Council of Inys had called it a tragedy, but given no particulars. Priessa sat down to read the other letters.

'There are details of some transactions and shipments,' she said. 'His Majesty purchased a bolt of Seiikinese watersilk from a merchant in Kantmarkt. He also granted a considerable pension to an Yscali seamstress.' She leafed through the small pile. 'The ink is faded. This must all have happened long before Fýredel woke, but ... they are all innocent purchases.'

'I would not be so sure,' Marosa said. 'My father despises the trade with the East. He craves the coin it brings to the West, but I cannot imagine him personally buying Seiikinese goods.'

'A bolt is enough to make a fine gown.' Priessa took the last few letters from the coffer, then reached into the bottom and held up a glass vial, as long as her finger. 'What is this?'

'Let me see.'

Priessa handed the vial over. The glass was thicker than any Marosa had ever seen, full of something translucent and slippery, with a yellowish tinge. She worked off the stopper with care.

A curl of steam escaped, releasing a faint, acrid smell. Sensing danger, she poured a few drops on to the corner of a table. It sizzled before it burned through the wood and dripped on to the floor.

She snapped the stopper back into the vial. A chill pierced her through as she slotted the pieces together.

She knew why Wilstan Fynch had come to Yscalin.

She knew why her mother had died.

Marosa

Of course, the idea had occurred to her, in the darkest hours of night. That her father had executed his queen consort in secret, then made up a lie to cover her death. King Jantar would likely have declared war on Yscalin if he learned that his sister had been harmed with intent.

I did it to protect you.

Words that made no sense, that never had. Marosa could think of reasons why Sahar might have taken her own life – to spare herself the indignity of exile and disgrace – but not how it would have protected *her*. How could the sudden loss of a mother ever aid her child?

So for years, the idea had seeped into her, like poison taken by the drop. That her father was a murderer, a fiend. But she could not flee the man who had sired her, so she had never dared to look her idea in the face. Instead, she had turned very still, trying not to be noticed.

For surely a man who killed his own queen could also kill his own daughter.

Now she could be still no longer. For the first time in a decade, the Knight of Courage, her patron, had overtaken her body, driving out the fear that had kept her silent for so long.

Marosa did not go to Fynch. Instead, she marched up the stairs to the Royal Apartments. Four of the Vardya guarded the doors, all wearing cloths over their noses and mouths.

'Let me through,' Marosa said.

'His Majesty is not to be disturbed, Your—'

'I am the Donmata of Yscalin. I can go where I please in my ancestors' halls.'

Something about her manner must have reminded them of the king, for both of them looked taken aback. She countered their gazes without blinking, turning the force of her eyes on them all.

'Your Radiance,' one said, 'His Majesty is … indisposed.'

'I am well aware.'

'Then take this, at least.'

She offered Marosa a handkerchief, which she accepted before sweeping past them.

King Sigoso lay on his canopy bed. The room smelled of bonfires and unwashed skin. The Royal Physician lurked in the corner, wearing a beaked mask with glass eyeholes, the sort that kept out the pestilence.

'Leave us,' Marosa said to her.

'Donmata, you should not be here.'

'I told you to leave us.'

The Royal Physician obeyed her without further protest. King Sigoso did not move, his grey eyes fixed on the ceiling. His face was blank and slack.

'I have long suspected that you murdered my mother,' Marosa said, very softly. 'Now I believe I know why.' She held up the vial in a gloved hand. 'This is basilisk venom. Is it not?'

'Yes.'

'And you somehow used it to kill Queen Rosarian.'

'I knew your mind was sharper than you wanted me to see. You truly are my daughter, though you look so much like Sahar.'

Marosa stiffened. She had not expected her father to admit to murder at all, let alone do it so quickly.

Perhaps the Draconic plague was rotting his wits, breaking down his judgement and inhibitions. He likely had a fever. And yet, for the first time in her life, Marosa thought she was seeing his true self. The underpainting of the man, leaking from beneath the royal portrait.

'Come, then, Father. Confess it all,' she said. 'It must have been hard to keep it a secret. Tell me how you did it.'

'A gown made of Eastern watersilk, which resists the corrosive nature of basilisk venom – as does Northern diamond glass, the substance used to make the vial. All so very expensive.'

He delivered all this – the specifics of murder – in a cold and impassive voice, not so different to the one he always used to address her. Her body prickled with chills.

'How did you acquire the venom?' she asked, forcing herself to sound calm.

'A merchant prince in Samana,' her father said, 'who purchased it, I believe, from a culler.'

'You *execute* cullers.' She chanced another step towards his bed, moved by her wrath. 'You have accused so many of heresy and wrongdoing, all while you have wallowed in hypocrisy for years. You have failed to adhere to the Six Virtues. Were you ever true to the Saint?'

'The truest of all.'

'You barefaced liar.'

'I have no need to lie to you, daughter. The Saint I loved so dearly has abandoned me.'

'You never loved the Saint. You only ever loved yourself.'

'I was his most devoted servant, willing to do what others would not. See how he rewards me?' He licked his cracked and bloody lips. 'The lining of the gown was impregnated with the venom. My Inysh ally could touch it, to conceal it in the Privy Wardrobe, but once it was on Rosarian … well, there was no getting it off. She burned like a heretic.'

His faint smile twisted her stomach. She saw the wood again, the venom eating straight through it.

'This ally. The Cupbearer,' she said. 'Who in Inys would kill a descendant of the Saint?'

'Someone who saw Rosarian for the shameless harlot she was.'

'You dare name *another* queen an adulteress?'

'This one spurned a king for bedsport with lordlings and commoners. Even pirates knew her well.'

'Enough with these baseless accusations. Did you seek revenge on her because she spurned your suit?' Marosa demanded. 'Saint on high, what did I do to deserve such a father?'

Her eyes were the proof, the eternal reminder, that she had been reared with no will of her own. To be no one while he still lived. His blood was in her veins, and she could not burn it away.

'Rosarian had lost the right to represent the Saint on earth. She contravened all of the Six Virtues,' her father said, unmoved by her outburst, 'but most of all, she indulged in carnal lust and conceit, defiling his house. Even a holy bloodline can be fouled by vice and bastardry.'

'Not hers. Her blood chains the Nameless One.'

'Rosarian had given birth. The next link in the chain was forged. What was her purpose after that?'

The words struck Marosa like a hammer to her chest, driving the breath from her.

'Did you think the same of my mother?' she forced out. 'Once she had given you an heir, was her life worth nothing to you, Father? Or less still, because she was not a Berethnet?'

'Sahar was a Southern spy, sent to my court to fill it with heresy.'

'You say this only because she found the same evidence I did. And drew the same conclusions.'

'She did,' King Sigoso said. 'Some might say I was foolish to keep the documents, but they were the proof of my love for the Saint. And I liked to imagine Rosarian dying.'

He had slashed her portrait long before Fýredel woke.

'Sahar believed that if I could kill a queen in Inys, I might also harm my own flesh and blood,' he said. 'She always was unable to control herself. A heathen to the end.' He sat up, so she could see that his eyes were grey, without the spark. 'Aryete Feyalda informed me that your mother was planning to leave, though she did not know why. I assumed Sahar had simply grown tired of the West ... but I could not let her abscond with the Donmata of Yscalin.'

Marosa, hurry, we must leave.

'After I had Sahar imprisoned, she pleaded to speak to me, to beg for mercy and forgiveness. I was fool enough to let her back into my bedchamber. I had not realised what she knew.'

Marosa watched him, heart thudding. She was there again, in the dark, glimpsing the red fire.

'And then, in her last act,' King Sigoso said, 'my bride took a knife she had concealed in her sleeve, and she ensured that you would be my sole heir of the body. She brought death on herself.'

'You killed her. With your own hands.'

'With my own hands.'

No block in a private chamber. No rope.

A brutal, human fight between a king and queen.

'Why have you kept me caged for ten years?' Marosa asked, close to losing her grip altogether. 'I knew nothing of this.'

'You guessed.'

'I did not want to believe my own father was capable of murder.'

'But your Ersyri uncle always has. Jantar threatened to abduct you to Rauca,' he said. 'He fears for your life, as well he might. No matter what your mother intended, she did not protect you. You are no Berethnet queen, Marosa Vetalda. The world will not end if you die.'

'That is true,' Marosa conceded, 'but you will die first of the two of us, Father. I am not the puppet here. And if I survive Fýredel, as you will not – if I remain – then Yscalin will be mine to remake. I will let the world know what you did to Rosarian. I will do to your image exactly what you did to hers. I will raise my mother back to glory, and bury your legacy in the dust.'

King Sigoso did not speak again. She turned away and left him to decay in his own company.

****

The Vaulted Gallery housed the foreign ambassadors. Marosa was slow to reach it, her mind seeming to drift in her wake. She had never believed that anything could frighten her more than Fýredel, but the evil in the mountains paled in comparison to the evil in her own home.

Fynch received Marosa in his apartments. As Dowager Prince of Inys, his were the finest quarters, with nine windows in the main chamber and a door leading to a roofed balcony.

'I have seen,' Marosa told him.

He lowered himself on to a settle, suddenly looking his age.

'When Fýredel called your father,' he said, 'I sensed it was the first and last opportunity I would ever have to get inside his cabinet – the one he built for secret and sensitive documents. That is where he kept the evidence. And where the poisoned gown was made.'

'Who told you about it?'

'His locksmith, who is faithful to the Saint above her king. She also showed me the water passages.'

'My lord?'

'The copper pipes that bring hot water run in narrow tunnels behind the walls. There are entry points for plumbers, so repairs might be made if the pipes leak or rupture. I have the key to those entry points. I doubt that your father knows, but one of them is in his bedchamber.'

A lifetime spent in this suffocating tower, and somehow, Marosa still did not know it.

'These passages,' she said. 'Will you show them to me?'

'Yes.' His gaze became distant. 'I was not there when Rosarian died, but our child was. I am still not sure how Sabran survived it. There was … almost nothing left of her mother to bury.'

Marosa thought of Sabran, a consummate queen, never showing weakness. All while she held that memory within her.

'I once believed my father was faithful to the Saint,' Marosa said. 'I do not know how he justified this.'

'Oh, I think Sigoso *was* devout, but I have long suspected him of harbouring a grudge against Rosarian for rejecting his suit. It is why I asked Sabran to make me her ambassador.'

'When did my father court Rosarian?'

'About five years before you were born, when Rose was still a princess. But the late Queen Jillian had wanted her to marry me. Rose respected her last wish.' He clasped his liver-spotted hands. 'During my inquiry, I discovered that your father once had ambitious plans for this kingdom. He hoped that, by siring a Berethnet with Vetalda blood, he could eventually move the seat of Virtudom to Yscalin. Rose inadvertently thwarted those plans. Later, it seems this Cupbearer convinced him that she was adulterous. In his mind, that allowed him to mete out punishment. By then, she had an heir. Her untimely death would not release the Nameless One.'

'It frightens me that our faith can be twisted so.'

'As all faiths can in the wrong hands.'

'Yes.' She watched his face. 'Who is this Cupbearer?'

'I still do not know.'

'My lady mother came upon the evidence. She realised my father was behind it,' Marosa said. Fynch looked at her. 'She tried to flee to Rauca, to protect us both from his madness. He killed her and tarnished her legacy, but she dealt him justice first, Your Grace.'

'How?'

'She ensured that I will be his only heir.'

'You mean that she ... damaged him?'

Marosa nodded once. Fynch released his breath.

'I always did wonder why your father never took another bride,' he said. 'Queen Sahar was a brave woman. I am sorry for her death, but I am not surprised to learn her last act was in your defence. A dove is a bird of peace, in the main, but it will protect its young to the last.'

Her vision blurred. She pressed a hand to her partlet, where the pendant was concealed.

'I still do not quite understand why he married her,' she admitted. 'There was no love between them.'

'To spite Rosarian, I imagine. She wounded his pride, so he forged an alliance with a country that did not acknowledge her divine authority. Clearly it was not enough to sate him in the end.' Fynch rubbed his face. 'Still, I do believe that fear of discovery – or the wrath of the Saint – has gnawed your father ever since. For years, he could not face my daughter. He avoided me. He knows that if King Jantar learned the truth, he would declare war on Yscalin.'

'My father believed he would steal me away. It is absurd,' Marosa said bitterly. 'Without proof of murder, why would King Jantar go so far to save a niece he never met?'

'Surely you know.' When she frowned, Fynch did the same. 'Your Radiance, King Jantar and Queen Saiyma do not yet have a child. It has been speculated that they never will. Unless they do, *you* are heir presumptive to the Ersyr.' She stared at him. 'I suspect King Sigoso has kept you close as surety, so your uncle can never move against him, nor take you to Rauca.'

Marosa hardly knew how to digest the revelation. She had never learned the politics of the Ersyri court, but not once had the idea occurred to her that she could be next in line to the throne.

'No doubt,' Fynch said, 'it also ensures that King Sigoso shapes you in a way he likes.'

'I am not clay to be moulded, my lord.'

'No, indeed.' Fynch sighed. 'Sabran knows what I suspected. As more and more Yscals succumb to despair – as they submit to the wyrms, knowing they will die if they do not – I fear that Virtudom will lose faith in this country. My daughter will have to declare holy war.'

'I mean to prevent that.'

'I recall that the Knight of Courage is your patron. If anyone can save Yscalin, I believe it is you.'

Marosa could feel the press of her patron brooch, hidden in the lining of her gown. Shaped like a shield, for courage was not only necessary for the clash of blades. It was also for defending those with no defences of their own.

Aubrecht

BRYGSTAD

FREE STATE OF MENTENDON

CE 1004

Aubrecht looked at the human skull on the table. It had been charred so badly that it was black all the way through. A grizzled Inysh mercenary stood before him, ashen and wayworn.

'I am sorry for our failure, Your Highness,' she said. 'We found the Pass of the Imperator. It was a hard climb, but we entered Yscalin and proceeded towards Cárscaro. Before we could reach it, we came under attack by all manner of unholy beasts. I was the only survivor.'

The skull seemed to stare in accusation.

'How?' Aubrecht asked the mercenary. 'How did you live?'

'I killed Draconic sleepers for a living before I came here. I knew their weak points,' she said, 'but there were so many. They overwhelmed us. It felt ... like stepping into the Grief.'

It was all true, then. All the things the intelligencers had reported.

'After the creatures had left,' the mercenary said, 'I pressed on for about two miles. I wanted to finish our task, to reach Cárscaro, but you need send no more of us, Your Highness.

The Pass of the Imperator is blocked. A rockfall, from the looks of it. I do not know if the Ersyri path is clear. Only that there is no longer any way from Yscalin to Mentendon.'

Aubrecht closed his eyes. His map was very old, but it had been his one and only hope.

'You have my gratitude for trying,' he said. 'And you will receive thrice the pay I offered you.'

The mercenary nodded, but her face was drawn. She never took her dark eyes off the skull.

'I couldn't find any of the others,' she said. 'By the time I returned to the place we were attacked, the creatures had taken their bones.'

'Their deaths honoured the Knight of Courage. I will pray for their safe deliverance to Halgalant,' Aubrecht said. 'Their families will be compensated.' He gestured to the skull. 'Take this to the High Sanctuary of Brygstad to be interred in the charnel garden. Tell them I sent you.'

'Thank you, Prince Aubrecht.'

She took the skull and left. Aubrecht lowered his head into his hands.

For months, he had tried everything he could imagine to extract Marosa from Cárscaro. The first and second groups of mercenaries had not been able to find the Pass of the Imperator. The third had vanished altogether. Aubrecht had organised search parties to no avail.

During the winter, he had not been able to risk sending more, given the snow in the Spindles. A fourth group had found no trace of the third, but turned back in fear when a quake shook the mountains. Now this fifth group had been killed, he knew what had befallen the others.

'No more,' he said softly. 'No more.'

****

He stood before his aunt that night, in the candlelight of her Privy Chamber. Liuthe did not chastise him, but he knew, from her tired expression, that she never expected his plans to succeed.

'You must request an annulment from Queen Sabran,' she told him in an undertone. 'It is only a matter of time until she declares holy war. Yscalin can offer us no more protection. And we cannot have the Hróthi using your betrothal to tarnish us by association.'

'There must be another way to Marosa. We could tell her uncle about the Pass of the Imperator.'

'No, Aubrecht. That would be too far,' Liuthe said. 'We have no quarrel with the South, but informing the Ersyris of a vulnerability in Cárscaro would betray the Chainmail of Virtudom.'

'Yscalin is no longer part of Virtudom.'

'Its people still deserve our fellowship,' she said. The fire crackled. 'Only a few of our intelligencers have been able to return. They tell me the wyverns are in every city, watching the people, spreading the Draconic plague, killing anyone who tries to leave. And you know as well as I do that Cárscaro is impossible to approach unseen.'

Aubrecht looked away, his jaw working.

'Why is this happening?' he said. 'Why are they trying to build a kingdom of their own?'

'The wyrms are likely weak from centuries of slumber. This must be their way of establishing a haven,' Liuthe said. 'Perhaps even a breeding ground for more Draconic things.'

'This is the beginning of the end, then.'

'That is not like you, Aubrecht. You are the most devout and hopeful of us all, and you must remain so, regardless of your grief.'

Aubrecht lifted his gaze. Liuthe returned it, as steely as ever.

'I will send a bird to Ascalon,' Aubrecht said. 'But as long as I live, I will never believe Marosa Vetalda is a willing servant of the Nameless One. I believe that we are abandoning her to her doom, and that I am failing her by ending this betrothal. The Saint will punish me for it.'

Liuthe gave him a sad, tender look.

'You are a kind young man, Aubrecht. You always were,' she said. 'Sometimes it pains me that you must rule.' She sank deeper into her seat. 'Leovart will die very soon. I imagine I will follow in due course.'

'You might yet live for many years, Aunt.'

'The sweating sickness never did release its grip upon my bones.' She cast a weary look towards the nearest portrait. 'And … I miss Edvart and Lesken. I am ready to join them.'

Aubrecht looked up at the portrait of his uncle, red-haired and bearded, with a small girl in his arms. Edvart the Second, the Laughing Prince. The man who was supposed to rule for decades.

'When we are gone,' Liuthe said, 'you will be the head of the House of Lievelyn, and you must be prepared to make the hardest decisions of your life. We Ments have survived a great deal. The Northerners drove us out first, based on naught but superstition. The Dreadmount forced us from Gulthaga, the flood from Thisunath, and the wyrms from Carmentum, but each time, we not only survived, but triumphed. When our ancestor Ebanth – displaced and alone – was shipwrecked on the locked isle of Seiiki, she did not accept her execution. What did she do instead?'

'She convinced the First Warlord to listen to her,' Aubrecht said, 'and together, they struck a bargain. Only the Ments could trade in Seiiki, though all other foreigners had been exiled.'

'And what did her descendant do a century later?'

'Aunt.'

'Tell me, Aubrecht.'

He had learned all of this in his youth from his tutors. His mother had told it to him before he fell asleep. The origins of Mentendon, from the snows of the North to the silver swan.

He was not a boy any more, but he did love his aunt.

'Kathel Lievelyn was her descendant,' he said quietly. 'She sailed to the West and petitioned for Mentish independence from the iron grip of Hróth. So began the Mentish Defiance.' Liuthe nodded. 'At last, Sabran the Eighth agreed that the stewardship had gone on for too long. She ordered the Queen of Hróth to withdraw her forces and granted the Ments the right to rule ourselves, so long as we retained a monarchy and remained true to the Saint.'

'And so we have,' Liuthe said. 'You think I treat you like a child by asking you to recite a story. But this is a dangerous world for us Ments, no matter if there are wyrms in the sky, or conquerors on the waves, and the story of us – the story of Mentendon – is the very foundation of our dynasty. You must tell your own subjects. You must remind your sisters. You must teach your own children, whenever they come. And they will come, Aubrecht. One day.'

Aubrecht wished he could believe her. Until that day, he would pretend.

'I hope that I will be a worthy storyteller,' he said. 'And honour you, Aunt. In all that I do.'

****

He walked the corridors in his bedgown, watched by concerned servants. His chest was tight, and cold sweat beaded on his face.

The mountain pass had been his only hope. Liuthe was right. Cárscaro was impregnable on the western side, especially with wyverns on the wing. He could not order thousands of Mentish soldiers to walk into the jaws of certain death. Neither could he go alone. Even though he was training with a sword, hoping to master the skills that befitted a monarch, he was no fighter. For all his bold talk before his family all those months ago, he no longer had any confidence in his own ability to reach Cárscaro.

The House of Lievelyn had to come first. He could not plunge his family into mourning yet again. Sorrow had eaten away at his aunt; he would not let it kill his sisters.

He reached the Marble Court, where he sat and gazed at the stars. Marosa knew a great deal about astronomy, having lived in a tower all her life. The Favour twinkled above the palace, mocking him with its brightness. That was the constellation that Ments hoped to see on the night of their marriage, for it was a sign of approval from the Knight of Fellowship.

Ermuna came to join him. From the ink on her fingers, she had been studying.

'I know you spoke to Aunt Liuthe,' she said. 'She wants you to annul the betrothal.' When he nodded, she laid a hand on his. 'I am so sorry, Aubrecht.'

Aubrecht nodded again. He felt as if a fire had burned him through, leaving only ash behind.

'The Yscali alliance was meant to protect us,' Ermuna said. 'Assuming a High Western does not destroy us all, you must still wed, to strengthen our dynasty. And there is one obvious match.'

'Who?'

'Queen Sabran. If you had a child with her, the next Queen of Inys would have Lievelyn blood. The Vatten would be pacified once and for all. You know this as well as I do, Aubrecht.'

'I thought Queen Sabran was attached to Lord Arteloth Beck. Granduncle says it is common knowledge.'

'Granduncle needed an excuse for why Queen Sabran turned down his suit,' Ermuna said. 'In truth, it is gossip at best, an inconvenience at worst. Inys stands to gain far more from a foreign alliance. Sabran needs to demonstrate the strength of Virtudom. We can fill the yawning gap that Yscalin has left in the Chainmail.' She leaned closer to him. 'The first Mentish prince consort to a Berethnet queen. Imagine our security.'

Aubrecht turned the thought over in his mind. In truth, he had never considered proposing to Sabran, assuming the Berethnets would only want to marry their older allies.

But Ermuna was right. Now Yscalin had fallen, Mentendon had a chance to rise.

'Not yet,' he said, nonetheless. 'I cannot ... move on so quickly, Erma. I cared for Marosa, even if I never had a chance to fall in love with her. I have lost the future I dreamed of having.'

'That is grief,' Ermuna said, 'and it is the luxury of men, not monarchs. The suit will be strongest when you are High

Prince, but that will be very soon. Granduncle will not recover from this illness.'

'Ermuna.'

'I sound cruel. But it is true, Aubrecht. His physicians think he has days, not weeks.' Ermuna tightened her grasp. 'Mourn your betrothal to Marosa for as long as it takes him to die, then write to Queen Sabran. Make her an offer before she accepts a suit from Hróth. You are the most eligible prince in Virtudom.'

She really was like steel, unbending.

'I vow to you that I will give it thought as soon as Granduncle passes,' Aubrecht said, 'but too quick an offer will make me appear inconstant and cold. Let us allow the dust to settle.'

Ermuna did not reply, but she stayed.

****

The next day, Aubrecht walked in silence to the Royal Aviary, where several piebald doves fluttered and cooed. He chose the one with the delicate gold collar, showing it knew how to fly to Ascalon.

He looked down at the letter. A request for an annulment, addressed to Queen Sabran, the highest authority in Virtudom. His suit would come later, when his family decided he had grieved Marosa for long enough.

The dove perched calmly on his wrist. As he tucked his letter into the holder on its foot, he thought once more of the princess in the tower, whose soul had touched his for twelve precious days. She might already be dead. Pushing down a surge of grief, he opened the shutters with one hand

and let the dove go. It swept over the courtyard, and then into the sky.

It was done, and it could not be undone.

Like a sleepwalker, he went to the Privy Sanctuary. He could not help Marosa – a failing for which he could never forgive himself – but he could pray for her safety and deliverance.

As he knelt before the statues, he found the plea refused to come. The Saint and his Holy Retinue, for all their strength in life, no longer held any power in Yscalin. They might not be able to see Marosa, trapped as she was in the shadow of evil.

Aubrecht knelt for some time, thinking.

Long before the Midwinter Flood – the event that preceded their forced conversion – the Ments had followed a far older religion. It posited a doomed love between the Smith of the Earth and the Smith of the Heavens, and their eternal battle for dominance. The Smith of the Earth had dwelled in a great forge beneath the Dreadmount, and when he was angry, the volcano rumbled.

Perhaps the Smith of the Earth was the same god the Yscals had once worshipped, known by a different name. But Yscalin no longer needed fire. Only the Smith of the Heavens – the silver queen of the sky – might save them.

'Hail, Smith of the Heavens,' Aubrecht said, his voice soft. 'If she is still alive, protect her.'

He made the sign of the sword, to cleanse his own vice, and walked away.

Marosa

Another year of smoke and brimstone. Little by little, the people of Cárscaro were losing their faith. The wyverns' eyes were too sharp, the Great Yscali Plain too wide. Gulthaga had chosen its outpost all too well.

In the city, things had taken a turn for the worst. Over time, Draconic monsters – the dreaded sleepers, now woken – had started to arrive. Now there were not just wyverns, but other vile beasts, stalking the streets in search of prey. Unlike the wyverns, they fed on flesh.

The city guard was still trying to keep the peace, but it was a fruitless endeavour. Anyone could be snatched up and carried to the crack in the mountain, never to be seen again. Without the sanctarians to guide them, and with all of their nobles serving the wyrm, some Cárscari had lost their fear of the Knight of Justice. Cutpurses and robbers prowled by the light of the Tundana. More than one person had been killed for sport. Clearly there were some who had been waiting for the Saint to fall, so they might indulge their vices. Worse still, several cases of the Draconic plague had been reported. The sick had been sealed in their homes.

Marosa tried her utmost to keep despair at bay, even after learning the truth about her father – even after telling Priessa, who had not yet found out if her own father had been complicit. Every plan to resist had failed, but they had started to sew gloves and handkerchiefs for the people, to be handed out in secret, with parcels of food and notes to bolster their spirits.

Within the walls of the Palace of Salvation, some of the Vardya had submitted to Draconic rule. They scoured the halls for any hint of rebellion, perhaps out of fear that Fýredel would burn the city if defiance thrived. But Ermendo, ever loyal, had ensured that some obeyed Marosa. She had sent two of them to scale Mount Fruma, to see if there was a way to drop gunpowder on Fýredel, to no avail. The Fell Door seemed to be the only way into his lair.

Hope was now a dying lamp, and hers only had a little more oil.

It almost went out on the anniversary, two years to the day since Cárscaro fell. She was gazing out of the window, hoping for the sight of a dove, when Ermendo entered her apartments.

'I have a message from His Majesty,' he said, his gaze low. 'Fýredel wishes to see you.'

Marosa slowly looked at him. In two years, Fýredel had never once acknowledged her.

Priessa rose. 'Fýredel has the king as his puppet. Why would he ask for Marosa?'

'I wish I knew, my lady.'

The number of people who had survived a close encounter with a High Western was very small. Marosa knew of only three. One was Glorian Shieldheart, the second was Gastaldo Yelarigas, and the third was her father.

'I see.' Marosa stood, her voice distant even to her own ears. 'I had better get ready, then.'

'No.' Priessa grasped her arm. 'Marosa, we can hide you.'

'Fýredel will burn us all if we do not submit.' Marosa smoothed her bodice. 'I doubt that he will kill me. What purpose would that serve?'

Priessa was turning pale. After a moment, her resolve seemed to stiffen.

'Fýredel will likely breathe the plague,' she said. 'If you must go, then let us armour you.'

****

It took some time. Marosa donned twice as many layers as usual, with a veil of the sort that mourners favoured. She would have worn a plague mask, but she imagined that Fýredel might want to see her face, her royal eyes. The veil was more a prayer than any real protection.

Ermendo lent her a breastplate, which she covered with a cloak, in case the wyrm perceived her armour as a threat. Last came a gold circlet forged by Oderica. When Priessa placed it over her veil, she felt as if she, like her ancestor, could survive being folded into the mountain.

The Palace of Salvation looked different. It had been discovered that the bile of Draconic creatures could be made into candles and torches, which burned for days with hot red flames, drawing the air even closer. Her father insisted upon their use. He had also forced a stoneworker to carve grotesques of Draconic beasts around the main doors of the palace, and commanded his court to refer to him as the Flesh King of Yscalin, servant to the Iron King.

Cárscaro had turned into the Womb of Fire. The realm of damnation, the cradle of iniquity. If any newcomer looked upon it now, they would believe its people loved their overlords.

And Marosa could do nothing but watch.

She descended the Grand Stair with her guards, bathed in a crimson glow. Despite the peril, she felt no fear. Perhaps the threat was simply too great to work its way inside her.

A coach waited outside the palace. When Marosa saw what drew it, she stepped back. Two monstrous beasts observed her with glowing eyes. From their furred lupine heads, these were jaculi – a melding of wyvern and wolf, each about the size of a carthorse.

They would ensure she heeded the summons.

'Saint.' Ermendo kept one hand on the hilt of his sword. 'Let me go first, Your Radiance.'

He approached gingerly and opened the door. The jaculi growled, but allowed them both to board.

The Cárscari watched the coach emerge. Their silence was unnerving in a city of forty thousand souls, but one wrong sound could draw fatal attention. Marosa wished she could make the sign of the sword, showing herself to be true to the Saint. Instead, she avoided their eyes, grateful for the veil.

They must think she was on her way to die.

Perhaps she was.

The coach jolted and rattled so badly her teeth clashed. The jaculi were swift, but clearly had no care for their passengers' comfort, nor for the safety of those around them. More than one person had to run out of their way. They loped between the guildhalls and grand basalt mansions and banking houses around the Palace of Salvation. When Marosa spotted a pair of red wings painted on a door, she pointed them out to Ermendo.

'What does that symbol mean?'

'The plague is in the house,' Ermendo said. 'Any afflicted families board themselves inside.'

Marosa closed her eyes after that. So tense was her body, she felt sore by the time she dared to look outside again. The coach had passed the merchants' rowhouses and crossed the Tundana twice. Now they were among the tenements that most Cárscari lived in.

They reached the eastern outskirts of Cárscaro, where the stonecutters dwelled. This was where the rockslide had ended, the night of the fall. Several cottages were almost buried in rubble.

'I was born here,' Ermendo said. Marosa looked at him. 'Most of the survivors have left this quarter, since no one wishes to live near the Fell Door. They've all moved closer to the cliffside.'

'What of your family?'

'My parents died many years ago, and I thank the Saint for it. I need not fear for them.'

At the foot of a slope, when the wheels could roll no farther, Marosa got out, her veil fluttering in the wind from the Spindles. For the first time in years, she could see the Palace of Salvation from a distance. The dark and sombre tower, illuminated by the sinister red of the Tundana.

Her riding boots slewed on loose fragments of rock. Ermendo steadied her as she began to slip. 'I must go alone. Fýredel did not summon you,' she said to him. 'Will you wait for me?'

'As long as it takes.'

He offered her a lantern from the coach. 'Thank you,' she said, 'but I read in a bestiary that fire can become ... unpredictable in Draconic lairs. I trust there will be a safe path.'

'Very well.'

Above loomed the Fell Door, dwarfing her. Relying on the full moon for light, she clambered up the wooden ramp that had been constructed, each step hard on her feet, even with boots. She was used to the smooth floors of the palace.

At last, she stepped into the cave. The cave from which many Cárscari had never returned.

Fýredel must have set humans to work in here. There were pickaxes and ladders around the entrance, as if someone had been trying to widen it. Not only that, but iron braziers and torches blazed, lit with red fire. Out of their reach, it was black as pitch. She nerved herself and stepped forward.

A hiss stopped her in her tracks. A grey beast emerged from the nearest shadows, its forked tongue lashing out. A culebreya – a winged serpent, like the amphiptere, with a hood like a cobra. They were believed to have come from Afelayanda Forest, hence the Yscali name.

Marosa managed to keep still. The culebreya retreated a short way, eyes aglow with hatred, before it moved its head into the light again. This time, its hiss was louder, scraping down her spine. When it repeated this swaying motion a third time, she realised that it wanted her to follow it. Praying her instinct was right, she placed herself at the mercy of a monster.

When she came near, the culebreya did not strike. Instead, it turned and slithered into a tunnel. Marosa shadowed it, keeping a safe distance. It was hard to keep her veil on, such was the overpowering heat. She could already see another brazier, but when they reached it, she wished for darkness, for the ground was strewn with bones. She had almost convinced herself they were animal until she noticed a human skull, bloody and missing its jaw.

Marosa began to shake uncontrollably. She had known the creatures fed on flesh. Bartian had guessed the fate that must have met the Cárscari who came here, but she had denied it to preserve her sanity. *Surely not all of them*, she reasoned with herself. *They would not eat their own labourers.* She forced herself to walk after the culebreya. *Please, let some of them have lived.*

Now she could hear a hammering. It distracted her and she misplaced her boot, stepping on something that caused her foot to roll. When she instinctively looked down, she saw the mound of bones she had disturbed, and then a human arm on the ground, still fresh, torn off at the elbow. She pressed her lips together, sweat trickling down her face.

A hot roar of light drew her attention back to the hammering. In a vast cave to her left, two wyverns lay alongside each other, surrounded by humans.

Marosa glanced at the culebreya, which had stopped to lick the blood from a skull. While it was distracted, she squinted into the cave again. Several of the humans were climbing on a wyvern, cloths over their faces. As Marosa watched, two women lowered a sheet of metal over a deep hole in its hide.

Her heart was beating harder than it ever had. The Cárscari were mending the wyverns' injuries from the Grief. Taking away those few hard-won weak points in their armour.

She tore her gaze away and looked across the rest of the cavern, straining to see through a haze of dust and smoke. A burly man was using hot water and a stiff broom to clean the filth off a basilisk, while another scrubbed rust from its patches of iron armour. It hissed at them both, but seemed to endure their ministrations. The sight of that great serpent chilled Marosa. If its venom touched either of those men, they would disintegrate, like Rosarian.

Even farther away, a group of Cárscari were chipping at the wall. The Fell Door was large enough for wyverns and Draconic creatures. These people could only be excavating more beasts.

The culebreya snapped at her. Marosa flinched and went after it, hot tears on her cheeks.

Her people were being forced to act as agents of their own destruction. To make worthless the sacrifices of their ancestors.

At last, her guide brought her to another cavern, where a hot wind made her veil flutter. A faint glow – lava, flowing somewhere nearby – lit its walls. She walked to the end of a long spear of rock, reaching the edge of a pit that seemed bottomless. The culebreya let out a harsh sound, which echoed through the darkness.

For a long time, Marosa could only shiver at the precipice. At last, she heard movement. A low rumble, followed by earth-shaking thuds, shards of rock skittering.

It took some time for her eyes to tell rock from scale, and to pick out the face of the wyrm.

The face of Fýredel.

A thousand stories could not have prepared her for a High Western. Even after reading eyewitness accounts, she had never imagined that he could be so immense, nor to look exactly as volcanic as he was. His scales were obsidian, though his throat was reddish, as if stained with blood. She could not even see all of him, but what little she did see dwarfed her.

The wyrm that had almost destroyed humankind. An abomination of the highest order.

If this was only an underling, she could not imagine the Nameless One.

Did Fruma look this way to Oderica?

His fiery gaze was nailed to her. A wonder that he could even see a small human. Marosa sank to her knees, unsure if she had done it on purpose, or if her joints had failed her.

'Who comes?'

His voice was so deep, it took her a moment to realise he was speaking Inysh.

'Marosa Vetalda, Princess of Yscalin,' she replied, her voice shaking. 'You summoned me.'

'You are the whelp of the Flesh King.'

'Yes.'

Marosa forced herself to look up again. She had to take the measure of the enemy. There were dents and scores in his black hide, but no missing scales, no obvious vulnerabilities. All wyrms had a weak spot under the wing – their hides were thin and supple there, allowing them to fly – but she doubted even a javelin, even there, could pierce a High Western.

'The fire burns through his body, though he does not perish yet.' Fýredel spoke Inysh with a strange inflection, forcing her to concentrate to understand him. 'Whenever he is too weak to rise, you will hearken to my commands in his stead. I will send them through the seneschal.'

The title had not existed for a long time, but the seneschal could only be Lord Gastaldo.

'Yes, my liege,' Marosa said, addressing him in an archaic manner. 'We are ready to serve.'

She loathed how meek and docile she sounded. If only she had the mettle to defy him, like the heroes of the Grief, but forty thousand lives hung in the balance. How could she risk them?

'There is a woman in your dungeons. Red her cloak and sharp her blade,' the wyrm said. 'In agony and fear she must die. The Flesh King will bear witness, so I might know the deed is done, hear the screams that mark her end. She must hang alive upon your gate of stone by dawn.'

He wanted this woman to be pecked and cut to death.

'It will be done,' Marosa said. 'Wh-who is this woman?'

Fýredel did not answer her question, but his gaze scorched into hers through her veil, like a brand. It took all her will to keep her eyes open, in case that was the way he seized a mind. She had lived for years as a figurine, to be moved as her father wished; she did not want to die as a puppet.

'Why do you do this?' she said. 'Why do you wreak such violence upon humankind?'

She did not know what possessed her to ask such a thing. Perhaps because she was one of the few who had ever come this close to a wyrm. Perhaps because Fýredel seemed, unexpectedly, to be listening.

'You doomed your own earth,' he said.

'How?'

When Fýredel was silent, Marosa forced herself to rise, even though her knees shook. A low growl resonated through the chamber.

'Majesty, I beseech you, give us your counsel,' she implored the High Western. 'Our ancestors slew your siblings. I know this. I see the scars upon your armour. But we fought you because you attacked first, because you did not tell us what you sought. If we have offended you, I am sure we can atone, but how can we put right a wrong we do not understand?'

Fýredel considered her. His eyes were like two great braziers beneath a pair of formidable horns.

And then Marosa did something that she knew was not only very foolish, but would surely enrage the Saint, who had risked his life to slay one of these creatures. She thought of her people in the other cavern, permitted to climb on the wyverns.

Before she could doubt her decision, she drew her pendant from her bodice and slowly held it up, showing it to the wyrm. Fýredel turned quite still, and she prayed that he could see a sliver of his own reflection, little though her mirror was. Perhaps he would be like the bird Denarva had brought from the Ersyr, unable to recognise its own image, courting itself in the looking glass. Even if he was too large to see himself, she hoped his curiosity would buy her time to speak.

She took a step towards the wyrm. Fýredel remained motionless. Slowly, she reached out her left hand, safe in its thick riding glove, and grazed her fingertips against his snout.

And Fýredel, the enemy of humankind, did not strike her down.

See yourself in others. She trembled violently as she felt his terrible heat through her glove, strong enough that it would surely make short work of the leather. Every breath moved through him like a slow rockslide. *Show them the same grace ...*

'Please,' she said. 'Tell me your purpose. Tell me how I can stop this.'

Another ominous rumble filled the room. She knew he was considering whether or not to kill her.

'Broken are the roots of chaos. Thrice cleaved,' Fýredel said, 'and never knit.' He bared his teeth, which gleamed like iron swords. She made out her own dim reflection in their polished surface. 'The fire beneath must rage above. All must burn, from shore to shore.'

Marosa tried to parse the words through the dizzying fog of her fear.

'Then you do mean to destroy Yscalin,' she said. 'Why do you stoop to this puppetry?'

Fýredel snarled at her. She fell hard on the ground before him. Still clutching the pendant, she stared into his mouth – at the second and third rows of teeth, and his forked tongue, dark as blood.

And there it was. The crimson light at the back of his throat, an ember from the Womb of Fire. It was hot and bright enough to cast a glow on her body, and to coat her face in sweat again.

'Forgive my insolence. I misspoke,' she stammered, 'but please, take no more of my people.'

'You do not command the fire,'

Fýredel told her. 'Go back to the Flesh King, and when he can no longer stand, don my aspect in his stead. Let them know whose decree resounds from the mountain.'

With a heavy *clang*, something fell at her side. Marosa picked it up with clumsy hands. Even through her gloves, she felt its warmth.

A helm of cast iron, shaped like the head of a wyrm.

****

She carried the helm with her from the cave. When she reached the Palace of Salvation, Priessa was there to wrap her in a mantle and embrace her. Marosa tried to still her shaking as Ermendo took the dreadful helm out of her sight.

'Your Radiance.' Lord Gastaldo appeared to her right. 'Are you injured?'

'No, my lord.' Marosa kept her left hand clenched against her breast. 'I am only shaken.'

She had thrown her glove into the Tundana. The evidence of her folly.

'I am relieved to hear it,' Lord Gastaldo said. 'Please, come to my study.'

'I must bathe first. Saint knows what Draconic filth I have brought.'

'Do not fear. The floor is cleaned with vinegar.'

Marosa followed him up the many steps to his study, torn between nerves and curiosity. Lord Gastaldo had always been a broad man, but in the weeks since she had last seen him, his face had turned gaunt.

In his study, Marosa took a seat, keeping her veil in place. Lord Gastaldo opened a window, while Priessa stood beside the door.

'Donmata,' Lord Gastaldo said, 'what did the wyrm say to you?'

'He said I must take over when my father can no longer stand.'

Priessa made a faint sound. Lord Gastaldo glanced at his daughter, his lips pressed into a line.

'Your Radiance,' he said to Marosa, 'I know you must resent me for keeping you away from the Privy Council, as your father always has, but I did it only to conceal you from Fýredel. I have tried my best to stop His Majesty visiting you when the wyrm looks through him.'

'The wyrm *does* look through him, then?'

'I have no doubt of it. I have stayed close to him in the hope that Fýredel would perceive me as his natural replacement. Until today, I believed I was succeeding.'

Marosa was momentarily speechless.

'You meant for him to sow the plague in you next?' she asked him. 'You would sacrifice your own life to his evil?'

'Better me than our Donmata.'

He was serious. She could see it in his eyes.

'You may know that Fýredel called me into the mountain some time ago,' he said. 'During our meeting, he made clear that he knew I was not a Vetalda. Perhaps it is a scent. He knows enough of our laws to understand that the throne must pass to someone of the same blood.'

'What was the purpose of the meeting?'

'He wanted to know why His Majesty was sleeping more often. I explained that he was unwell. The plague has been afflicting him with fevers, which leave him too weak to rise, even when Fýredel compels him to do so. The Royal Physician has also given him dwale, which keeps him in a deep stupor for hours. That must be why the wyrm called you today. He wanted to see who is next in line. To make sure they are young and strong enough to bear his fire.'

'What cares a wyrm for the petty laws of humankind?'

'I suspect that he wants to use Vetalda authority to make this invasion appear legitimate.'

'How long do you think I have?'

Marosa asked the question in a detached manner, as if it were of no more import than the weather.

'The Royal Physician is working around the clock to keep your father alive. The longer he endures, the longer you are safe,' Lord Gastaldo said. 'His deterioration appears inevitable, but so far, it is mercifully slow. He can still walk. So long as he does not refuse food or water, he should not die.'

'How much of his mind remains?'

'It is difficult to say. When his eyes are unlit, I think that he is both himself and Fýredel – as if the wyrm is asleep, but their memories blur. He dreams of things he has not seen.' He rubbed between his dark eyebrows. 'Stay away from him, Donmata. Let us hope that Fýredel will forget you are there.'

Marosa thought of asking him if he had known about Queen Rosarian. If he was the one who had taught the cypher to King Sigoso.

In the end, she decided that she would prefer not to know.

'I must go,' Lord Gastaldo said. 'Your father has called a meeting of the Privy Council.'

'Are you trying to stop this, Lord Gastaldo?' Marosa asked him. 'Are you trying to free our people?'

'I am. But in my opinion, there is ... not a great deal to be done, Your Radiance. Not without condemning all of Cárscaro.'

'Then I suppose we have nothing further to discuss. Goodnight, my lord.'

'Goodnight, Your Radiance.'

****

In the relative safety of her apartments, Priessa helped remove her reeking layers, which the laundress meant to burn. For once, Marosa wanted the bath as hot as she could bear it. Once she was in, Priessa scrubbed her scalp and used the last of the rosewater to banish the smell of wyrm.

'Did you know of this?' Marosa asked her. 'Did you know that your father was shielding me?'

'I guessed.' She wore a mask of indifference, but Marosa could see the conflict behind it. 'I cannot stop wondering if he knew about Queen Rosarian. My father is not perfect – he can be unfeeling and vainglorious; perhaps he is even cruel – but I believe that he is loyal to your dynasty. So is my mother. All of us would give our lives without question.'

'As I would give mine for you.'

Priessa poured clean water, rinsing the suds away. 'Was Fýredel as ghastly as they say?'

Marosa looked down at her left hand.

'Like nothing you can imagine,' she murmured. 'He is so much larger than the wyverns, but I think that is why he has not yet emerged. It will take him longer to regain enough strength to fly.'

'But he does have his flame?'

'Yes.'

Hot enough to make her sweat, even before he breathed.

'We should try to slay him while he is grounded, to spare the world another Grief.' Priessa reached for a cloth and soap. 'As soon as he takes to the sky, all of humankind is doomed.'

'None of our weapons could get near, except when he is slumbering. Even then, scores of his creatures stand guard. It would be death to attempt it. Perhaps if we could pack his lair with gunpowder, but even then ... I doubt it would kill him.' Marosa closed her eyes as Priessa washed the grime from her face. 'Do you know if there are any new prisoners in the dungeons?'

'Only the Duchess of Ortégardes and Sir Robrecht Teldan, to my knowledge.'

They had both confessed to imagining the death of the king. Even in his changed state, her father did not forgive acts of treason. There had been other prisoners, but they had already been killed.

'Fýredel has told me there is someone else down there,' Marosa said. 'She is to be hung upon the Gate of Niunda by dawn.' Her temples were pounding. 'Do you know how long the Privy Council will be in session?'

'An hour or two, I should think. His Majesty wishes to share more of his plans for this Draconic kingdom.'

'Then I must go now, to visit this prisoner.' Marosa rose. 'Do not wait for me, Priessa.'

****

Five centuries ago, Queen Rozaria had built a palace from the rock and glass of the Dreadmount. Now Marosa felt certain that Fýredel had some unholy connexion to it. She imagined herself as an insect, trapped inside his gullet; that he felt her every footfall, heard her every breath; that she glimpsed his serpentine eyes in the slivers of black glass around the palace. She imagined that, even as the wyrm slumbered for all those years, his ears had been open.

The dungeons of the Palace of Salvation were close to the wine cellars, with no windows to banish the darkness. Three guards flanked the entrance, sweating in the light of the red torches.

'Your Radiance,' the nearest said. 'Good evening.'

'I wish to speak to the newest prisoner,' Marosa said. 'How long has it been since she came here?'

'Almost a week,' another guard said. 'A wyvern brought her to the steps of the palace.'

'Is she an Yscal?'

'From the weapons she was carrying, we assume not. They look to be of Southern origin,' he answered. 'The wyverns must have found her on the plain, or perhaps in the Spindles.' He glanced at the door. 'She hasn't made a sound, even though the Jackal used the iron boot on her.'

One of the interrogators Lord Gastaldo had brought to the palace, known for her brutality.

'Very well,' Marosa said. 'I will not be long.'

'Don't step too close to the bars,' the first guard warned. 'The woman put up a mighty resistance, Your Radiance. Even thirsty and weak, she killed five of us before we could overpower her.'

'Which cell is she in?'

'The last.'

Marosa stepped through the doors, entering the dungeon for the first time in her life. Her mother had not been kept here, to her knowledge, but Denarva likely had. Finding the right door, she lifted the latch and pushed with her shoulder, scraping it open.

Beyond was a row of iron bars, behind which sat a woman in a stained white tunic, no more than thirty years old. Sweat and blood mingled on her brown skin, and dark curls fell into her eyes, which were puffy and bruised.

Her right foot was horribly mangled. Marosa had known that Lord Gastaldo allowed the Jackal to maim certain people – suspected traitors, murderers, the cullers he despised so much – but seeing the aftermath shortened her breath. The straw was soaked in blood.

She was not naïve enough to think she would never have enemies when she was queen, but there must be a better way to treat them. Surely the Saint would not condone this cruelty.

'Do you speak Yscali?' she asked, receiving a wary look in return. She tried Ersyri: 'What is your name?'

It had been a long time since she had spoken Ersyri, but recognition sparked in those brown eyes, alert and unclouded after days of torture. The woman sat up straighter, but said nothing.

Perhaps the Jackal had torn out her tongue. Either that, or she thought Marosa was another torturer. Marosa took out the small bottle of red wine she had brought from her apartments.

'To dull your pain,' she said, still in Ersyri. 'And help you sleep.'

The guard had told her not to get too close to the bars, but she risked it, offering the bottle. The woman slowly reached out and took it, sniffing the neck before testing a drop on her tongue. Apparently satisfied that she was not being poisoned, she took several deep gulps.

'Jondu.' Her voice was hoarse. 'My name is Jondu.'

'Where did you come from?'

'I was on my way to Oryzon,' Jondu said. 'To find a ship to Lasia.'

'That is not what I asked.'

'No.' Jondu shifted a little closer to the bars, her face tightening as she moved her mutilated foot. 'Are you Princess Marosa, daughter of Sahar Taumargam, Princess of the Ersyr?'

'Yes.'

Jondu released her breath. 'A mercy,' she said. 'The Mother is good.'

'Why were you in the Spindles?'

'The wyverns and their offspring are all over this country. I decided to make my way to the South through the mountains, to stop the creatures sensing me. It did not work.' She fixed a steady look on Marosa. 'The torturers informed me that Fýredel has wakened here. Is it true?'

'Yes,' Marosa said. 'In a cave to the east.'

'And where is Denarva uq-Bardant?'

It was such a sudden and drastic change of subject, Marosa hesitated. 'You knew Denarva?'

'Tell me where she is.'

Marosa was not used to being given orders, but Jondu spoke with such authority, she obeyed by instinct.

'Denarva has been dead for years,' she said. 'She tried to help my mother flee this city, after she learned that my father had Queen Rosarian of Inys murdered.'

Jondu slumped against the wall again, gazing at the opposite side of the cell. Her cheeks were damp, either with sweat or tears.

'It is as we feared,' she said to herself. Marosa stepped closer, her brow creased, and Jondu looked back at her. 'Denarva was my friend. I cannot say from whence I come, but I am a protector of the South, loyal to the House of Taumargam, known and trusted by your uncle, Jantar the Splendid. Can I trust you, Princess Marosa?'

'If you were a friend of Denarva, you are mine as well.'

'Very well.' Jondu glanced at her foot, which had started to bleed again. 'Your Vardya seized a box from me. If you value human life, you will find a way to get it to Chassar uq-Ispad.'

'Chassar uq-Ispad,' Marosa echoed. 'The Ersyri ambassador?'

'Yes.'

'What he has to do with your box?' she asked. Jondu did not reply. 'I would imagine that His Excellency is in Rauca.'

'More likely at his estate in Rumelabar.'

'It makes little difference. None of us can leave Cárscaro.'

'There is a way out through a lava tunnel, which leads farther into the Spindles. From there, you can take the old Pass of the Imperator to the Ersyr. A horse trail laid by the Gulthaganians,' Jondu said. 'I am sure that is the path Denarva would have used to get you to safety.'

'How do you *know* any of this?' Marosa said, frustration surging up. 'I have lived here all my life, and never have I heard of this tunnel. Even if I could find it, the Spindles are swarming with Draconic creatures.'

'They will not attack a person who carries the plague.'

'But the plague would kill anyone who contracted it.'

'Not immediately. It steeps in the body for some time before the bloodblaze takes hold. And if the person you send forth is able to reach Chassar … he will be able to cure them.'

Marosa stared at her.

'Ambassador uq-Ispad has a cure to the Draconic plague?' She grasped the bars. 'Hundreds and more of my people may have it, after two years of occupation, and he dares to withhold a remedy?'

'It is not my place to say the reason.'

Marosa tightened her grip. It took her a long moment to master the anger that had risen in her.

'This lava tunnel,' she finally said. 'How would I find it?'

'It adjoins the foundations of this very building. If you still have the plans, you should find a stairway leading there, likely hidden in some way. But Denarva would have opened it.'

'And what is in the box?' Marosa asked her. 'If I am to risk enraging Fýredel – to gamble with the lives of every person in this city – then I must know why.'

'It is the key to a weapon. A weapon that may help defeat the wyrms.'

'A mangonel, a springald?' Marosa pressed. 'What in the name of the Saint can you mean?'

'I do nothing in *his* name,' Jondu said, with such open contempt that Marosa stiffened. 'Princess, you are a daughter of the Ersyr, heir presumptive of the House of Taumargam. You have my sisters' respect and protection. I put my faith in you to finish my assignment.'

'Who are your sisters?'

Jondu shook her head. Marosa had the sense of being caught upon a root she could not see.

'Donmata,' a guard called, 'are you well?'

'Yes,' Marosa called. 'Thank you.' She stood. 'I can make no promises, but I will do what I can.'

'Wait,' Jondu said, stopping her. 'My cloak. Has Fýredel seen it?'

Red her cloak and sharp her blade.

'Yes,' Marosa said. 'What is special about your cloak?'

'It is dyed with Draconic blood.'

'Are you a culler?'

'Of a sort.' Jondu raised her chin. 'I know that I will die here, but let it not be at the jaws of a wyrm. Fýredel will make an example of me. Better it was swift and clean.' Marosa turned back to her, and Jondu read her face with unexpected ease. 'He has already given you orders.'

'He will not kill you himself, but he wishes to witness your death. To hear your screams.'

'Your torturers could not win one from me,' Jondu said, her smile tight, 'but I would still rather that my death was not to satisfy a wyrm. He will likely have me fed to his creatures. I would prefer to die in battle.'

'Are you asking to fight me?' Marosa said, returning the grim smile. 'I am not strong.'

'That cannot be true. You are a Taumargam. But no, I will not fight you, Princess.'

Marosa did not carry anything sharp. She had never been permitted, after the way her mother had supposedly died. Another lie her father had used to control her every move. There was dwale in the palace – a potion for reducing pain, too much of which could kill – but she would not find it before dawn.

All she had was the vial of basilisk venom.

If she handed it to Jondu, she would bear responsibility for the death of at least one person, whether that was Jondu herself, or the guards outside. The Knight of Justice would condemn her, but there was no justice in what Fýredel planned for this woman. A knight was supposed to prevent suffering. That was why, in ancient days, they had worn blades for mercy killings.

How easy it was to gamble with her place in Halgalant when a living woman sat before her, asking for help and compassion. As her conscience battled her faith, she remembered.

See yourself in others.

A clarifying thought, soothing in its simplicity. She slid the vial from her bodice and placed it between the bars.

'This is basilisk venom,' she said. 'Do not use it to cause your own death, but to melt your way from this cell.'

Jondu picked up the vial and turned it several times.

'I cannot cross the Spindles. Not with my foot like this,' she said. 'The arch is shattered.'

'Then fight the guards. This time, they might be able to subdue you,' Marosa said. 'You can die in battle, as you wished.'

After a long and silent moment, Jondu nodded.

'This is a kindness. A gift,' she told Marosa. 'I hope your Saint will not punish you for it.'

Marosa unlaced her partlet, revealing the pendant that sat below her neckline. Jondu beheld the mirror with clear recognition.

'I do not only follow the Saint,' Marosa said quietly. 'If I am ever in your place, I hope to be shown the same mercy.'

Jondu smiled, cracking her lips.

'You will make a mighty Queen of the Ersyr,' she said. 'I would have been honoured to be your protector. In my stead, may the Mother watch over you, Princess Marosa.'

Marosa did not ask who she meant. She had her own mother to watch over her.

She left the dungeon and returned to the guards. 'Tell me,' she said to them, 'where are prisoners' effects kept?'

'In there, Your Radiance. On the bench to the right.'

'Is there anything especially unusual among them?'

'She did carry a strange box. We haven't been able to open it.'

Marosa went through the door they had indicated. Beyond was a storage room, lined with instruments of torture. There was the iron boot on the floor, crusted with blood, turning her stomach.

And there, the iron helm that Fýredel had given her.

She stopped in her tracks at the ominous sight. Ermendo must have put it down here, so she never had to look at it. It was mounted on a stand, as if it were part of an ordinary suit of armour.

At first, she had assumed that Fýredel had forged the helm. Now she looked again, it was obvious that one of the captive Yscals was responsible. She wondered if the blacksmith had known that it was meant for her. The vacant eyeholes seemed to stare into her soul, and she could not break their gaze. It was as if she looked upon her own casket, made to her measurements.

Before she could stop herself, she put it on.

Inside, all was dark. Her neck immediately started to ache. As sweat broke out on her forehead, she tried looking one way, and then the other. She could see through the eyeholes, but not well. She could breathe, but not with any ease.

Was this how Fýredel felt when he looked through her father? The thought made the helm even harder to bear. She wrenched it off with clammy hands and put it back on to its mount.

Jondu had been carrying more weapons than a hired killer, all worth a queen's ransom. A crossbow with folding limbs. A fine Ersyri scimitar, its ornate white scabbard encrusted with pearls. Several other blades, the origin and type of which she did not recognise.

And there was the box.

It looked to be made of iron. An oblong at the bottom, with a lid shaped like a pyramid, all swirled with intricate engravings, which could be patterns or a language. There was a ring at the top of the lid, so it might be attached to a saddle or girdle. It was light in comparison to the helm.

The guards had not followed her. She hung the box from the back of her own girdle, so her cloak would cover it. When she returned to the guards, she wore an imperious expression.

'There was no box in the room,' she said. 'Do you mean to trick me?'

'Donmata, I will investigate.'

Marosa nodded and walked away, the box heavy against her hip.

She waited in her apartments all day, watching the mantel clock. At last, Ermendo came to her.

'Your Radiance,' he said in an undertone, 'a woman escaped from the dungeons today. She didn't get far – her foot was injured – but she fought. One of the guards slashed her throat by mistake.'

Marosa suspected it had not been a mistake, even if the guard had not meant to do it. Jondu had clearly known how to fight.

That meant she also knew how to die.

'Tell Lord Gastaldo she died of her wounds,' Marosa said. 'Be sure that is what His Majesty hears, Ermendo. All of our fates may depend upon it.'

'It will be done, Donmata.'

✳✳✳✳

It was not for several days that Marosa was made to understand the consequences of her actions. During those days, she found the way that Jondu had described, tucked in a corridor with a dead end. She found the stairs that lay beyond it, twisting into the depths of the palace. Though she dared not risk it yet, it comforted her to know that escape might truly be possible.

After some thought, she decided to share the discovery with Ruzio and Priessa, and to show the latter the box as well, in case Priessa had any ideas. Priessa pondered it for hours – she even took a small hammer to it – but could not get inside.

The next day was colder than most. Priessa was about to try a different tool when King Sigoso arrived. She curtseyed to him, hiding the hammer from sight. Marosa stepped in front of her.

'Your Majesty,' she said. 'How are you feeling?'

Her father wore a silver mask, but she knew him by the smell of bonfires, the reek that always seemed to emanate from him. Likely the mask was to cover his blisters.

'Come outside, daughter,' he said. 'Come with me.'

Some of the Vardya were behind him, all with cloths over their faces. Marosa had little choice but to follow.

Sigoso had not emerged from the tower since Fýredel had summoned him. His infirmity was becoming too obvious. The Vardya ushered him into one coach, Marosa into another, and escorted them through the streets on horseback, keeping the people at bay with halberds.

Once more, Marosa observed her subjects through her veil, absorbing their silent hatred, their hollow cheeks, the plague masks that must be making them sweat in the oppressive heat of the Tundana. *Where is the Saint?* their eyes seemed to ask. *Where is the Knight of Justice now?*

The coach stopped at the Gate of Niunda. Marosa allowed the Captain General to help her down, then beheld the great arch of green stone. The paving stones beneath were dark with blood.

She tensed when she saw a creature nearby, circling the gate – about seven feet in height, with feathered wings and scaled legs ending in talons. It possessed a long tail, like a wyverling, but also a beak and a coxcomb, like a rooster. Its eyes were twin embers.

A cockatrice. It lowered its awful head and licked the ground with a forked tongue.

'Look up,' King Sigoso said. Marosa could only do as he ordered.

Jondu hung from the gate by her wrists. Her white tunic was bloody where the Vardya had cut her throat.

To her left was Ermendo Vuleydres.

His armour, came a distant thought. *I have never seen Ermendo without his armour.*

His face was intact. The rest of him was charred and withered, and his legs ended at the knee, one longer than the other. Next were Sir Robrecht Teldan and the Duchess of Ortégardes, flanked by the two Hróthi ambassadors, who had clearly been dead for several days longer. The beasts had jabbed and torn at their flesh, leaving gaping holes in their bodies.

Last in the row was Yscabel Afleytan, brown hair fluttering in the wind.

Two more cockatrices soared on to the Gate of Niunda. The one below called out to its kin – a sinister clucking – and winged up to join them. In unison, they began to peck at Yscabel.

And Yscabel made a weak sound.

Marosa almost fell to her knees. She turned away from the arch with a gasp of denial, but her father caught her upper arm, his fingers bruising. There were three layers of cloth between his skin and hers, but his touch still flooded her with fear. Even in his enfeebled state, she knew she could not have broken his grip if she fought him for the rest of her life.

Against her will, she imagined this hand on her mother.

'No. Look up,' her father sneered. 'See what you have done, Marosa.' Yscabel let out anguished sobs, making Marosa shudder. 'See what your defiance has brought upon your subjects.'

For once, she wished the veil was thicker. She willed her tears to dull her sight.

'Fýredel gave you an order, and you disobeyed him,' King Sigoso said. 'Did you not think I would find out that the bars in the dungeon were melted with venom? Do you think I am blind and deaf in this state?' His hold tightened painfully. 'No. I see and hear more than ever.'

Someone shoot her, Marosa willed the city guards, barely hearing her father. *End her pain.* But the guards only watched as the cockatrices began to feast. They would not risk being next.

Yscabel did not suffer for long. All the Draconic creatures were hungry, after centuries of macerating in their sleep. Soon there was more blood on the stained ground, and all was quiet again.

Like a tomb.

At last, King Sigoso let go of Marosa. Her ears rang and the world slanted, and there was no Ermendo to steady her. She feared she would fall to the ground, but she could not. Some of the Cárscari had followed the coaches here from the palace, and even if the guards were keeping them away, they could still see her posture, if not her bloodless face. She could not show any sort of weakness in front of her despairing subjects.

'If you try any other tricks,' King Sigoso said, 'the Dowager Prince will be next. I have no further need for ambassadors.'

Stand firm. Marosa locked her knees, and the wave gradually passed. *Hold still, as you always have.*

'Forgive me,' she rasped. 'Forgive me, Father.'

'It is not for me to forgive you.' He shoved her towards the coach. 'Now only Fýredel can.'

Marosa sat in numb silence as they returned to the Palace of Salvation. All the way back, she held in her grief, but it was so large, so wild, that it threatened to split her. Her father left her alone in the entrance hall, where she swayed like a blade of grass, her sight dimming.

First her mother. Now this.

How much loss could one soul bear?

For only the third or fourth time in her life, Marosa ascended the steps of the tower alone, without Ermendo. She could not even begin to fathom how she would break this news to Ruzio.

When she finally reached her apartments, drained and aching from the climb, she doubled over and vomited on to the floor. Each surge wrung icy sweat from her in rivulets.

'Save us,' she choked out. 'Anyone, I beg you, help us. Saint, Dawnsinger, Smith of the Heavens—' She groped for the pendant. 'Mother, I beg you, help me. What now can I do?'

She sobbed until she made no sound. At last, Priessa returned, her chest heaving.

'Marosa?'

'I killed them,' she choked out. 'Ermendo and Yscabel. I killed them.'

'No, Marosa.'

'Yes.' She looked up at Priessa, her face tearstained. 'Where is Ruzio?'

'Ruzio is gone.' Priessa pressed a note into her hand. 'She was with her lover in the kitchens when the Vardya came. That is why she was not taken.'

'Her lover?'

'Lord Bartian,' Priessa said quietly. Marosa stared at her. 'They have been having an affair for some time. Ruz was even with child by him once. I am sorry for not telling you, but … I felt it was her business, even if it was a vice, so I looked the other way.' She closed her eyes. 'I do not understand why I was spared. I can only think that my lord father protected me.'

'Fýredel has never seen you with me. He did see Yscabel and Ruzio.'

Marosa unfolded the note. Ruzio had clearly written in haste, and the ink was smudged in several places.

> *Yscabel is gone. I cannot bear the suffering. My lady we have dressed warmly & gone to the tunnel you found. They will arrest us as well if we stay, knowing we are your friends. Better they cannot use us against you. Saint protect & keep you in adversity. We will try to reach Prince Aubrecht. I pray we return, but if not, I trust to embrace you again in Halgalant.*

'No.' Marosa started to rise, more tears spilling down her cheeks. 'They will not survive the mountains. Essa, we must stop them—'

'We can't.' Priessa caught her by the waist. 'They are gone, Marosa.'

Marosa sank back to the floor in despair. Priessa embraced her, and they both wept bitterly.

****

Ruzio did not return. In the small hours, Marosa pored over maps of many ages, trying to work out how long it would take a person to reach Mentendon on foot. As Jondu had said, there had once been a Gulthaganian path through the Spindles, known as the Pass of the Imperator, but surely nothing remained of it now. Even if it did exist, it would be deep under the snow at this time of year.

The longer Marosa looked, the more she suspected that Ruzio had known there was no hope. That her friend had simply wanted to die on her own terms, with the man she loved, beyond the stranglehold of occupied Cárscaro. In that moment, Marosa was tempted to do the same.

But Queen Sahar would not have wanted that. She would wish, above all, for Marosa to live. To learn to be a flower that, deprived of water, kept growing. A flower that could bloom in fire.

Stand firm, like a desert rose, and you will yet be queen.

She pictured her mother now. Her broad smile and her warm brown eyes. Sahar Taumargam, who had discovered the murder of an Inysh queen, a fellow woman, and refused to ignore it.

And Marosa Vetalda knew what to do.

Marosa

CÁRSCARO

DRACONIC KINGDOM OF YSCALIN

CE 1005

She went to the Vaulted Gallery, where the doors to the Inysh rooms were unlocked. Wilstan Fynch was alone on his roofed balcony, gazing out at the desolation. Still in the grey of mourning, refusing to let go, even after fourteen years. Marosa took the empty seat beside him.

'Good morrow, Donmata,' he said. 'How do you do?'

'Your Grace.' She folded her hands in her lap. 'I have learned of a way to escape Cárscaro.'

'Truly?'

'A lava cave runs from beneath the palace and emerges in the Spindles.'

'By the Saint. Perhaps we are saved.'

'Perhaps.' She paused. 'Your Grace, has my father ever seen you when his eyes are aglow?'

'Not to my knowledge. Why do you ask?'

'Because it means that Fýredel does not know you. Your absence would not be noted as quickly as mine. The way through the mountains is dangerous, but ... it is the only plan I have.' She paused once more. 'Lord Wilstan, would you be willing to leave Cárscaro, to seek help from Virtudom?'

Fynch had looked hopeful, but now misgiving filled his face.

'Your Radiance,' he said, 'I am honoured that you would trust me with such a grave responsibility, but I am not as strong as I once was. I would not be able to conquer the Spindles.'

'I do not ask you lightly,' Marosa said, 'but you are one of the few I still trust. My father has murdered all of my other allies in the palace, with the exception of Lady Priessa and Lady Ruzio, and the latter … succumbed to grief for her sister.'

'May the Saint receive her.'

They both made the sign of the sword.

'Priessa would be missed,' Marosa said, 'but I need some-one I can trust, Your Grace. And you have always been a true friend to Yscalin.' She looked him in the eyes. 'There is another reason I ask you to go. For your own safety. My father has openly said he has no more use for ambassadors. I fear he may wish for you to share the same fate as the others.'

His face hardened.

'The Knight of Courage is not my patron,' he said, 'but … perhaps the Saint will lend me his sword and shield, even in my silver years.' He took a slow, deep breath. 'When would I leave?'

'As soon as possible,' Marosa said, 'but before you return to Inys, I must ask you to carry out a task for me. A task of great import, to honour a promise I made to the dead.' Fynch listened. 'There is a way to the Ersyr through the

Spindles. I need you to deliver an item to Chassar uq-Ispad. He may be at the court of Rauca, or at his own estate in Rumelabar.'

'I remember Chassar. A virtuous man, for a heretic,' Fynch said. 'What is this item, Donmata?'

'A box. I am told it contains the key to a weapon. Something that can help defeat the wyrms.'

'Who told you this?'

'A woman in the dungeons. Her cloak was dyed with Draconic blood.'

'A knight-errant, then?'

That was the name the Inysh used for cullers. Queen Sabran rewarded them handsomely for their service.

'A brave one,' Marosa said. It seemed the simplest explanation, even if Jondu had never confirmed it. 'Before you leave, you must armour yourself. I think it very likely that wyverns and their offspring are all over the mountains. The only way to survive them, to my knowledge, is to afflict yourself with the Draconic plague. But I am told Ambassador uq-Ispad has a cure.'

Fynch was silent for some time.

'There is no cure. None was ever recorded,' he eventually said. 'The plague was eradicated by careful isolation of the sick.' He pulled at his collar. 'Even if there *is* a cure, I repeat my point about my age. It takes the old and frail more quickly than it does the young.'

'I know,' Marosa said softly. 'I know what I ask, and how futile it seems. But I have nothing else, Your Grace. I have tried everything I can think to do within the city.' She placed a hand on his shoulder. 'Leave this accursed place while you can. Save your body and your soul.'

Fynch had started to tremble, just barely.

'If I were to agree,' he said, 'how must we proceed?'

'We can use the water passages to reach my father. I will drug his wine to make him sleep, so Fýredel will not see you. All you need do is lay your hands upon his skin. You will contract the old form of the plague.'

He looked back once more at the Great Yscali Plain – as if he was giving one last thought to the possibility of crossing it. The land that stretched to the horizon without shade or shelter.

'Tell me,' he said, 'can your father still speak with his own tongue?'

'Yes.'

'Then I want his confession.'

'Your Grace, if Fýredel sees you—'

'If his eyes are lit, I will not risk it. But if they are only grey, I will hear the words that damn him to the Womb of Fire. This is my price, Donmata,' Fynch said. 'I hope you understand.'

And Marosa could not deny him, for she had wanted exactly the same.

****

When night fell, Fynch showed her a small ebony door concealed behind a tapestry, impossible to find by chance. He used a key to open it. Together, they slipped into the secret tunnels, past the scalding pipes that wormed like veins behind the walls.

At first, Marosa had wondered if Queen Rozaria had never considered the risk posed by these passages, which must run past the rooms of the most important people in Yscalin. But as soon as she was inside one, she knew. It felt like a space not meant to be entered. Anyone who found an entry point, even if they were inquisitive, would not risk going far into this darkness.

Fynch carried a Draconic lantern. Marosa thought she would never be free of the sweltering heat, the heavy damp. He led her up slick black steps, almost too narrow for her slippers. At the top, he unlocked another ebony door, and they both stooped to go through it.

The Flesh King was sound asleep.

They moved in silence towards the bed. As expected, the Royal Physician had left her provisions close to her charge, including a flask of dwale, which Marosa picked up. When she was young, she had seen Aryete taking dwale to promote sleep. A drop or two would be enough.

'Your Majesty,' she said, keeping her voice low. His guards would be close. 'Sigoso Vetalda.'

King Sigoso slowly opened his eyes. There was no light in them.

'Sahar?'

Marosa stiffened. He drew out the *s* in the name, like a snake.

'No. Sahar is dead,' she said coldly, 'but I am here.'

'I dreamed of a woman holding a shield,' King Sigoso whispered. 'I dreamed of a star that shackled my wings.'

Marosa looked at the fresh linen at his bedside, used to cool his brow. 'You know the Dowager Prince of Inys has long sought an audience with Your Majesty,' she said. 'I have granted it.'

'Lord Wilstan,' came the soft reply. 'Have you worked it out, as my clever daughter did?'

'To my own dismay.' Fynch wore a cloth over his mouth and nose, despite the nature of their plan, but his eyes held more than a decade of banked sorrow. 'I will have it from your own forked tongue, Sigoso. Tell me how it was done.'

'As you wish. I have nothing to hide.'

Fynch listened to the sordid tale. Little by little, Marosa could see his younger self emerging. The man who had loved the Queen of Inys. The spy who had ventured to Yscalin in search of justice. When the Flesh King had confessed all, Fynch gave her the smallest nod.

'Here, Father,' Marosa said. 'You must be thirsty.'

The Flesh King finished the wine in three gulps. They both watched as he fell asleep.

'I will afflict myself,' Fynch said hoarsely, 'but I would sooner you did not see it, Donmata. I am still afraid, and would not have you see me at my weakest, now the Saint tests me anew.'

Marosa watched his face.

'If I leave you alone,' she said, 'you will not kill him, Your Grace?'

'No. I will not sacrifice my own place in Halgalant for his sake.'

****

Time was of the essence. They used the water passages to bypass the locked door to the armoury, where Marosa gave Fynch furs to wear, along with an alpenstock and cleats, a crossbow, a firesteel and a sturdy blade, all so he could hunt and keep warm in the Spindles.

She gave him the posy ring from Aubrecht. It had pained her to work it from her finger, but it was the only jewellery that could be soundly identified as hers, so Virtudom would know she was faithful. Lastly, she gave him a bundle of letters, written over the course of a year.

Deep in the bowels of the Palace of Salvation, they stood before the entrance to the cave, both holding torches lit with red fire. He wore the satchel containing the box, with the strap across his chest.

'Go to Rauca first, my lord,' Marosa said. 'If Ambassador uq-Ispad is at his estate in Rumelabar, I am certain King Jantar will help you reach him. Tell him what has happened here.'

'I will, Your Radiance.' Fat beads of sweat lined his forehead. The plague must already be making him too warm. 'I feel rather like Sir Wulfert Glenn, forging into the frozen North. Perhaps it is only right that I have an adventure in my winter years.'

Marosa returned his weak smile, wishing she could embrace him. 'Goodbye, Lord Wilstan,' she said. 'The Knight of Courage is with you. So is the Saint.'

Even with plague reaching its roots through him, he bowed. 'Goodbye,' he said. 'My lady.'

She watched him walk into the darkness, small but steady, lit by his Draconic torch. When his footsteps had gone too far to be heard, she ascended the steps and went to her apartments. For the first time in months, she dared to play music, plucking 'The Swan Song' on the harp.

When she tried to sleep that night, her mind wandered back to the tunnel. Something about the farewell had troubled her. She shook herself, but the feeling persisted, quashing any chance of sleep.

She lay awake until sunrise, listening to Priessa breathe. At last, she dressed in a clean shirt and kirtle. Taking a torch, she returned to the tunnel, heart almost thumping out of her chest.

In the cave, the volcanic glass reflected her torchlight. Its walls yawned around her, black and silent as a tomb. Marosa had not walked so much since she was a child; it seemed as if she would never stop. Down here, deep under the ground, time seemed out of joint.

The farther she ventured, the more she thought she was being foolish. Fynch had the plague. He was protected.

A spot of daylight far ahead, growing by the moment. She quickened her step, only to slow when she made out a shape on the ground. When she knelt, the red glow of her torch revealed it.

'Saint,' she whispered.

It was the box. Leaving it behind, she ran and ran for the end of the tunnel, and at last, her boots crunched into deep snow.

A bitter wind ripped at her veil. She took it off, blinking in the sudden, dazzling glare. The sky above was clear and blue, and there, in all their glory, were the mountains. When she looked behind her, Mount Fruma blocked any sight of the city.

For the first time in five years, she was outside Cárscaro. Had she not been so afraid, Marosa would have laughed in sheer relief.

As it stood, she had to keep her wits.

Her breath escaped her in white plumes. Never had she been so cold. She clutched her cloak around herself and shielded her eyes with the other hand. The tunnel had brought her to a narrow pass, with steep walls on either side, leading deeper into the mountains.

'Lord Wilstan,' she shouted, but the wind stole her voice. 'Lord Wilstan!'

It took her a moment to notice the footprints. When she followed them with her gaze, she finally made out the small, distant mound in the snow. It could be a snowdrift, except that it was crimson.

Before she could think better of it, Marosa left the safety of the overhang above the cave. By the time she reached the corpse, her legs burned with exertion, and hot tears lined her eyes.

The snow was stained with blood and gore. Fynch had not met with a gentle death. One of his arms had been ripped off, and his skull was caved in on one side. Marosa collapsed to her knees.

She was no culler or historian, but she had read chronicles of the Grief. Straight after his death, the Draconic plague should have turned his hands red, and his body ought to smell of brimstone. Little by little, she peeled off his gloves, so she could see his fingers. They were still pale.

Fynch had never touched her father.

In that moment, Marosa considered forging on, even without the sickness. She considered making the journey to her uncle, carrying a box that could mean and contain nothing.

Then she saw two skeletons, farther ahead, strung up on a cliff. Like some dire warning.

Ruzio and Bartian had got no farther than Fynch.

Her stomach heaved, just as a strange hiss stiffened the hairs on her neck. She froze in place. To her right, a monstrous creature was emerging from a crack in the pass, its tongue flickering.

Its thick legless body led up to a head like that of a snake. A pair of leathern wings unfolded, and it bared a pair of terrible fangs, each slick with the blood of the Dowager Prince of Inys.

Marosa almost fainted in fear. She maintained her clarity just long enough to reach into the pouch Fynch had been carrying. Inside was the posy ring. Her last reminder of Aubrecht.

She jammed it on to her finger. The amphiptere slithered towards her, and she ran, almost stumbling in the snow. Even when she reached the cave, she kept running. Behind her, the amphiptere screeched in fury as she snatched up the box and clutched it to her chest.

At last, she reached the steps to the palace, where she buckled. Everyone who had tried to take the Pass of the Imperator was dead. If Aubrecht had sent anyone to save her, they would have long since perished. She did not even know what lay inside the box, or how to open it.

Her sobs echoed through the darkness, unheard.

Aubrecht of the House of Lievelyn, Crown Prince of Mentendon, has sought annulment for his betrothal to the Donmata Marosa, Princess of the Draconic Kingdom of Yscalin, for her country has broken faith with the Saint.

Let it be known that His Virtuousness, the Arch Sanctarian, and Her Majesty, Queen Sabran of the House of Berethnet, who is the blood and heir of the Saint, hereby grant this annulment with the blessing of the Saint. Let it be known that Prince Aubrecht is now at liberty to marry whomsoever he desires.

Marosa

Priessa Yelarigas stepped into the Privy Chamber. Beside an open window, Marosa Vetalda sipped from what might be the last cup of perry she would taste in her life. The red pears had died, defeated by the foul air on the streets, worsened by the wyverns' breath and the Draconic plague.

For the first time in two years, there were newcomers in Cárscaro.

Lord Gastaldo made the announcement to the court first. On the orders of Fýredel, the capital was now admitting any person who wished to serve the Draconic Army of their own free will, though they could never again leave Yscalin, except with royal permission. Fýredel had allowed him to send a consignment of letters by coach, inviting all of humankind to join the House of Vetalda in worship of the Nameless One. A post road had been opened from Cárscaro to the northern coast, where ships would be permitted to bear them elsewhere.

Marosa wished Lord Gastaldo could have used a cypher to conceal other messages in the letters, but her father still read every one, both with and without the embers in his eyes. Not only that, but jaculi and cockatrices pulled the coaches.

She had not expected anyone to answer the summons. Instead, the population of Cárscaro had swelled to sixty thousand.

Perhaps it ought not to have shocked her so deeply. In recent months, several Draconic sects had sprung up throughout Yscalin, including the Cult of the Iron King, which worshipped Fýredel as a primordial god. They wore red and black to mirror his armour – a fashion that had quickly spread across the capital. A temple was being raised where the Great Sanctuary of Cárscaro had once stood, built in the Gulthaganian style, with columns and enormous hearths.

Marosa wanted to ask the cultists if they had always reviled the Saint, or if their outward devotion was only a means of surviving their new circumstances. Either way, they were overtaking her city. Now it would be even harder for the faithful to fight back.

'My father asked me to tell you,' Priessa said. 'Aubrecht Lievelyn has broken your betrothal.'

Marosa did not weep. Instead, her body turned numb by increments. It was its only means of self-defence.

'I see,' she said. 'How does your father know?'

'We still have intelligencers in other countries. Now a post road is open, some of them sent word.' Priessa lowered her gaze. 'It also seems the High Prince intends to marry Queen Sabran.'

'High Prince?'

'Leovart died.'

Aubrecht was not just a crown prince now, but the ruler of the Free State of Mentendon, as he should have been for years.

He could not maintain a betrothal with someone whose king-dom was pledged to the Nameless One. Neither could she blame him for seeking a second betrothal. Mentendon still needed a strong alliance with another country in Virtudom.

But the thought of their future in Mentendon – their life, their children, the world they would build – had been her last thin shred of hope. She had clung to the memories of their courtship.

Now her only future was the inside of the iron helm.

She could take her own life to deprive Fýredel of a puppet. In the dark hours after Fynch died, she had considered it. But the wyrm might burn Cárscaro in retribution for her defiance, and she would not condemn her people to that fate. Her folly had already killed her friends.

If her soul was the price for Yscalin to be safe, she would pay it.

The box remained hidden under her bed. Another source of hope, perhaps, if Jondu had been right.

She could not stop seeing the mountains beyond Cárscaro. She saw them in her dreams, in her nightmares, even when she was awake. For a few heartbeats, she had been on the verge of freedom. She had seen the sky of her childhood, blue and wide, without the constant haze of the Tundana. It had been the sweetest sight in the world, and a poison to her soul.

Priessa sat opposite her. She studied Marosa, reading her thoughts.

'I know we have discussed this,' she said, 'but I could still go to the Ersyr. You know I would not fail you.'

'No.' Marosa continued to look out of the window. 'You are all I have left, Priessa. You are my sanity.'

'There may be another way.'

'What do you mean?'

'Not long after the post road opened, a letter arrived at the Customs House of Perunta, addressed to His Majesty. It was from Lord Seyton Combe, the Principal Secretary of Inys. This letter was apparently courteous, seeking to restore diplomatic ties with Yscalin. He offered to send two ambassadors. Their names are Lord Arteloth Beck and Lord Kitston Glade.'

'What of other countries?' Marosa asked her. 'Will they send anyone?'

'No word yet from the South. I imagine they are debating what to do,' Priessa said. 'Mentendon and Hróth have demanded that their existing ambassadors are sent back to them safely before they will treat with us.' Marosa clenched her jaw. 'Fýredel has sanctioned the Inysh embassy.'

'Inys is the last country I would have expected to send one, and not just on religious grounds. After her father vanished here, why would Queen Sabran want to risk any more of her courtiers?'

'To see inside Cárscaro. To find him,' Priessa said. 'Lord Wilstan would not do what was needful, but Her Majesty must have faith that these ambassadors will be strong and shrewd enough to learn the truth and escape Yscalin. Perhaps they can be persuaded to make the journey in our stead.'

'And if they break our trust, like Fynch?' Marosa asked her. 'If the box is lost for good this time?'

'They must have great courage, to enter a Draconic land by choice.'

Marosa finished her drink, rolling the perry around her mouth.

'Lord Arteloth is a close friend of Queen Sabran,' she murmured. 'Perhaps you are right.' She put the cup down. 'The box may be empty, or filled only with dust. All of this could be false hope.'

'That is better than none.' Priessa took her by the hands and sought her gaze. 'Let us say that we succeed in convincing these men to go. While they make their way to Ambassador uq-Ispad, you must appease the cultists by emphasising your descent from Oderica the Smith.'

'Why?'

'They venerate her as an early oracle and worshipper of Fýredel.'

'I will never be one of them.'

'No, but the fact of it will protect you. There are more and more of them arriving by the day. Securing their respect will keep you safe and allow you to maintain control of Cárscaro. And if you appear loyal to the cause, Fýredel may not see any need to make you his puppet by force.'

Her gloved hand resting on his scales. His eyes searing into hers, as if he recognised her.

'This is about surviving long enough for help to come, as our ancestors did. The Grief of Ages was not won by the sword, but through endurance,' Priessa said. 'The Saint will forgive us.'

Marosa set her jaw. Even if the idea of such a performance was repulsive, she saw the wisdom in it.

'Find out as much as you can about the Cult of the Iron King,' she concluded, 'and I will attempt to mirror its followers. Let them bow to the heir of Oderica.'

****

The candles were burning, red and intense, when her guard disturbed her three nights later. Once a member of the Knights Defendant, he was now a nameless cultist of the Iron King. Marosa had never seen his face, for he covered it with a mask, like all the others.

'Lord Gastaldo is here,' he informed Marosa. 'With your permission, Your Radiance.'

Marosa gave him a nod. Once the guard had retreated from the Privy Chamber, Lord Gastaldo strode into it, wearing a black cape that rode on one shoulder.

'Your Radiance,' he said, bowing to her. 'Fýredel will speak with you again this night.'

'At the Fell Door?' Priessa stood at once. 'If so, let me go in her stead.'

'No,' Marosa said to her. 'Fýredel would realise the deception, Essa.'

'Perhaps not if I wear your clothes and carry a vial of your blood, so I smell of you. We can ask the Royal Physician to—'

'The Donmata is right, daughter. The Iron King sees all,' Lord Gastaldo said. 'It is time to give up our thoughts of resistance. All of it has come to naught. There is no Saint to keep us safe, no Halgalant to receive us. That much has become apparent.'

He walked to stand beside the hearth, gazing into the flames that danced there.

'It is clear that our ancestors, the early Yscals, had it right. They saw a god in Mount Fruma,' he said. 'Now that god has revealed himself to us, just as he did to Oderica the Smith.'

As he spoke, Marosa took in his fine garments again. His black cloak had a red lining. Priessa tensed as she, too, grasped the danger. She had known about the cultists, but not that her own father had joined their ranks.

'Yscalin should always have rejected the Saint, Donmata. He is an Inysh god, not ours,' Lord Gastaldo said. 'Galian Berethnet was forced on us by your ancestor, Isalarico the Betrayer. But you are not just *his* descendant. You are the scion of Oderica, with eyes lit by a holy fire.'

Marosa maintained her composure as Priessa sent her a glance.

'I believe,' she said, 'that we understand each other, my lord.' She rose from her settle. 'You are right. If there was indeed a Saint, he has abandoned us in our hour of need. He is unworthy of devotion.' She forced a smile. 'Let us embrace our roots as Yscals, and our independence from Virtudom, by worshipping the Iron King.'

Lord Gastaldo listened in rapt silence. So did the cultist by the door.

'Too long have we been chained to the Queendom of Inys. Oderica drove out the Gulthaganians; let us do the same to the usurping Saint,' Marosa said, her tone commanding. 'If we are loyal – if we aid him – then Fýredel will spare us when fire rages from shore to shore.'

His face relaxed. Some part of him must have needed her approval, so he could persuade himself that succumbing was the right decision. In the absence of the Saint, Gastaldo Yelarigas needed to believe in something else. He needed to be reassured that he was not a monster.

'Radiance,' he said, raising a gloved hand to his chest. 'We are ready to serve.' He nodded to the doors. 'Fýredel does not ask you to come to him in person. He will speak through His Majesty.'

She expected to be escorted upstairs. Instead, the Flesh King entered the Privy Chamber, out of bed for the first time in weeks. Two masked Vardya stood on either side to him, close enough that they would catch him if he fell. His eyes had the piercing embers in them.

'Donmata of Yscalin. Glassbearer,' he ground out. 'Do you hear me?'

'Yes, my liege.' Marosa sank into a low curtsey, her skirts fanning around her. 'I hear.'

It was easy to act in front of her father.

'The Queen of Inys sends envoys to my kingdom. Perhaps she wishes to treat with me,' Fýredel said. His puppet coughed, blood and spittle leaking from the corners of his mouth. 'I will grant her desire, for I owe the seed of Shieldheart a death.'

His loathing of Glorian Shieldheart had not waned in five hundred years. Marosa went over his words again.

'Then you mean to leave us?' she asked him. 'To go to Inys?'

'Not for long.' Fýredel looked into her eyes. 'Enact my will in Yscalin. Do not seek to escape or resist, or flesh will burn as flowers do, all across this land. You know what is expected.'

The iron helm, wrought like a wyrm.

'Yes,' Marosa said. 'I understand, my liege. You will find no disobedience in Cárscaro.'

'So be it.'

The Flesh King crumpled. While Lord Gastaldo and the Vardya tended him, Marosa left the Privy Chamber, her skin turning cold, and rushed to her balcony for the first time since Ermendo died. She had not been able to bear walking that familiar path without him.

In the distance, she heard the first screams, followed by cries of joy.

It was not yet dawn, so she only saw Fýredel when he passed over the lava, which lit his colossal form. The architect of the Grief of Ages, free of his lair in Mount Fruma, taking to the sky for the first time in centuries.

His wings stretched wide enough to plunge Cárscaro into shadow. Now she saw that he had four legs rather than two, separate from those wings, and his tail was as broad as the trunk of a stone pine, with spikes at the end, each twice as long as she was tall.

Every scale looked as hard as a shield.

As he passed the Palace of Salvation, his gaze scraped hers for a moment. She gripped the balustrade as he soared towards the Great Yscali Plain, watched by all who were awake. With three mighty sweeps of his wings, the wyrm disappeared into the night.

Marosa slid to the ground, strands of hair blowing free of their braid. Priessa came to kneel in front of her.

'And so a second Grief begins,' Marosa said softly. 'If he kills Queen Sabran, all is lost. The Nameless One will rise. This time, humankind will be extinguished. Not even bones will remain.'

Priessa cupped her face. Marosa searched hers for hope, for salvation.

'I care not if my father is a cultist,' Priessa said, her voice taut. 'We two may be quite alone, but we are Yscals. We are strong.' Her freckled cheeks glistened. 'I believe Queen Sabran will survive Fýredel, as Glorian Shieldheart did. And I believe in you, even above the Saint himself. One day, you will be Queen of Yscalin. The Marosan era will heal this scarred country.'

They pressed their foreheads together.

'The Knight of Fellowship is good,' Marosa whispered, 'to have given me you, at the end of our days.'

They stayed there until the sun rose, bleeding its light on to the dead and barren plain. At last, a chirp made them both look up in surprise, their faces tearstained. After two long years, the serin – that lovely, merry little bird – had dared return to Cárscaro. It cocked its head, seeming to look Marosa in the eyes, before it flew away again.

****

Outside, the Tundana kept flowing. The wyverns kept their constant watch. Under the eye of Lord Gastaldo, the Privy Council fell to the cult. Meanwhile, the Flesh King rotted in his bedchamber, dreaming of flight and scarlet fire, of a woman with the sun in her grasp.

By the time the new Inysh ambassadors arrived in Cárscaro, Fýredel had not returned, but Marosa stood ready. They might only have a small window of time to send the box away once more.

Priessa had gone to meet the *Rose Eternal*, the ship that had brought the pair to Yscalin. By feigning her devotion to the cult, convincing her father that she was loyal, she had earned the freedom to leave Cárscaro.

And soon Marosa stood at a hidden entrance to the Presence Chamber, wearing a black gown with a red sash, pinned by a brooch showing an iron tongue of flame. The Privy Council would be in the audience. They looked to her now, instead of her father, just as she had once desired.

If only it had not happened like this.

The Inysh ambassadors waited for her. Lord Arteloth Beck and Lord Kitston Glade, two men who did not know that she would soon ask them to risk their lives for her people – but who had risked their own, by choice, by coming to a harrowed land the Saint had forsaken. And she – a puppet, a prisoner, a princess – would remain on the throne, unable to leave, until the day that Fýredel fell, as he had once before, on the last day of the Grief of Ages. She wore her suit of armour, made up of her fear and pain, but underneath, she was still burning.

She donned the head of Fýredel, and inside, all was quiet. Watched by her court, and by the two men, she took her place on the obsidian throne, carved from the Dreadmount itself.

'Lord Arteloth and Lord Kitston,' she said. 'My beloved father and I bid you welcome to the Draconic Kingdom of Yscalin.'

Your Majesty, I scarce know how to describe the misfortune that has befallen Yscalin, nor my anguish as I choose the words to convey it to you.

A second Grief of Ages is upon us. Fýredel, that cunning old foe, has woken in Mount Fruma. Glorian Shieldheart defied him upon Cenning Moor; I pray you will exhibit the same courage and aid my people as best you may. As I write, they face the mighty wrath and vengeance of his wyverns.

Cárscaro was lost in hours. Our mountain city was a prison once; so it has become again. Alas that we did not foresee the enemy within. I cannot escape, nor resist Fýredel, with thousands of innocent souls held to ransom – but no matter the lies my father has sent, Yscalin remains faithful.

I pray that Ambassador Fynch will survive his journey across the Spindles; that your father, gentle as he is, will inform you of the grave evil that mine did in these very halls. It seems our shared grief in the loss of our mothers had only one root, and his blood is my own. I would question how to live with the knowledge, but I doubt that I will survive for much longer, though I will fight as long as I may.

Should any of my family escape this new Draconic kingdom, I ask you to grant them shelter and kindness.

Know that I was loyal to the end.

Yours in everlasting faith,

Marosa Taumargam Vetalda, Donmata of Yscalin, Crown Princess of the Ersyr

Timeline

BEFORE THE COMMON ERA (BCE)

BCE 2: The First Great Eruption of the Dreadmount. The Nameless One emerges from the Womb of Fire and settles in the Lasian city of Yikala, bringing with him the Draconic plague. The Nameless One is later vanquished and disappears

THE COMMON ERA (CE)

CE 1: The Foundation of Ascalon by Galian I of Inys, also known as the Saint

CE 279: The Chainmail of Virtudom is formed when Isalarico IV of Yscalin weds Glorian II of Inys

CE 480: The catastrophic Midwinter Flood strikes the northern coast of Mentendon, drowning thousands and destroying its capital, Thisunath

CE 481: The Hróthi raider Heryon Vattenvarg takes advantage of the Midwinter Flood, which has destroyed Mentish coastal defences. His aim is to settle the country, claiming it for himself and his clan. Taken by surprise and unsupported, the Ments are soon forced to give up their fight and submit to Vattenvarg. He founds a new capital, Brygstad

CE 483: Heryon Vattenvarg pledges allegiance to the new King of Hróth, Bardholt I, and is named Steward of Mentendon. He converts to the Virtues of Knighthood, bringing Mentendon into Virtudom. Both the Ments and the Hróthi are forced into conversion by their leaders

CE 509: The Second Great Eruption of the Dreadmount births the five High Westerns and their wyverns, led by Fýredel, who breeds the Draconic Army

CE 511: The Grief of Ages, or Great Sorrow, begins, and the Draconic plague returns to the world

CE 512: The Grief of Ages, or Great Sorrow, ends with the arrival of the Long-Haired Star, also known as the Saint's Comet

CE 953: Sigoso Vetalda is born to Idreiga V of Yscalin and her companion

CE 954: Sahar Taumargam is born to Mezdat VI of the Ersyr and her spouse. She has one sibling, Jantar, who is approximately two years her senior

CE 955: Rosarian Berethnet is born to Jillian VI of Inys and her companion, Ranulf Heath the Elder

CE 970: Idreiga V of Yscalin dies, and her son is crowned Sigoso III

CE 971: Aubrecht Lievelyn is born to Paltar Lievelyn and Fralet Dabanon utt Kantstad

CE **974**: Jillian VI dies, and her daughter is crowned Rosarian IV at the age of nineteen. She receives offers of marriage from across Virtudom, including from Sigoso III of Yscalin, who has already pressed his suit for over a year

CE **975**: In accordance with her late mother's wishes, Rosarian IV marries Lord Wilstan Fynch, the Duke of Temperance

CE **976**: Ermuna Lievelyn is born to Paltar Lievelyn and Fralet Dabanon utt Kantstad

CE **977**: Princess Sabran is born to Rosarian IV. A month later, Sigoso III marries Sahar Taumargam, Princess of the Ersyr, who is crowned queen consort of Yscalin

CE **978**: Marosa Vetalda is born to Sigoso III and his queen consort, Sahar Taumargam

CE **979**: Estina Melaugo is born to Rozia Melaugo and Azgo of Vazuva

CE **980**: Queen Rosarian gifts a magnificent ship named the *Rose Eternal* to Gian Harlowe, who becomes the youngest naval captain in the Inysh fleet

CE **985**: Bedona and Betriese Lievelyn are born to Paltar Lievelyn and Fralet Dabanon utt Kantstad. Fralet dies soon after

CE **991**: Queen Rosarian dies shortly after a poisoned gown is placed in her Privy Wardrobe. Sabran IX is crowned and enters her period of minority

CE **992**: Melaugo, now an urchin in the Port of Oryzon, is taken under the wing of Gian Harlowe, who pays her fee for a smithing apprenticeship

CE **993**: The Brygstad Terror – an outbreak of the sweating sickness – kills many members of the House of Lievelyn, including Edvart II. His paternal uncle, Leovart, becomes High Prince of Mentendon

CE **994**: Queen Sahar of Yscalin dies, apparently by suicide

CE **995**: Gian Harlowe begins smuggling goods to and from Yscalin

CE **998**: Aubrecht Lievelyn and Marosa Vetalda are formally betrothed

CE **1000**: A celebration of a millennium of Berethnet rule takes place in Ascalon. Marosa is among the guests

CE **1003**: *Among the Burning Flowers* begins in the spring. Aubrecht is 32, Marosa is 25, and Melaugo is 24

The Persons of the Tale

LIVING PERSONS OF THE WORLD

THE STORYTELLERS

Aubrecht Lievelyn (the Red Prince): Heir apparent to the Free State of Mentendon. He is the eldest of four children born to Paltar Lievelyn – secondborn of Aubrecht I – and his companion, Fralet Dabanon utt Brudstath.

Estina Melaugo: An outlaw born to peasant winemakers in the Groneyso Valley. Formerly a smuggler in the notorious Greenshanks gang, she went on to become a culler of Draconic sleepers.

Marosa Vetalda: Donmata (heir apparent) of the Kingdom of Yscalin, the only child of Sigoso III and Sahar Taumargam. She has rarely left the Palace of Salvation, her ancestral home, since she was sixteen.

THE ERSYR

Chassar uq-Ispad: An ambassador to Jantar I and his consort, Queen Saiyma.

Jantar I (the Splendid): King of the Ersyr. Firstborn of Mezdat VII and brother to Princess Sahar Taumargam. Like many of his ancestors, he styles himself the King of Kings.

Saiyma Taumargam: Queen consort of the Ersyr and spouse of Jantar I.

FREE STATE OF MENTENDON

Aleidine Teldan Utt Kantmarkt: Dowager Duchess of Zeedeur. A member of the Teldan merchant family, she was ennobled upon her marriage to Jannart utt Zeedeur. Her paternal aunt was consort to Aubrecht I.

Bedona Lievelyn: Princess of Mentendon. Sister to Aubrecht, Ermuna and Betriese.

Betriese Lievelyn: Princess of Mentendon. Sister to Aubrecht, Ermuna and Bedona. She is the youngest of the siblings, born just after Bedona, her identical twin.

Clothild Lievelyn: A noble of the House of Lievelyn, fourth cousin to Aubrecht. Her mother is a Hróthi chieftain of Clan Ókyrr.

Ermuna Lievelyn: Princess of Mentendon. She is second in line to the Mentish throne after her older brother, Aubrecht.

Gaspart Lievelyn: A noble of the House of Lievelyn. He is a third cousin, once removed, to Aubrecht.

Henselt Lievelyn: The baby son of Gaspart Lievelyn and his companion.

Leovart I (the Grey Prince): High Prince of Mentendon and paternal granduncle to Aubrecht, Ermuna, Bedona and Betriese.

Following the Brygstad Terror, Aubrecht was next in the line of succession, but Leovart persuaded the Council of State that he ought to be the one to take on the burden.

Liuthe Dabanon utt Brudstath: Dowager High Princess of Mentendon. Born into the Dabanon banking dynasty, she was the companion of Edvart II and mother of his heir, Lesken Lievelyn.

Sennera Yelarigas: Yscali ambassador-in-residence to Mentendon. The daughter of Oryzoni merchants, she was ennobled upon her marriage to Gastaldo Yelarigas. She was formerly First Lady of the Bedchamber to Queen Sahar.

KINGDOM OF HRÓTH

Raunus III: King of Hróth and current head of the House of Hraustr.

Skuldir Vatten: The current head of Clan Vatten. He is a descendant of Heryon Vattenvarg, who conquered Mentendon.

KINGDOM OF YSCALIN

aryete Feyalda: A noblewoman of the Feyalda family, a cadet branch of the House of Vetalda. She was formerly Third Lady of the Bedchamber to Queen Sahar of Yscalin.

Bartian Feyalda: Count of Orzyon, currently a courtier in Cárscaro.

Comptroller of Perunta: This title refers to an official who oversees the collection of taxes on foreign imports to Yscalin. In *Among the Burning Flowers*, the position is held by a member of the Afleytan family.

Ermendo Vuleydres: Personal bodyguard to Marosa Vetalda.

Gastaldo Yelarigas: Secretary of State and third cousin to Sigoso III.

Jondu: A mysterious prisoner in the Palace of Salvation.

Liyat of Nzene: A dealer of antiquities, who secretly recovers and protects forbidden artefacts. Liyat is a member of a consortium of smugglers, pirates and other lawbreakers.

Orentico Feyalda: A bastard son of Princess Darica Vetalda, first cousin to Sigoso III, from her liaison with a member of the Feyalda cadet branch. While Sigoso despises bastards, he has kept Orentico close as his decoy.

Priessa Yelarigas: First Lady of the Bedchamber and fourth cousin to Marosa Vetalda. She is the daughter of Gastaldo and Sennera Yelarigas.

Robrecht Teldan: Mentish ambassador-in-residence to Yscalin. Paternal uncle to Aleidine Teldan utt Kantmarkt.

Ruzio Afleytan: A Lady of the Bedchamber to Marosa Vetalda. Older sister to Yscabel.

Sigoso III (the Pious): King of Yscalin and current head of the House of Vetalda. Father of Marosa Vetalda.

Suylos the Hinderling: A smuggler and former pirate, based in Lovers' Cove near Perunta. As well as being the head of the notorious Greenshanks gang, he leads a consortium of lawbreakers who work on the Yscali coast. His epithet refers to a contemptible wretch – a title he proudly adopted after the Comptroller of Perunta described him as such.

Ussindo Vetalda: Younger brother of Sigoso III and Princess Viterica.

Viterica Vetalda: Archduchess of Hart Grove and High Princess of Yscalin. Younger sister of Sigoso III. She is married to Oscardo Vuleydres and has four children – three by him, and one by her previous companion.

Wilstan Fynch: Dowager Prince and Lord Admiral of Inys, head of the Fynch family, and Duke of Temperance. The companion of the late Rosarian IV and father to Sabran IX, he is now the Inysh ambassador-in-residence to Yscalin.

Yscabel Afleytan: A Lady of the Bedchamber to Marosa Vetalda. Younger sister to Ruzio.

QUEENDOM OF INYS

Arteloth 'Loth' Beck: Heir apparent to the wealthy northern province of the Leas in Inys. Closest friend of Sabran IX.

Gian Harlowe: An Inysh naval officer with a mysterious past. He is captain of the *Rose Eternal*, a man-of-war given to him by Rosarian IV of Inys.

Kitston Glade: Poet at the court of Sabran IX of Inys and friend of Lord Arteloth Beck.

Sabran IX: Thirty-sixth Queen of Inys and the only living member of the House of Berethnet. Her dynasty is said to bind the Nameless One, preventing him from returning to the world. She is the daughter of the late Rosarian IV and her companion, Lord Wilstan Fynch.

Seyton Combe (the Night Hawk): Duke of Courtesy, Principal Secretary, and spymaster to Sabran IX of Inys.

Denarva uq-Bardant: The former Second Lady of the Bedchamber to Queen Sahar, who accompanied her from the Ersyr to Yscalin. She was executed for abetting treason.

Dumai of Ipyeda (Noziken pa Dumai): The firstborn child of Jorodu IV of Seiiki, who presided over a rival court to her half-sister, Empress Suzumai, during the Great Sorrow. Like many of her ancestors, she was a dragonrider, bonding closely with a Seiikinese dragon named Furtia Stormcaller. She and Furtia are believed to have died in battle against Taugran the Golden in CE 512. Later Seiikinese rulers had differing attitudes towards Dumai, resulting in some misconceptions about her life and importance.

Ebanth Lievelyn (the Briar Rose of Brygstad): A Mentish noblewoman and courtesan. Following the Hróthi invasion, she fled to the Republic of Carmentum and became a consort to its leader, Numun. After Carmentum fell, she sailed east, only for her ship to wreck on Seiiki, where she struck a deal with the First Warlord.

Edvart II (the Laughing Prince): The previous High Prince of Mentendon. He died of the sweat during the Brygstad Terror of CE 993.

Fralet Dabanon utt Brudstath: A member of the Dabanon banking dynasty. Mother of Aubrecht, Ermuna, Bedona and Betriese. She died after giving birth to the twins.

Fruma: A god in the old religion of Yscalin. Along with his siblings, Fruma was a stone giant who emerged from the goddess Erto, the personification of the world. He carved the first Yscals from clay before he fell into a deep slumber, becoming Mount

Fruma. The Gulthaganians later built on his slopes, angering the Yscals, including Oderica the Smith.

Galian Berethnet (the Saint): The first King of Inys. The religion of the Virtues of Knighthood, which Galian based on the knightly code, professes that he vanquished the Nameless One in Lasia, married Princess Cleolind of the House of Onjenyu, and with her, founded the House of Berethnet.

Glorian II (Glorian Hartbane): Tenth Queen of Inys. She married Isalarico IV of the House of Vetalda, which brought Yscalin into the faith of the Six Virtues.

Glorian III (Glorian Shieldheart): Twentieth Queen of Inys. She came to power at sixteen after her parents were murdered by Fýredel. Despite her youth, she led Inys through the Grief of Ages and is remembered as the most famous and beloved queen of the House of Berethnet.

Idreiga V: Mother of Sigoso III and paternal grandmother of Marosa. She had three children – Sigoso, Viterica and Ussindo – by her companion, Lorento Yelarigas.

Kathel Lievelyn (the Defiant): The first High Princess of Mentendon. A direct descendant of Ebanth Lievelyn, she was born in Orisima, the only Western trading outpost in Seiiki. In her twenties, she sailed to Mentendon and led the Mentish Defiance against Clan Vatten.

Kuposa pa Fotaja: The River Lord of Seiiki during the reign of Jorodu IV. As a high-ranking nobleman and the maternal grandfather of Jorodu's daughter, Princess Suzumai, he enjoyed a great deal of power and prestige at the Seiikinese royal court, but came into conflict with Princess Dumai, the rightful heir to the throne. He died in CE 512 after bonding with Taugran the

Golden, to whom he sacrificed a number of Seiikinese royals, including his young granddaughter.

Lady Nikeya (Nadama pa Nikeya): The only child of Kuposa pa Fotaja, Nikeya was a Seiikinese noblewoman and talented writer who lived during the reign of Jorodu IV. She married her father's political rival, Noziken pa Dumai, without his permission. In CE 512, Nikeya became Dowager Queen of Seiiki and the first monarch of the new House of Nadama. She styled herself Warlord of Seiiki.

Lesken Lievelyn: Daughter of Edvart II and Liuthe Dabanon utt Brudstath. She died of the sweat during the Brygstad Terror of CE 993 when she was still a child.

Oderica the Smith: The first Queen of Yscalin. As a young woman, Oderica – a fierce warrior – was imprisoned by the Gulthaganians in their mining outpost, Karkara. It was said that Fruma, the god in the mountain, swallowed her into himself and taught her to smelt iron. This skill allowed her to drive out the Gulthaganians and found her own dynasty, the House of Vetalda. Fruma later taught her descendant, Dreigo Vetalda, to forge steel using the bones of his enemies.

Paltar Lievelyn: Secondborn of Aubrecht I and father of Aubrecht, Ermuna, Bedona and Betriese. He died of the sweat during the Brygstad Terror of CE 993.

Rosarian IV (the Merrow Queen): Thirty-fifth Queen of Inys, mother of Sabran IX and companion to Lord Wilstan Fynch. She died suddenly.

Rozaria III: Queen of Yscalin during the Grief of Ages. She was the older twin sister of Guma Vetalda, companion to Glorian Shieldheart.

Sabran VIII: The thirtieth Queen of Inys. The daughter of the progressive Rosarian III, she supported ending the Hróthi stewardship of Mentendon.

Sahar Taumargam: Princess of the Ersyr, younger sister to King Jantar. A follower of the Faith of Dwyn, she publicly renounced her religion and converted to the Six Virtues in order to marry Sigoso III of Yscalin, whereupon she became his queen consort.

Suttu the Dreamer: The legendary founder of the House of Onjenyu. She led the Joyful Few to Lasia, crossing the Eria – a great salt desert – from a distant civilisation named Selinun. The Joyful Few were made up of Selinyi and Pardic people.

NON-HUMAN CHARACTERS

Fýredel: Leader of the Draconic Army, loyal to the Nameless One and known as his *right wing*. He led a ruthless campaign against humankind in CE 511, known as the Grief of Ages, after emerging from the Dreadmount in CE 509.

Nameless One: An enormous red wyrm, thought to have been the first creature to emerge from the Dreadmount. His confrontation with Cleolind Onjenyu and Galian Berethnet in Lasia in BCE 2 became a fundament of religion and legend the world over.

Taugran the Golden: One of the five great wyrms – known as the High Westerns – that emerged from the Dreadmount in CE 509. In CE 512, Taugran was defeated by Queen Dumai of Seiiki and her dragon allies.

Glossary

Braiding cap: An Yscali headdress. A net is worn on the back of the head and attached to either a hollow tube of silk, into which the hair can be fed, or ribbons the hair can be plaited around. They are fashionable among noblewomen in Cárscaro, particularly within the Palace of Salvation.

Commendation: The formal introduction of a young noble into society. The custom originated in Inys, where it has since died out, but is still observed in Yscalin.

Companion: The word used to describe a spouse in the religion of the Virtues of Knighthood.

Culebreya: A Draconic creature that originated in Yscalin. It resembles a large winged cobra.

Culler: A person who kills Draconic sleepers for a living. In Inys, they are referred to as knights-errant. The practice is outlawed by the Act of Restraint in Yscalin, but glorified in the rest of Virtudom.

Donma: A title used by female knights in Yscalin.

Donmata: A title granted to a female Yscali heir apparent, literally meaning *greatest lady*.

Draconic Army: A collective name for the wyrms and wyverns that emerged from the Dreadmount, as well as all creatures made by the wyverns, such as lindworms and basilisks.

Grief Laws: A series of laws made in Virtudom after the Grief of Ages, to prevent loss of life and damage to buildings in the event of the wyrms returning.

Halberd: A two-handed pole weapon.

Halgalant: The afterlife of the religion of the Virtues of Knighthood, said to have been built in the heavens by Galian Berethnet after his demise. A beautiful castle in a bountiful land where King Galian holds court at the Great Table with the righteous.

High Prince: A title used by male rulers of the Free State of Mentendon. In deference to the last High Queen of Mentendon, who was murdered by Clan Vatten, Mentish monarchs do not refer to themselves as kings or queens.

High Westerns: The five wyrms that emerged from the Dreadmount in CE 509: Fýredel, Valeysa, Orsul, Dedalugun and Taugran.

Holy Retinue: A name for the six companions of the Saint, who each represent one of the Virtues of Knighthood.

Intelligencer: Spy.

Kirtle: A one-piece sleeveless gown. May be worn on its own or as an extra layer beneath a more formal garment.

Mangonel: A catapult-like device. Once used as a siege engine, it was repurposed for use against the Draconic Army in the Grief of Ages.

Pardic: A term used to refer to both a language and a people from beyond the Eria, the salt desert to the south of Lasia.

Partlet: A Western garment that covers the shoulders and part of the neck, often used as an infill for a low neckline on a gown.

Patron: At the age of twelve, children of Virtudom choose a member of the Holy Retinue as their patron knight and receive a brooch to show their devotion. Only the Queen of Inys may take the Saint himself as her patron.

Pestilence: Bubonic plague.

Preventers: A smugglers' term for customs officers.

Rock dove: A homing pigeon, used for carrying letters.

Saint's Comet: The Yscali name for a comet with an orbital period of five hundred years, which holds an important place in history and legend. In CE 512, it ended the Grief of Ages by stripping the wyrms and wyverns of their fire and forcing the Draconic Army into a deep sleep.

Sanctarian: A religious officiant in the religion of the Virtues of Knighthood.

Sanctuary: A religious building in Virtudom, where those who believe in the Virtues of Knighthood can pray and hear teachings from a sanctarian.

Settle: An upholstered wooden seat, not unlike a sofa.

Six Virtues: Also known as the Virtues of Knighthood, this religion is modelled on traditional values taught to knights of ancient Inysca. The eponymous virtues are courage, courtesy, fellowship, generosity, justice, and temperance.

Spill: A slender piece of wood, used to light pipes.

Stickelchen: A Mentish padded headdress, consisting of a jewelled or beaded silk cap over a layer of sheer linen.

Sweat: A contagious disease, also known as the sweating sickness. Its cause is unknown, but it is highly contagious and fatal. Most people who contract it die in days, or even hours.

Verdugado: An Yscali hoop skirt stiffened with whalebone, worn beneath gowns to give them a bell-like shape. In Inys, where the fashion has caught on, this garment is called a farthingale.

Virtudom: The collective name for the four countries in Virtudom: Inys, Yscalin, Hróth and Mentendon. Also known as the Chainmail of Virtudom.

Womb of Fire: The core of the world. It is the birthplace of the Nameless One, the High Westerns, and the wyverns.

Wyrm: A scaled and fire-breathing creature of imposing size, with four legs and two wings. The term is usually applied to the five High Westerns, though the people of Virtudom also erroneously use it to describe Eastern dragons, despite the differences between the two species.

Wyverling: A small wyvern. When on the ground, they stand on two legs with their wings folded at their sides, unlike larger wyverns, which often use their wings to crawl.

Wyvern: A two-legged, winged Draconic creature. Like the High Westerns, the wyverns came from the Dreadmount and can breathe fire. By unknown means, the wyverns created the foot soldiers of the Draconic Army by warping livestock and wildlife. Each wyvern is bound to one High Western. Should the High Western die, the flame in its wyverns will go out, as will the flame in every creature descended from those wyverns.

Acknowledgements

If this was your first step into the Roots of Chaos universe, welcome. I hope you'll want to explore it further. If so, *The Priory of the Orange Tree* and *A Day of Fallen Night* are waiting for you, with more adventures to come.

If you're returning, welcome back to a world of chaos. Thank you for joining me on this journey to the Kingdom of Yscalin and the Free State of Mentendon – two countries I've been itching to explore in more depth since I wrote *The Priory of the Orange Tree*. Many Roots of Chaos readers have told me how much they loved Marosa, and I'm grateful to have been able to tell you more of her story.

Thank you to everyone at my agency, David Godwin Associates – David Godwin, Sebastian Godwin, Aparna Kumar, Bianca Rasmussen – and to everyone at Bloomsbury and my other publishing houses across the globe, including: Adam Kirkman, Áine Feeney, Amy Donegan, Ben Chisnall, Ben McCluskey, Benjamin Kuntzer, Beth Maher, Carmen R. Balit, Carrie Pitt, Charlotte Webb, Craig McKerchar, Cris Caserini, Danielle Rudasingwa, David Mann, Deborah Ogunnoiki, Emily Russell, Emma Allden, Fabrice Wilmann, Faye Robinson, Genevieve Nelsson, Grace McNamee,

Gráinne Reidy, Hannah Temby, Ian Hudson, India Arzoo Robinson, Inês Figueira, Inez Maria, Isi Tucker, Jack Birch, Janis Lardeux, Jess Stevens, Jillian Ramirez, Joanna Vallance, Joe Roche, Julien Ricard, Kai Papafio, Kathleen Farrar, Katie Vaughn, Katy Follain, Kenli Manning, Lauren Molyneux, Lauren Moseley, Lauren Elizabeth Moseley, Lauren Ollerhead, Lauren Wilson, Leah Robert Packer, Lily Watson, Lorraine Levis, Lucie Moody, Lucy Dixon-Peel, Maike Anderson, Maisie McCormick, Mariafrancesca Ierace, Marie Coolman, Mpumi Mgidlana, Natalia Facelli, Nigel Newton, Paul Baggaley, Phoebe Dyer, Rachel Wilkie, Robyn Enslin, Sam Halstead, Sara McLean, Sam Rioult, Sarah Rucker, Sharona Selby, Sudipto Mookherjee, Thea Hirsi, Tom Skipp, Trâm-Anh Doan, Volodymyr Feshchuk.

The warmest of thanks to the artists who have made *Among the Burning Flowers* so beautiful: Rovina Cai for the stunning illustrations, Emily Faccini for the maps and chapter headings, and of course, Ivan Belikov, whose covers are second to none. Thank you to the teams at the Broken Binding, Forbidden Planet, Goldsboro Books, Illumicrate and Waterstones for their gorgeous special editions.

Among the Burning Flowers is the inaugural book in the new Bloomsbury Archer imprint, spearheaded by the extraordinary Vicky Leech Mateos. I'm honoured to be the first author to be published under this imprint, and to be working with Vicky, who is both a brilliant editor and a beacon of kindness in the industry.

The amount of love and support I've received for this series over the last few years has changed the course of my life and career. Thank you.

And remember, you are enough.

PS: This one is dedicated to my kind and hilarious brother, Alfie, who always shows up to support me at my events in London. Aubrecht Lievelyn loves his younger siblings fiercely, and I was so lucky to be able to draw on a deep well of that love from my own life when I wrote about his relationship with Ermuna, Bedona and Betriese. Thanks for being you, pal. I'm so lucky to be your big sister.

A Note on the Author

Samantha Shannon is the million-copy bestselling author of The Bone Season and The Roots of Chaos series. Her work has been translated into twenty-eight languages. She lives in London.

samanthashannon.co.uk / @say_shannon